This novel is a work of fiction. Any resemblance to actual events, corporations or people, living or dead, is entirely coincidental. References to office holders or other people in the Secret Intelligence Service (MI6), the Serious Organised Crime Agency, Europol, the police - British or otherwise - or any other body, organisation or company anywhere are also fictional and are not intended to relate to any actual person who may have been in any similar post or position mentioned at any time.

Copyright © by Jo Calman 2024
All rights reserved.

www.jo-calman.com

ISBN 979-8-3441-0814-8

An Act of Faith

by Jo Calman

Love thyself last:
cherish those hearts that hate thee:
Corruption wins not
more than honesty.

Shakespeare, Henry VIII

Chapter 1 – Shepherd's Bush, West London, Spring 2009

Tallboy lay back in the barber's chair, his head wrapped in a hot towel. Marlon was preparing the razor to shave him. Tallboy relaxed as he listened to the buzz of the shop. Three or four guys new in from Jamaica bantered in patois; Tallboy barely understood what they were saying - he had forgotten all the patois he once spoke fluently. He was London now; he spoke London. Tallboy heard the door go, the ding of the bell.

"Yo! Marlon, 'sapnin?" a new voice hollered. Tallboy recognised it, and he smiled to himself. "Who ya got wrap in there, man? 'Zat Tallboy? I seen his shoes."

"Yo! Gol'fella," Tallboy spoke, "Is me. Howzit?"

"Cool, chill, I was lookin' f'you. You come see me after, yeah? Marlon, Tallboy shave on me, okay?"

"Sure t'ing, Gol'fella," Marlon said, "he be done quick now."

"Na rush, man, do 'im real fine, yeah."

Tallboy heard the door go again as Gol'fella left the shop. He smiled again to himself as Marlon continued. Marlon unwrapped Tallboy's face and set about lathering. He stropped the cut-throat on his leather strap and went to work. Ten minutes later Tallboy was done. His face shone - his cheeks now as smooth as his shaved head. He grinned, his gold tooth glinting.

"Nice one, Marlon. Feels good, man," Tallboy unfolded himself from the chair and reached for his coat. One of the Jamaicans handed it to him, saying something in patois. Tallboy responded and reached out to shake his hand.

"Stay cool, bro," Tallboy said, and he sauntered out of the shop.

Gol'fella's yard, ostensibly a music studio, was a few blocks away. Tallboy sauntered, enjoying the rare London sunshine.

In the observation post a camera shutter clicked.

"Tango Plus on the move," the surveillance man said into a radio, "going the same way as Tango Kilo."

"Blue four, I've got eyes on, blue four over," a crackled voice came over the waves, "Tango Plus entering Tango Kilo's premises. Over to you, OP2."

"Roger, blue four," said OP2, "Tango Plus is inside and mounting the stairs. Lost sight now. Standing by, over."

In the Operations Room at Scotland Yard the Ops Manager made her notes.

"What's he doing?" the Irishman asked.

"Don't know," the Ops Room Manager said, "we'll find out later."

"If he's talking to Gol'fella it could be the break we've been waiting for," the Spaniard said. What's the latest from Jamaica?"

"The Serious Organised Crime Agency have information that Adda himself is coming to Europe, may be using Gol'fella to make arrangements," this from the Detective Inspector from the Met Police Organised Crime Team. "The SOCA guy will be at the briefing later today; we'll know more then. Let's go grab a coffee, Tash can give us a call if anything happens."

The three detectives, part of one of the new-fangled Joint Investigation Teams now springing up all over the European Union, rose as one and trooped out to one of the trendy coffee shops dotted around New Scotland Yard.

******

In Gol'fella's office above the studio a large rum was poured and handed to Tallboy. Tallboy looked at the man; he was large, running to fat. Four of his teeth were gold, and he dripped with the stuff. Bracelets, rings, chains, a massive Rolex, all gold, which was how he got his street name. He just loved gold. Gol'fella had dismissed his crew and there were just the two of them in his large, plush room. Once they were alone he dropped the street chatter and spoke plainly.

"You know Adda? You was one of his boys back in the day, in Kingston?"

"Long time back, Gol'fella, not seen him in years."

"But you got no beef with him, right?"

"No beef, no. We parted as friends. I went a different way, is all. Went on the cruise ships."

"Why zat?" Gol'fella asked.

"We was living in Trench Town, across the street from the jail and just up from Tivoli Gardens. I ran with Adda and his crew for a time, but too many kids was getting wasted. The filth, the Shower Posse, anyone, shooting up the place all the time. I had family up in the north, St Ann, and a cousin workin' at one of those hotels at Ocho Rios. He made good money and didn't get shot or cut, so I went up there. Got into cooking and ended up on the cruise ships. Been doin' that for a few years now."

"Doin' what?" Gol'fella asked.

"I started out in the kitchens, galleys they called, but man it's tough and hot and hard an' long. After a few trips I asked to get moved to the restaurants, waiting tables. It don't sound much but there's benefits, lots of benefits. Plus you still ain't getting shot all the time. It's easy work, you get to go places - no one eats on the ship when you in port so you get a vacation two, three times a week, on a beach someplace with a ladyfren', someone's ladyfren', anyway. And on the ship, man, some of the ladies are *keen*, an' I mean *keen*. Easy work, easy money, easy pussy, or getting shot and shook down by the filth? No brainer, namzain?"

"Get your point, Tallboy. Why you ain't on a ship now?"

"A misunderstandin', no big t'ing. How's I to know they was mom and daughter? I got kicked off at Southampton. They said to give it a few months then go back on a different ship. So I'm jus' chillin' for now. Usin' a shipmate's crib in this hood."

"How you pay your way, bro?" Gol'fella asked.

"Duck and dive, some cheffin'," Tallboy said. "Why? Got somethin'?"

"You in England all legal? No beef with anyone, no po-lice, no immigration, no nuthin'?"

"No suh, no beef with nobody. Got a Brit passport years back, always polite to Babylon, kinda pay my taxes. Why?"

"Need someone clean to do a job, drivin' mostly. You can drive?"

"I can drive anythin'."

"Clean licence? No points? I want real clean, an' also someone I can trust and who Adda can trust. Is that you?"

"Adda?"

"Yeah. He comin' soon. Got some t'ing to take care of. He need a guy he can trust but who don't got no business with the filth, who going to drive him nice and careful, no red lights, no bad parking, all nice and peaceful, so he don't get attention. You do that?"

"How long?"

"Week, ten days top."

"How much?"

"Three hundred a day."

"I can do that, Gol'fella. When do I start?"

"Tomorrow morning." Gol'fella passed Tallboy a slip of paper. "You go there at ten, see Dawson and get the keys to the Benz we hired. Make sure it's nice inside and looks good. No junk car. Make sure it's real good. Then come back here."

"Yes, Gol'fella. I'm on it."

"While you work for me, it's *Mister* Gol'fella."

"Yes, *Mister* Gol'fella."

Chapter 2

The Austrian took a tram from near the run-down warehouse in District IX back towards the centre of Budapest. It was a dark night, wet too, and there weren't many people about. He was anxious but didn't look it. At Ferenc Körút he got off. The smell of damp bodies and the steamed-up windows were starting to bother him. He walked. The city was becoming less insalubrious, more touristy - safer. He took a few turns left and right, and he was soon beside the well-lit Central Market where it was never quiet and where there were always plenty of police, the *Rendörség*, hanging around. The Austrian started to relax.

He crossed the main street and entered the very end of Váci Utca, the long shopping street that ran from near the market all the way to Vörösmarty Tér and the upscale hotels and eateries. Váci Utca was useful. It was always packed; there were plenty of places to wait and watch. It was good for the Austrian's team to watch his back. He slowed his pace to a casual stroll and politely declined the many offers of company he received from scantily clad girls and a few boys too.

Just outside the entrance to McDonald's he saw his handler. She dropped a drink carton on the pavement and crushed it with her foot before bending to retrieve it. She slipped it into the waste bin and walked off down Váci Utca in the opposite direction. It was the signal that he was clear, no tail, no worries. He relaxed even more and picked up his pace. His car was parked in an underground car park not far from Vörösmarty. Now that his meeting with the Hungarian and his Croatian and Bulgarian associates was over, and they had shaken hands on the deal for a hundred kilos of best Afghan heroin, he was going home. Home to his nice apartment and his nice wife in one of the up-and-coming areas not too far from the river in Vienna.

His car was where he had left it, the key hidden in the exhaust pipe. He unlocked it. He threw his damp jacket onto the passenger seat and started the engine. He reversed out of the parking space and drove slowly towards the exit ramp. He relaxed even more. As the car started to ascend the exit ramp it might have been possible for him to hear the click of the mercury tilt-switch as the liquid metal completed the circuit that had been primed as soon as he turned the ignition key.

A few blocks away, at the near end of Váci Utca, his team heard the unmistakeable sound of the bomb. As one, they ran towards the underground car park and saw the plume of smoke, heard the shrieking of car and shop alarms, smelt the burning.

******

In the seaside town of Portimão on the Algarve, a Dutchman was finishing his morning coffee. The Algarve was fast becoming the resort of choice for the northern European gangsters and drug traffickers and bandits who once favoured the Spanish Costas as their preferred sunny operating bases. The Costas had become infested with cops and grasses, and the Spanish had too much invested in the tourist industry to keep extending the generous favours of times past to well-paying fugitives seeking privacy. So they were on the move. Just a few at first, but these days in larger numbers. The Portuguese had not yet caught up. Which was why the Dutchman was here.

He had found himself a nice villa with a pool, just a bit inland, with a private gated driveway and no near neighbours. He had found suitable places for the others too, and the equipment was on its way. Soon they would be ready to start work. There were operations ongoing, targets identified, phone numbers grabbed. While the operation was nominally under Portuguese control, the Dutchman was really the one in charge. The operation was multi-national; there were the Brits, of course, the Spanish and the French were in on it too. The Portuguese were there to keep appearances straight. It was their country, after all.

The Dutchman made a call to the French representative, Corinne. They had made a connection, not yet consummated but, he felt, not too far off now. He shouldn't really have called her, but they were both using local pay-as-you-go mobiles. She giggled softly as they chatted and he tried his rusty French for a while. In the end she called a halt and reverted to English.

"Let's have dinner," Corinne suggested, "at Praia da Rocha, that seafood place right on the beach."

"Seven this evening?" he asked.

"Sure, why not. See you then."

Just before seven, the Dutchman took a seat at the table he had reserved. It was on the terrace, under the awning. It was still spring and not so warm, but it had been a sunny day. He ordered a drink and let his mind roam among the erotic possibilities of the night ahead with the enticing Corinne. He was mentally approaching fulfilment, and thoroughly enjoying it, when a man approached him from behind and shot him twice in the head.

Chapter 3

Julia Kelso closed the front door as she left her rented house beside a large park in The Hague. She smiled as she heard Mel trying to calm little Freddie who, at nearly two years old, definitely did not want to eat his breakfast slop quietly. The arrangement was working reasonably well. Mel and Freddie had a big bedroom and a bathroom on the ground floor, Julia had the upstairs rooms and a shower. They shared the kitchen / diner and kept each other company. Julia even found herself enjoying little Freddie - when he wasn't having a tantrum.

She rode her bicycle, like a proper native *Haagenaar*, to the Europol building a couple of kilometres away, using the extensive network of cycle tracks. It was okay exercise, and it gave her a few minutes of private time to think, and to grieve. In nearly two years she had heard nothing of or from Ferdinand. He hadn't suddenly reappeared as she had so desperately wanted; there had been no news, good or bad. No messages, no coded emails. She and Mel had stopped talking about him now, but he was always there, in her head.

She parked her bike with all the others in the small Europol car park and went to her office. It was on the second floor, with all the other Directors' and senior managers' rooms. None were large, except the Director General's, but spacious enough to hold small meetings or to work in peace. Today she would spend most of her time in the Directors' conference room to sit through briefings on the progress or otherwise of the many Joint Investigation Teams she oversaw, and to hear submissions from Member States' representatives wanting to launch new ones. JITs had been around for a few years, and they were growing in popularity as police services more used to competing with each other started to see the benefits of collaboration. JITs weren't without their issues, though. There were many disconnects between evidential rules and surveillance procedures in most Member States - particularly the UK - which required diplomatic intervention, usually by Julia, to make sure the bad guys did actually end up in a jail somewhere.

Julia spent some time in her office checking her emails and messages and drinking a decent cup of hot coffee before heading for the conference room. There was nothing startling in her inbox.

The first briefing had been set up. It was not good news. The team was headed by Austria, and the country rep reported that there had been a fatality. The Austrians' key asset, an undercover police officer, had managed to make contact with a heroin-smuggling gang and had obtained intelligence of an incoming cargo of one hundred kilos via Bulgaria, Croatia and Hungary. A meeting had taken place between the respective gangsters in a warehouse in a run-down part of Budapest, successfully monitored by the Hungarian police. The undercover police officer had extricated himself and had thought he was clear and safe. Then his car had exploded as it left an underground car park in central Budapest, killing him instantly.

The operation had been aborted and the JIT was being dismantled. A murder investigation was underway, with the Hungarian CID demanding access to all the JIT files and subpoenaing the officers deployed in Hungary as potential witnesses.

It wasn't the first Joint Investigation Team to have ended in failure, but it might be the first to have been successfully disrupted by the targets, assuming they were responsible for the murder.

Julia asked the team leader to provide her with a comprehensive report so she could see what could be salvaged, if anything. The team trooped out, disheartened, and made their way to their next meeting with the Europol lawyers.

Julia's second briefing was no better. A multinational operation targeting fugitive offenders settling on the Algarve was being established in Portimão, complete with an interception suite, surveillance facilities and skilled investigators. Arrangements were progressing well, or had been, with an experienced operational team leader, provided by the Dutch police, and participants from the UK, Spain, France and, of course, Portugal. There had been a set-back. The Dutch team leader had been killed in an apparently random shooting on the terrace of a restaurant on the sea front at Praia da Rocha. So far, there was no evidence to indicate that it had been a targeted attack or that the operation itself had been compromised. It had, however, set the operation back considerably as all the arrangements for accommodation, vehicles, every-day administration and so on had all been made by the dead detective in his assumed name. They would have to start all over again.

Julia went back to her office as the briefings paused for coffee. She was uneasy. To have not one but two fatalities, each one a personal tragedy of course but also with a significant impact on major law-enforcement operations, was unusual to say the least. Coincidence?

Possibly, but Julia Kelso didn't hold with coincidence. She picked up the phone.

"Mel? It's me, how are you doing?" she asked.

"I'm covered in rancid slop and I stink of baby sick. I think I've got it in my hair. Want to swap?" Mel said.

"I wouldn't mind, not this morning. I wish you'd come and work with me, I think I might have a problem brewing."

"We've discussed it, Jake," Mel replied, "apart from Freddie taking up all my time I'm not sure I've got it in me anymore. I am getting properly fed up with baby sick though. What's happening?"

"I don't know. Can we talk later, when I get home?"

"Are you making an appointment, Kelso?"

"No, just trying to make sure you'll still be awake when I get home at six."

"Let me check my diary," Mel said, "bathtime at four, feed at five, another bath at five-thirty, then a shower for me to get rid of the debris, I should be clear by six. See you then."

Julia hung up. She still couldn't get used to Mel Dunn being a mother, especially of the apparently late Alan Ferdinand's child. Julia wished it had been her - she was the one who loved him, after all. Mel still maintained she didn't love anybody, but it was clear that little Freddie was changing that, just a little bit, day by day.

She finished her coffee and went back to the conference room. Next up was some better news. The Brits were leading a JIT targeting a Class A importation and distribution organisation based in Jamaica but operating in Spain, Ireland and the UK. The Serious Organised Crime Agency had persuaded the Metropolitan Police to participate, in itself no mean feat, and by all accounts they were on track to infiltrate the organisation with an undercover officer. All was going well and according to plan. The next phase was dependent on the safe arrival in the UK of the organisation's main man, a diminutive and particularly nasty gangster known as Adda, as in Puff Adder. The Europol liaison in Kingston had just reported that Adda had successfully departed Jamaica by convoluted means and was believed to be *en route* to Europe, probably to the UK and London. It was a nice change to have some good news at last.

The afternoon was given over to submissions and applications, a complex and bureaucratic, but nevertheless necessary, process to make sure all the legal t's were crossed and i's dotted. Three out of five passed the test, two were sent back for more preparation before Julia could give them Europol's blessing.

Shortly after five p.m. Julia closed her files and powered down her computer. As she was about to leave the office her personal mobile phone rang.

"Julia? It's me, Abigail, from Hugh's office."

Julia froze. Abigail Ukebe, Hugh Cavendish's new right hand at SIS headquarters in London, had been the MI6 caseworker on Ferdinand's last operation. The operation had led to the successful MI6 takeover of a sophisticated global money laundering operation, which was still producing Grade A intelligence.

"Hello, Abigail, it's been a long time," Julia said, trying to sound calm.

"Can we meet?" Abigail said. "I'm in The Hague, at the Carlton Ambassador. I've got some news."

"I'll see you in the Carlton bar in twenty minutes," Julia said.

Chapter 4

Julia almost ran to the Carlton Ambassador Hotel, completely forgetting her bike. She arrived at the plush hotel and scoured the elegant lobby bar before taking the stairs to the bustling basement pub. She found Abigail seated in a corner, on her own. Abigail waved and lifted an empty beer glass.

Julia ordered drinks for them both and went to Abigail's table. Abigail smiled at her as she approached.

"Good to see you, Julia," Abigail said, accepting the proffered glass.

"You too, Abigail, it's been a while," Julia paused and took a seat. "I don't want to seem rude or abrupt, but you said you had news?"

"I do, not particularly good I'm afraid, but I wanted to come to tell you myself. It may help you move on."

"Is he dead? Alf I mean, Ferdinand?"

"I don't know for definite, but I do think he is. Let me tell you what I know."

"Please," said Julia.

"A few weeks ago, a British passport was handed in to the High Commission in Abuja by the Nigerian police. It was the one Ferdinand had been using on his last trip into Port Harcourt, the one in the name of Eric Milton. Milton was eventually reported missing, incidentally, by his employer. So, the passport was recovered by the police from a prisoner who had been arrested for robbery in Kaduna, that's a town about two- or three-hour's drive north of Abuja. The prisoner was languishing in Kaduna jail.

"When I heard about the Milton passport being found - I had flagged it so I was notified when it was handed in - I asked Abuja station to go and speak to the prisoner. They did. It turns out that the prisoner was one of the Italian Agent's security team. When the Agent was killed at Dankama, the prisoner and the rest of the team went back to the guy's house in Katsina to ransack it before the police got there.

"The prisoner - his name isn't important - used to be a policeman, and he knew that dead white folks tend to attract a lot of police attention. There were already two of them in Dankama, and when our man got back to Katsina he said he found another one in the Agent's house. That was where he found the Milton passport. I'm certain the person the prisoner saw there was Alf. He said Alf was completely still and cold.

"He took the body out to a pick-up truck they had and threw him in the back. The prisoner said he heard a groan come from the body, just one. It doesn't mean he was alive though, Julia. Anyway, the prisoner decided the best and quickest thing to do with the body was to drive it over the border into Niger. The border is extremely porous, in fact the only people who take any notice of it are the Nigerian police, and that's only to make life easier for themselves.

"The prisoner said he drove a few kilometres into Niger and dumped the white guy by the side of the road. Judging by the prisoner's description of the place, Abuja station thinks it was somewhere near Dan Issa, off the main road up to Maradi. The prisoner said that was the last he saw of him.

"Abuja made some enquiries with the embassy in Niamey - we don't have a station there - and they couldn't find any trace of a European man being found, alive or dead. Abuja station doesn't think it is much of a surprise that the finding of a body hasn't been reported. If the locals did find one, they would probably just bury it to avoid getting involved with the police and officialdom.

"Look, Julia, you knew Alf much better than I did, so you know that if he was physically able to contact you or Mel he would have done so by now. I know you have a means of communication set up. So either he is dead, sadly, or he just can't make contact. From what the prisoner said about his injuries, the European, assuming it was Alf and if he was actually alive, he was in a pretty bad way. Loss of blood and injuries to his head. I think you have to let go."

Julia sat quietly for a few moments.

"Thank you, Abigail. I hear what you say, but for me, it's not enough. I can't let go until I know, know for sure. In some ways I want you to be right, to say he's dead and gone. I should go to Niger, try to find him."

"No, you shouldn't," Abigail said firmly, "it's a dangerous place, especially for someone like you."

"What do you mean, someone like me?"

"You are an attractive, blonde European woman. Do I have to spell it out?" Abigail asked.

"Yes!"

"There are gangs roaming around there, robbers, rapists, terrorists. No one who isn't local goes there without an armed convoy. With an armed convoy protecting you, you won't get near anyone who might have any useful information for you. Without an armed convoy protecting you, you won't come out alive. You would be wasting your own life. If, and it is an if, Alf was alive when he was dumped by the roadside on the edge of the Sahara, what are the chances that he could have made it? He was badly injured. There is no water, no medical facility, no anything for miles. It touches forty degrees at midday and drops to around ten degrees or lower at night. If he was in the open, how long could he last?

"There are animals, wild dogs, hyenas, roaming around. How long do you think he could last? I'm sorry, Julia. Accept it, I'm begging you. Let him go."

Julia felt her cheeks getting damp as tears fell slowly. She knew Abigail was right; knew it but did not want to believe it.

"Let me get you a drink, Julia," Abigail said.

"A large Jameson, with a little ice," Julia said.

"Was it his drink?"

"His favourite."

******

It was late by the time Julia got home. After a few drinks with Abigail, Julia had taken herself off to one of the Indonesian restaurants that she had been to with Ferdinand. She chose a *nasi goreng* dish he liked, extra hot, and had nearly choked as the fiery spices hit her throat. She drank more whiskey. She cried in the taxi.

Mel Dunn was asleep in a chair in her living room. She opened one eye as she heard Julia come in.

"So much for a six o'clock date, Kelso," she said.

Mel looked at Julia.

"Jake, are you drunk?"

"I think so. Why?"

"What's up?" Mel asked.

Julia held out her arms to Mel and pleaded silently for a hug, some contact. Mel rose and took her friend in her arms, held her wordlessly, stroked her head.

"What is it?" she asked again gently.

"I saw Abigail," Jake said, "she came over to see me. She says Alf is dead."

Julia started sobbing again. Mel held her.

"Tell me what she said," Mel commanded softly.

Julia did, between sobs and gasps. When she had finished Mel said nothing. She went to the cupboard for the whiskey bottle and poured out two large measures. She added a little ice. She put a glass in Jake's hand.

"A drink to Alf, wherever he is," Mel said.

They drank in silence.

Chapter 5

Adda reclined in his usual seat at the front of the Gulfstream Five. He stared at the bulkhead, not speaking. The only other passenger was at the rear of the long cabin. He still wore his bright red padded jacket, his black beanie and his wrap-around shades. Adda had taken his off. Leaving Jamaica had been easy, as usual. A fistful of dollars to a lazy policeman at the remote airfield, the rented private jet, a stooge dressed in ridiculous clothing. The Gulfstream was halfway across the Atlantic, not Adda's usual direction of travel. South towards Colombia or Venezuela or west toward the States were his regular headings, but he needed to go to Europe. There was a problem.

A few hours later the Gulfstream touched down in eastern France, the pilot having told French ATC that he needed to check something on the outside of the plane as a matter of urgency, hence the unscheduled stop. The jet was on the ground for less than five minutes. As soon as the door opened, Adda and the other passenger, both now identically dressed, alighted and were replaced by two other men of similar build and dressed in exactly the same way. The Gulfstream took off, calling French ATC to say all was well and they were continuing to Brussels, their stated destination.

Adda and the other guy climbed into a smaller aircraft, a Piper Malibu with a British registration, and they were airborne within minutes.

At Rochester airfield in Kent, Tallboy sat behind the wheel of the hired Benz while Gol'fella paced anxiously outside. Tallboy watched as a single-engine plane came in to land and taxied across the grass runway towards the car park. It came to a halt. Tallboy saw Adda for the first time in many years, and the sight caused him to shudder involuntarily. Adda was a small man, tight and compact. He shrugged off the ugly red coat as he approached Gol'fella and handed it to him. Underneath he was dressed in an Armani suit, dark grey, his hair was neat and short, he wasn't smiling. Tallboy recalled the fear he had always felt in Adda's presence. The small man exuded menace. His eyes seemed to smoulder as he stared at you like you were prey. He reminded Tallboy of a snake, the nasty venomous snake he took his nickname from.

Gol'fella held out his arms to embrace Adda, but Adda blanked him. Walking past, he went towards the Benz. Tallboy leapt out to open the rear passenger door. Adda stopped and stared at him.

"Tallboy?" Adda said after a second, "long time no see. You with Gol'fella crew now, eh?"

"Just short-term, Mr Adda," Gol'fella interjected, "you wanted someone clean in the driving seat while you was here."

"I do, Gol'fella. Tallboy will do, I know him before. Get my bag from the plane, Tallboy, put it in the trunk," Adda said. "Let's go, no time to waste."

Gol'fella and Adda were in the back. Tallboy waited for instructions.

"You wait outside, Tallboy," Adda ordered, "I want speak in private to Gol'fella here."

Tallboy obeyed and stood beside the car.

"So, how was your journey?" Gol'fella asked uneasily.

"Pain," Adda replied, "I don't want to be here but I need to come. There's a problem, maybe more than one."

"What's that?" Gol'fella asked.

"Rats," Adda said, "we got rats. Rats in the crew, your crew. I want you to get a place, a place I can *see* the rats and *exterminate* them, get me? A place no one knows you. You get it soon - tomorrow - and make it good. I mean plastic sheets on the floor and walls, two plastic chairs, soundproofing and some loud music. You do that?"

"Yes, Adda. I got somewhere in mind. You know the rats? Who they are?"

"I know one for sure, I'll tell you when I'm ready. I got filth, you get me? I got filth in me pocket, big filt'. Filth who know stuff. He go tell me tomorrow who the other rat is. When I know, you know. We deal with two rats at one time, you hear me?"

"'Course," Gol'fella said nervously.

"It's bad, Gol'fella. Not one rat but two rats, two rats in your crew, which is *my* crew, make you look like you got shit fo' a brain. Which make *me* look bad. I don't like that, Gol'fella. You an' me, we need to talk when the rats are *exterminated*, you get me? I said *you get me?*"

"Yes, yes, Adda, I get you," Gol'fella stammered.

"Get Tallboy back in," Adda demanded.

"London - Canary Wharf," Gol'fella told Tallboy once he was seated.

Tallboy nodded and engaged drive. He pulled away smoothly, not talking.

Silence reigned in the large quiet car as Tallboy drove smoothly towards the city, the skyline of Canary Wharf and Docklands already in sight. Gol'fella regained some of his composure and told Tallboy to drive to an expensive hotel right by the river. Adda held out his hand and Gol'fella gave him an envelope. Adda extracted a passport, a pile of cash and a hotel booking confirmation in the name shown on the passport. He nodded.

"Good," Adda said, "I'm going to rest. Tallboy, you be back here tomorrow, nine a.m. Bring two brand new phones, one for you, one for me. Get them in the morning, brand new, no used crap, and sealed in original packs. An' bring me the receipt with date and time. Make them basic, no GPS." Adda passed Tallboy two one-hundred-dollar bills. "Get going, Gol'fella, you got work," he said.

Adda hefted his small bag and strolled into the hotel without a backward glance.

******

Later that evening, the Joint Investigation Team at New Scotland Yard were elated. They had had an initial debrief from the handler, with more to follow once the source had an opportunity to speak at length. A small surveillance team was left near the Canary Wharf hotel, just in case Adda made a move before the morning.

The Operations Room Manager raised an action to be completed by the day shift to contact the hotel security manager, swear him or her to secrecy, and find out everything there was to know about the recently arrived guest. That done, the team leaders adjourned to the Buckingham Arms in Petty France for a few beers, leaving the night shift to it.

Chapter 6

That evening in her office in The Hague, Julia Kelso was reviewing the case file for the Jamaican operation that had now sucked in the British, the Irish and the Spanish. The primary target, a major and well-established criminal gang leader named Norbert Brown, known widely as Adda, was making a rare trip to Europe. A year earlier, the Jamaica Constabulary Force had infiltrated an informer, a Covert Human Intelligence Source or CHIS, into Adda's crew. They had shared this vital information with Europol but not the British, Irish or Spanish police, so that Europol could keep a remote eye out for their valuable and rare asset.

She found a recent note in the file, placed there only a day ago, that mentioned a new CHIS in Gol'fella's circle, a Brit undercover police officer, details to follow imminently. Gol'fella was Adda's London-based lieutenant. In Julia's position, she was one of the very few people who knew the real and assumed identities of all informants and undercover law-enforcement officers deployed within Europol-managed Joint Investigation Team operations at any given time. Such information was highly sensitive and disclosure could literally mean life or death for the individual concerned. Needless to say, it was extremely well protected within a segregated section buried deep inside the Europol Information System.

It was getting dark outside and a light rain was falling. Julia decided to work for a little longer before heading down to the basement gym for a workout on the way home. She was half hoping that Mel and little Freddie would be fast asleep by the time she got there.

She loved them both, she really did, but sometimes she just needed her own piece of silent space.

She got herself a large glass of water and opened the police reports on the two fatalities in Hungary and Portugal. It had been a few days since they had happened and the initial investigation reports had been forwarded to Europol. Julia read them both quickly. The bombing in Budapest was being treated as an organised crime assassination, the sort of thing that had once happened routinely in the first two or three years after the collapse of communism. It had become a rarity in more recent times. The Hungarian police had dragged a few old-time cops out of retirement and were picking their brains for names of likely perpetrators who might still be about and active. Tests had identified the explosive as Czech-manufactured Semtex. The Semtex had to be at least a decade old, given the stringent restrictions placed on its manufacture and export by the Czech government following its highly publicised reputation as the terrorists' explosive of choice in the late 20th century. The Hungarians were thinking it may have been part of a shipment stolen by a Serbian organised crime gang from a demolition site near the southern city of Pecs in 2001. In any event, it was obvious that it was still as potent as it ever had been, as evidenced by the extensive damage caused to the car park and to several innocent bystanders, as well as the apparently intended and very deceased target.

The identity and true role of the target had been shared only with the most senior investigating officer, and so far the media had no inkling of foreign law-enforcement connections. Julia made a mental note to call Niall Morton, the former Scotland Yard Special

Branch officer who was now the well-established UK Police Liaison Officer in Budapest so that she could get a view on what the Hungarians were actually thinking.

The shooting in Praia da Rocha remained unsolved and the Portuguese police were making slow progress. There were a few eyewitnesses who had seen very little. There was hardly any forensic evidence, apart from the two bullets recovered from the head of the victim, whose identity was being withheld, for now. The bullets themselves would be useful if and when a weapon was ever recovered. Initial ballistics database searches suggested that the weapon used had not been fired in any recorded crime anywhere in Europe where spent rounds had been recovered. There were no shell cases at the murder scene in Portugal. Between themselves, the senior investigators were of the opinion that this had been a professional assassination, once virtually unheard of on the sleepy Algarve but which had become more common since the migration of sunburnt bandits from the Costas had started. They thought it unlikely that a suspect would ever be identified.

They knew that the victim had been part of a covert law-enforcement operation, but one that had not started work yet and as such had had no impact on resident criminals or their organisations. The other members of the operation team had all been hastily withdrawn from Portugal and all their arrangements had gone back to square one.

In her office in The Hague Julia was weighing up the probability of coincidental killings versus coordinated assassinations, or at least assassinations that were linked by the same motive. She thought that both scenarios were unlikely, but nevertheless there were still two dead covert law-enforcement officers. She would make a point of speaking to the British Police Liaison Officer in Lisbon, an old acquaintance, to see what light, if any, she could throw on the Algarve killing.

Julia closed the files and signed off from her desktop before closing it down. She removed her Europol identity badge from the reader attached to the computer, without which it would not operate at all. The badge was on its extendable lanyard and attached somehow to her as its only permitted user. When inserted in the badge reader on her computer it would allow her access if the correct digital code was manually entered. Even when protocols were followed, the machine would turn itself off if no keys were touched for ten minutes, something which users found immensely annoying but which added to the intrinsic security of the Europol Information System. The badge was also needed to enter or leave the building, or certain parts of the building, and the Europol Information System could not be accessed by any person whose badge was not recognised as being in the same space as its purported user. It was all meant to ensure that no one had access to anyone else's information, or to anyone else's user permissions. It was how they kept information secure.

Julia changed into her sports kit in her office and badged out of the management area. She went down to the basement gym, knowing it would be almost empty at this time of night. There were a handful of other staffers in there, mostly on their own but with one pair running on treadmills side by side. She chose a vacant treadmill and programmed a 10k run. As her running rhythm became settled her brain switched off and she let her mind wander through happier times, times with

Ferdinand and Mel Dunn, when their exciting experiment as unorthodox corruption-fighters was still fresh. Before Mel had been so badly hurt; before Ferdinand had got himself killed.

It was almost nine p.m. when Julia got home. Mel's rooms downstairs were quiet, the main lights off and just a glow of a nightlight from Freddie's sleeping area. She found Mel upstairs, in her living room, with a bottle of wine open on a side table. Julia smiled at her. Mel smiled back and poured. She held out a glass.

"In a bit, I'm just going to take a shower," Jake said. "How are you?"

"Usual," Mel replied, "same as yesterday and the day before. You?"

"Fair," Julia sighed.

"Let's talk later, shall we?" Mel suggested.

"Yes, let's."

Chapter 7

Tallboy sat in the car and waited. It was just after nine. At eleven-thirty Adda emerged, fresh and neat. Tallboy leapt from the car to open the rear door. Adda ignored him and got in the front passenger seat.

"Get in," Adda commanded.

Tallboy did so. He passed Adda the two unopened, brand new, mobile phones together with the timed receipt. Adda took them without a word. He opened both boxes. From his jacket pocket he took two new SIM cards, throwing the ones that came with the phones out of the window. He turned on the phones and saw that there was some charge in their batteries.

"Let's go get charging cables," Adda said. "Good mornin', by the way."

"Good morning, Mr Adda," Tallboy said softly, "you have a good night?"

Adda did not reply. Tallboy started the car and drove towards the City. He pulled in at a filling station on The Highway and bought two car phone charging leads. By the time he returned to the car, Adda had moved to the back seat. He held out his hand and took one of the leads, which he plugged in to the socket by the door handle. Adda dialled the number of the other phone, and when it rang he killed the call and handed it to Tallboy.

"Now we in contact, Tallboy. You don't use this phone to call anyone else but me unless I tell you, got me?"

"Yes, Mr Adda."

"Good. Now we go see Gol'fella at his yard."

Tallboy drove smoothly and carefully. Adda seemed oblivious to the London traffic, slow moving as ever. He sat silently on the back of the big Benz staring straight ahead. Tallboy checked the rearview mirrors constantly, alert for any sign of followers. The ride to Gol'fella's yard took almost an hour. Adda got out.

"You wait here," was all he said to Tallboy.

Tallboy sat for a while, then stood to stretch his legs. He went into the building to use the toilet. He was getting hungry and thirsty, but he still waited patiently. The spring air was cool and fresh, even in London. The clocks hadn't yet gone forward, and by the time Adda finally emerged, followed closely by a very worried-looking Gol'fella, the sky was already dark.

"Dorchester Hotel," Adda said.

Adda and Gol'fella sat in the back. Gol'fella tried to make small talk.

"Shut yo' mouth, Gol'fella, will you?" Adda said quietly. "Yo' noise making my head hurt. I tol' you we goin' to see my man. I go get the name of the second rat from him, full name, an' real name too. Then you got work to do and you can make plenty noise then. But for now you stay shut, get me?"

"Yes Adda, if you say so," Gol'fella mumbled.

Minutes passed. Gol'fella couldn't do silence, and after a while he spoke again.

"So rat number one, the name you gave me, what you want me to do?"

Adda sighed.

"When we know who rat number two is, we know who we got left. Then we go get both of them and take them to the place you fixed. 'Cep I don't go - you go. Tallboy take me someplace and then come find you.

When the rats are finished with you tell him and he tell me. Then I can go home away from this rathole. You get me?"

Silence returned as the car slid through the evening traffic towards Park Lane. Tallboy pulled into the drop off point in front of the Dorchester Hotel, Gol'fella went to open his door.

"You stay here," Adda hissed. "You wait!"

Adda stepped out and walked towards the hotel's main doors. Tallboy manoeuvred the car so he could see the entrance and turned off the engine. Gol'fella sat in the back, looking glum.

"Wha's goin' on?" Tallboy asked.

Gol'fella looked up at the back of Tallboy's head.

"Adda sayin' we got rats, two rats. He tell me one is Shawny. You know him?"

"Don't think so, Gol'fella."

"Don't suppose you would. He jus' come from Jamaica couple months back. Mean fucker too."

"What you go do wit' him?"

"Never you mind, Tallboy. Now Adda go get the name of the second rat. He say he got big filth in he pocket."

"Big filth? Here in London?"

"Look like. Now be quiet. When you done with Adda you come to this place an' wait for me."

Gol'fella slipped a folded piece of paper to Tallboy, who looked at it. It was an address in Harlesden. Underneath were another two words, 'Spell Man'.

"What this mean, Gol'fella, 'Spell Man'," Tallboy asked.

"Gimme that," Gol'fella barked, "you didn't see that, jus' remember the address, okay?"

"Okay, Gol'fella, go easy yeah."

Tallboy passed the paper back to Gol'fella.

"Is there time to take a leak, you think?" Tallboy asked.

"Make it quick!"

Tallboy got out of the car, taking the car key with him. Gol'fella sat in the back, looking even more miserable.

Tallboy walked through the hotel lobby. On a signboard there was a list of that evening's events. Tallboy read the list quickly. He looked up, and in the distance he saw a door open. Adda came out, followed by a tall man wearing a smart suit. Tallboy had seen all he needed to.

He walked swiftly past the toilets and out of a side door into Deanery Street. He bent and dropped the car key through the grating over a drain. In South Audley Street, Tallboy started to run.

******

As Tallboy ran towards Piccadilly, an angry Adda stormed out of the main entrance of The Dorchester. He tore open the passenger door of the Mercedes and pulled a startled Gol'fella out, dumping him on the tarmac.

"Where Tallboy go?" he yelled.

"'E go for a piss, Adda, waas up?" Gol'fella stammered, struggling to his feet.

"He a fuckin' rat! A cop, you stupid fuck! You hire a cop to drive me? Fuck sake! Go get him, an' give me the keys to the ride, now!"

Gol'fella opened the driver's door and stared at the empty space where the key should be.

"No key, Adda. Tallboy must have it." Gol'fella braced himself for another verbal onslaught, but Adda just simmered.

"You call your crew, Gol'fella. I want four boys to go to this place in Streatham, bring back Tallboy." Adda passed a piece of paper to Gol'fella. "Another four to get Shawny, take him to the place you fixed and wait."

"Yes, Adda," Gol'fella said.

"And then get me some wheels, you dumb shit!" Adda spat at Gol'fella.

******

In Piccadilly, Tallboy kept running towards Green Park station. On the way he called Steven from his new temporary phone - he knew the number well. He told Steven to pack a few things and get himself and Sasha ready to move. It was urgent!

Twenty-five minutes later he emerged from Brixton tube station and started running again, this time southward towards Brixton Hill and Streatham.

He was panting heavily when he shoved open the street door of a large, imposing apartment building and took the lift to the fourth floor. He hammered on a door with his fists. The door opened. A red-haired man looked at him, askance.

"Steven," Tallboy panted, "get your stuff, we've got to go - now! Where's Sasha?"

"She's in her room. What's going on, Errol?"

"Big trouble. We've got to get out. We've talked about it. Get your bag."

Tallboy pushed past and opened a bedroom door. A younger woman was on her phone. He snatched it from her.

"Sasha, we've got to go. There's trouble. We don't have much time, get your things."

"Okay, bro. Gimme my phone back and I'll get my bag. This better be good!"

Tallboy rushed to another bedroom and rummaged in a drawer. He took out a passport and a wallet, together with a phone. He reached under the bed and pulled out a holdall. He quickly checked the contents before zipping it up again. By the time he emerged, Sasha and Steven were waiting by the front door. He pushed them out, checked that the lights were out and pulled the door closed.

"Take the stairs," he said.

The three of them sped down the stairwell and emerged in the dark street. Tallboy hissed at them to stay in the shadows as he looked around. The yellow light of a vacant taxi, a rare sight in South London after dark, shone fifty yards away.

"Get the cab, Stevie," Tallboy said.

Steven stepped into the light of a streetlamp and held up his arm.

"East Croydon Station," he told the driver through the open window as he held open the back door for Sasha and Tallboy.

"I'm not going that way," the cabbie protested.

"Yes you are," Tallboy said, showing the driver a Metropolitan Police warrant card. "Just drive!"

The reluctant cabbie did a U-turn, swearing quietly as a blacked-out BMW full of mean looking people tore down the road and screeched to a halt. Three large men, all dressed in black and wearing beanies, ran towards the apartment block the three of them had just vacated.

Tallboy slumped back in the seat.

"Fuck, that was close!"

Chapter 8

On the train towards Brighton, Detective Sergeant Errol Spelman, previously Tallboy, used Adda's throwaway phone to call the police emergency number. He gave the operator the address of the place Gol'fella had set up in Harlesden and said that a serious assault was in progress. He killed the call and tossed the phone, wiped clean of any fingerprints, out of the train window. He tried to relax but he was in turmoil.

"Are you going to tell us what this is all about, Errol?" Steven asked gently.

"When we get somewhere safe. I just need some time to think," Errol said. He squeezed his sister Sasha's hand gently. Errol closed his eyes and appeared to sleep.

Steven called a hotel he knew near Brighton and booked rooms for them for three nights. They took a taxi from the station towards Hove. They walked a couple of blocks and found another cab rank and took a fresh taxi to the hotel. Sasha went to her room, Steven and Errol to theirs. Errol fell onto the bed, exhausted.

"Get a shower, Errol, then let's go meet Sasha for a drink downstairs and we can talk. We need to."

Errol nodded in agreement and rose wearily from the bed. Half an hour later he wandered into the bar where Sasha and Steven were already seated at a corner table. Errol ordered a large rum from the waiter. When it arrived he looked at the others with sad eyes.

"Okay," he started, "as you know, sometime back I did an undercover job. A few years ago they sent me to Jamaica and for a while my cover nickname was Tallboy. I ran with a nasty guy called Adda - tough, mean, ruthless. When my time in Jamaica finished I came back to London and mostly forgot all about it. Then a few weeks ago I had a call from someone in Covert Policing. They wanted me to go back into cover as Tallboy. They said they'd heard that Adda was planning to come to London and would be wanting a clean skin to drive him around, and Covert Policing said it would be good if that person could be Tallboy. I agreed to do it and we set it up. We knew that a guy called Gol'fella was Adda's main man in London, so I started hanging in places I knew he went. It worked well, and a few days back Gol'fella asked me to do the driving job.

"All was going well, as planned and as we hoped. It turned out that Adda was coming over to deal with a 'rat', a traitor in his, or Gol'fella's, crew. He needed a clean skin driver for an alibi when the 'rat' was being punished. Which means killed, of course, but not quickly.

"I found out the name of the rat, but I also learned that there wasn't just one. There were two. I took Adda and Gol'fella to The Dorchester in London where Adda was going to meet someone he had referred to in conversation with Gol'fella as 'his filth', meaning a bent cop. Gol'fella showed me a piece of paper in the car when Adda went into the hotel. It had an address in Harlesden that had been set up as a slaughterhouse. But also on the paper were the words 'Spell' and 'Man'. I went into the hotel saying I needed a pee. I saw a list of events on a signboard. One event was 'MPSELT Dinner' in a named room. Now, MPSELT stands for Metropolitan Police Service Executive Leadership Team, all the top dogs in the Met."

"So, you put two and two and two together?" Sasha asked.

"I did. Looks like someone high up in the Met could be in Adda's pocket, and that person could have told Adda that informants have been placed in his organisation. Not only that, someone, let's assume it *is* a bent senior officer in the Met, must have also given Adda my real name and home address, as well as my cover name, alongside the cover name of the other 'rat'. There's no other explanation."

"Fucking hell!" Sasha stated. "What are you going to do?"

"I have no idea," Errol replied. "not knowing who the real rat is, I can't take this to the top. I need to find out who knew. Who knew about me and about the other one, who I don't think was from the UK. He had just arrived from Jamaica, apparently. I think it's unlikely that anyone in the Met would know that there was a Jamaica-based source in play, or who it was. So maybe Adda has more than one piece of filth in his pocket, who knows?"

"So, as of now, we're effectively on the run?" Steven asked.

"Consider it a sudden vacation," Errol said, trying to smile again. "I'll think of something, don't worry."

But Errol was worried. Someone, someone very high up, had deliberately endangered not just him, but also the two people he loved more than anything in the whole world. His sister - his only living relative - and his life-partner, his Steven.

Later, Errol lay in bed listening to Steven's soft snores. He was wide awake, his head full of fears and doubts. It was a long, long night. As dawn broke, Errol went to the bathroom and made a call.

"Niall?" he asked when the call was picked up. He heard a grunt. "It's me, Errol. I need help, mate, I mean I really need it."

"What's up?" Niall Morton, the UK's Police Liaison Officer in Hungary, asked.

"Can't say on the phone. Can we meet?"

"I'm at the Liaison Officers' conference in The Hague this week. I could pop across, or you could come over to Holland."

"I'd better come to you. Cheers mate, I appreciate it."

"Stay safe. You know where I am if you need me."

Errol cut the call and went back to the bedroom. Steven was awake; he had been listening.

"Who was that?" he asked.

"An old friend," Errol said, "someone I know I can trust. I need to go away for a while, later today. Can you look after Sasha, just until I come back with a plan?"

"Of course," Steven said, "but I want you to know you can trust me too. You do know that?"

Errol took his hand.

"I do. I do trust you. I'll make this all okay, believe me."

"Come back to bed, it's too bloody early. And do me a favour, will you? Lose that gold tooth!"

Chapter 9

They met at one of the open-air coffee shops on the Plaats in the centre of The Hague. Errol hardly recognised his old friend, who was now smartly dressed in a well-tailored suit. Errol remembered him habitually wearing a shabby anorak and scuffed trainers.

"Gone up in the world, Niall?" he asked.

"Diplomat now, aren't I? On paper anyway, got to look the part. How are you doing?" Niall asked.

"I've been better, to be honest."

They waited for a server to bring the coffees, then Errol started.

"There's a problem, mate, a big problem. An undercover job I was working on was blown, deliberately blown. Someone told the bad guys that there were two sources in play and named them both. I was one of them. They knew my cover name and my real name, address and all.

"The target of the job was a guy known as Adda, he's a Jamaican gang-boss, a real piece of work. He went into the Dorchester Hotel in London; I went in after him and saw him near a room where the Met Police Executive Leadership Team was having a get together. I didn't see him talking to anyone I recognised, but I'd already twigged that he knew my real name. I'm assuming he was being given my cover name too, maybe by someone in the MPSELT room. I didn't hang around to find out."

Errol pulled a newspaper from his backpack. He showed Niall an inside page. The story, complete with a large photograph, was about a major fire at a block of flats in Streatham.

"That was where we lived, Niall. We got out minutes before Adda's guys arrived, I knew some of them as being from Gol'fella's crew - he's a London hood, one of Adda's underlings. They probably tore my place apart before torching it. It took all night to put the fire out. It spread to other flats, at least one of my neighbours was killed and others hurt; everyone in the block is homeless now. I heard that the other source, a guy called Shawny, had it worse than me. The press says they found him, what was left of him, in a flat in Harlesden. That had been torched too."

"So," Niall said, "any idea where the leak is?"

"It's got to be high up. I wasn't really involved in the investigation, just had a walk-on part as a U/C. I'm guessing that the only people who would have known that there were two of us in play, and who we were, would be the SIO and the liaison person in Covert Policing. You know how tight this sort of thing is, Niall. I didn't know about the other source, don't know if he was an informant or another U/C, but apparently he was a recent arrival from Jamaica. It's possible that no one in the Met knew about him, not if he was a Jamaican police asset."

Morton sipped his coffee.

"I'm glad you made it through, Errol," he said, eventually. "I think you're right; there is a problem. But I don't think it's just a Met Police one. Was there any international involvement in the operation you were on? Apart from the Jamaican angle, I mean."

"You mean like a Joint Investigation Team?"

"Just that."

"It's possible, but no one would have told me, not necessarily. Why?"

"I think yours was a JIT. I know someone on the Spanish end of it. It could be that your job was the third one to be kyboshed on purpose. There was one on my patch, in Budapest. An Austrian undercover cop was blown to bits by a car bomb. My information is that a Hungarian organised crime group was behind it. The U/C was part of a Joint Investigation Team operation going after a load of heroin coming up through the Balkans. The targets were Bulgarians and Croatians mainly, with some input from a Hungarian gang to facilitate logistics. The gear was destined for Austria and on into Germany. Austria, Hungary and Germany were all represented on the JIT."

"Are you saying it was deliberate? Someone in the JIT gave up an undercover?" Errol asked.

"I don't know for definite," Niall replied, "but there's another one as well. I didn't know until yesterday. The UK Liaison Officer in Portugal, Laura, is an old friend. We had a drink last night and she told me that another JIT was disrupted on the Algarve. They were setting up a covert unit, interception and surveillance capabilities, to target the crims migrating to the Algarve from the Spanish Costas. It was at a very early stage, still laying the foundations. Seems the lead officer, a Dutch bloke, had arranged to meet another team member for dinner, all very short notice. While he was waiting for her at a restaurant in Praia da Rocha he was shot. It looks like a professional hit, two rounds close range to the head. The killer got away, no useful witnesses, not much forensic."

"And you think that was another betrayal? A deliberate act to blow a JIT operation?" Errol asked.

"Again, I don't know for sure, but it is a bit of a coincidence don't you think? Three Joint Investigation

Team operations disrupted, all in the space of a few weeks and all with fatalities. It's never happened before, not to my knowledge."

"How do Joint Investigation Teams work?" Errol asked.

"You need two or more EU member states to want to cooperate. There's a process to get the teams set up, they include law enforcement, prosecutors, examining magistrates if one or more of the states concerned have them, and anyone else who's needed. The JITs are coordinated and supported by Europol HQ, the Operations Directorate. Teams are set up for a specific purpose over a specific timeframe. The one in Portugal was a little unusual as it was a long-term thing, meant to run for years. Mostly, JITs are fairly quick in and out jobs intended to put international criminals away as efficiently as possible. They tend to work quite well."

"How could they be compromised?"

Niall considered his answer.

"I don't know. There are plenty of checks and balances built in. Of course, the chances of an operational blow-out are always there, and it does happen, as you well know. A deliberate leak? It's possible, I suppose, but the identities of human sources are kept very secret. Even the use of human sources is kept super tight. A source identity might be known to the Senior Investigating Officer from the country concerned, but it's not likely that the identity of a source from another participating country would be shared. No reason to. The deliberate compromise of source identities is almost unthinkable, but maybe a technical attack on Europol systems by some hostile actor could have happened."

"A hack?" Errol said. "A hack aimed at disrupting criminal investigations? Feasible, I guess, but why? Why would they bother?"

"I have no idea," Niall said. "I just don't want to contemplate another answer."

"That someone high-up in Joint Investigation Team coordination is bent?"

"It's one possibility. There must be others."

"Alright," Errol said, "so let's think about the others. You said that a team comprises prosecutors and examining magistrates? Would they know the identity of sources?"

"I guess so, but only in the Joint Investigation Team they are specifically working. They'd need to know, to ensure the integrity and admissibility of evidence."

"Could one of them be working across all three jobs that have been blown?"

"Looking at the three operations, there isn't a common denominator. The one you were involved in, which I think could have been a JIT, would have had British and probably Spanish input if it was a coke job, maybe another EU country as well, depending on who was involved and where any cargo was going to or through. I wouldn't know how a Jamaican source could be identified, it shouldn't be possible, not in theory anyway.

"The JIT in Budapest had Hungarian, Austrian and German members. The one in Portugal had more participants - Brits, French, Spanish, Dutch and Portuguese, but they are more on the intelligence side. So there's no clear common link that I can see."

"It looks like it's coming back to Europol then, as the coordinator, for the compromises in Hungary and Portugal," Errol said.

"It does, doesn't it?" Niall sighed. "More to the point, what are we going to do about you?"

"I was going to get round to that," Errol said. "As far as the Met is concerned, I'm AWOL. I haven't contacted them at all, apart from giving them the Harlesden address where the other source was found. My sister Sasha and Steven have called in sick. They're in a hotel in Sussex just now, but they can't stay there too long."

"I'll give you a key to my place. I've left it empty while I've been in Budapest, just popping back every couple of months. It's between Ruislip and Northwood - you can hide out there for a bit if you want. I'll call the neighbours to warn them that friends are staying - you won't want a visit from the cops. And when I'm done here I'll go to London to try to find out what your position is. Who was your handler in Covert Policing?"

Errol gave him a name.

"That's good, I know him, he's okay. Leave it with me. You got a number?"

"I've got a pay-as-you-go." Errol wrote a number on a napkin. "Emergencies only though."

"Understood," Niall said. "Look, I've got to get back. You go and get Sasha and Steven and wait for me to show up or get in touch, alright?"

"Thanks, mate," Errol said, genuinely relieved.

Niall Morton rose, paid the bill and walked off. He was preoccupied, anxious. What he hadn't shared with Errol was the fact that one of the very few people in the Europol command chain who would know who covert sources were and who therefore might possibly be responsible for the leaks was someone that both he and Errol knew quite well. They had both worked with her before, and he had spoken to her on the phone just a few hours ago.

Chapter 10

Errol Spelman arrived back at Gatwick later that afternoon. He felt that a weight had been lifted; he knew that his friend and former team partner would help him. He moved steadily and unobtrusively through the airport, concealed by the throng as far as possible, tagging on with groups of black travellers where he could. He took a train to Brighton, and from the station he called Steven on the hotel landline from a call box. He issued precise instructions and then walked to the Royal Pavilion to find a place to wait.

It took two hours for Steven to appear, walking in a determined way towards the café where Errol had said he would meet him. Errol approached him from behind, not speaking until he was just a few feet away.

"Steve!" he whispered urgently.

Steven almost jumped out of his skin.

"Jesus, you scared the shit out of me!"

"Did you get a car?" Errol asked.

"Yes, from one of the rental companies near the station. Sasha's waiting in it down the road."

"Good, let's go."

Steven led the way back to the hired car, an anonymous looking hatchback.

"Best I could afford," Steven said.

"It's fine," Errol reassured him.

"Where are we going?" Steven asked.

"North-west London, near Ruislip."

"You're not giving much away, are you?"

"Sorry Steve, I'm just in my zone. I'll explain everything when we're on the move."

Sasha was sitting in the back seat. She looked scared and confused. She didn't speak when her brother got in the car. Steven drove.

It was dark by the time they arrived at Niall Morton's house. It was a small Edwardian semi with no off-street parking. It would do nicely. Errol let them in. Steven carried their small bags, while Sasha brought in the carrier bag of provisions they had stopped for along the way.

"It belongs to a friend," Errol announced, "he said we could hang out here for a while, just until we have a better idea of what we're dealing with. Look, I'm really sorry to have brought this down on us, on you two. I didn't see this coming."

"Obviously," Sasha said. "We know you haven't done this on purpose," she reached out for his hand. "We'll get through this. I could do with a few days off work anyway," she smiled.

"Shall I get us a drink?" Steven suggested.

Errol set about preparing a meal for them all, Sasha sorted out the bedrooms. They hadn't yet discussed their situation, or asked Errol any questions, such as what happens next?

******

While Errol, Steven and Sasha sat it out in a borrowed house, a murder was happening in another part of suburban London. Adda's rage had overwhelmed his usual icy ruthlessness. He had maintained his liberty and status by being cold and calculating; often suspected of heinous crimes but rarely arrested and never convicted. Now, in a strange and alien country surrounded by people he barely knew and certainly didn't trust, he was having to take chances. He had decided to punish Gol'fella personally.

He had ordered Gol'fella to deal with the rat Shawny, and he had heard it happening on a phone. Gol'fella had given Shawny an appropriately hard time and it had taken a good twenty minutes to finish the job. Nevertheless, Adda was not satisfied. Gol'fella had let the other rat, the worst rat, slip through his slimy fingers and get away. Adda had sent Gol'fella's crew out looking for Tallboy, but he was nowhere to be found, not anywhere. Adda had ordered Tallboy's, or rather detective Errol Spelman's, crib to be ransacked and burnt out. It had been done. He had sent Gol'fella's boys to find out who else lived there, and what they did.

Adda's boys went to the ambulance station where the rat's batty boyfriend worked, he was not there. Adda's boys went to the IT company where the rat's sister worked. She also was not there. At home in Jamaica he could find anyone he wanted, anytime, but not here - and it infuriated him.

Gol'fella had failed. He had also made him, Adda, look foolish and bad. So now Gol'fella was tied to a tree in Epping Forest where his life was ending painfully and slowly. Adda was unmoved by Gol'fella's cries and tears. As he inflicted the final blow, the one that would eventually prove fatal - but not for a while yet - he let his face break into a hideous smile. He had sent the boys away but had made the youngest member of Gol'fella's crew watch what he did, and he punched him hard when the boy threw up and tried to look away.

"This what happen when me crew fail me, boy," he hissed at the terrified youth. "Now I done. You drive me now, and you don't tell no one never what you see jus' now. 'Nless you want it happen to you too."

Adda made calls on Gol'fella's phone, fixing his pickup at Rochester airfield. Adda was getting out, going home. The terrified youth drove cautiously, managing not to wet his pants until they got to Rochester and Adda had walked away to the small plane. Adda put on the ugly red coat and his silent travelling companion, who was waiting in the shadows, fell in behind him. The two men boarded the plane and a few moments later it climbed wearily into the air from the short grass runway.

It was early the following morning, as Adda's rented Gulfstream was approaching Jamaican airspace, that a dog-walker came across the grizzly sight in Epping Forest and called the police.

******

At Scotland Yard, the JIT operations room was closing down but others were opening up. The Met's undercover officer, Detective Sergeant Errol Spelman, was deemed missing in action. Efforts to trace him had produced no news or leads as to where he might be. That his home had been burnt out was obvious, but his whereabouts and those of his cohabitees - they had learned that two other people apart from DS Spelman lived at the address - remained unknown. The remains of an Afro-Caribbean man had been found in another burnt out property in Harlesden, and post-mortem examination was showing signs of torture and mutilation. A call had been made from a pay-as-you-go phone located somewhere near Croydon by an anonymous person, just after Spelman's address in Streatham was torched, stating that a serious assault was in progress at the Harlesden address.

The Homicide Team was talking to Covert Policing, thinking that the two matters might be linked. Now calls were coming in that another body, also of an Afro-Caribbean male and also showing signs of mutilation and torture, had been found tied to a tree in Epping Forest. Also linked? Almost certainly, especially as the latest body had been tentatively identified as being that of a known career criminal who went by the street name of Gol'fella.

The Senior Investigating Officer cursed quietly and hoped that this was the end of the matter, rather than the start of another bloody turf-war.

Chapter 11

Niall Morton was worried, very worried. His friend had had a close call, which was bad enough, but that close call had to be the result of an act of betrayal. He couldn't think of any other explanation. For the opposition to get to know the identity of an informant, a CHIS, was unfortunate but it did happen - often because of errors, bad practice or simple bad luck. For the true identity, including a home address, of an undercover officer deployed against a criminal target to become known could not, did not, happen, ever! It just couldn't, not unless someone either hacked into computer systems - several computer systems - or unless someone with access to that very sensitive information deliberately told the crims.

If Errol was the only victim of such a gross betrayal it would be serious enough, but Niall Morton was starting to suspect, to fear, that Errol was not the only one. Furthermore, the Joint Investigation Team operations that had been blown in recent months, and which, in his opinion, had also been deliberately compromised, only had one common link that he knew of with the case that Errol was working on. And that link was Europol.

Morton thought about his next steps, thought long and hard for several worried days. He could think of only one person who could help unravel the mystery, someone at the heart of Europol. Someone in a position to both solve the problem and also *be* the problem. One of the very small number of people in Europol who would know, or be able to find out, the real names of

Covert Human Intelligence Sources and undercover agents in play in Joint Investigation Team operations.

The conference Niall had been attending drew to its wordy close. He cried off the final end-of-conference party, claiming to have a migraine coming on, and he spent a long sleepless night alone in his hotel room. By morning he had made up his mind. He would have to take a huge risk.

Later that morning, Niall Morton took a flight to Heathrow and rented a car. He drove the short distance to his own house in Northwood. The curtains were drawn; the house was quiet. There was no sign of movement. He used his own key to open the front door cautiously. Inside it was gloomy, no natural light.

Niall suddenly felt cold pressure on his neck; a long blade was pressing down on his carotid artery.

"Jesus, bro," Errol panted, lowering the knife, "you scared me there!"

"Likewise," Niall said, "what are you doing sitting in the dark like that?"

"Not much else to do round here, is there? Sometimes we sit in the dark, sometimes we sit in the light. Living the dream, mate. Not that I'm complaining, we do appreciate this."

"Let's have a coffee; we need a chat," Niall said.

They found Sasha and Steven in the small kitchen. Errol did the introductions and shooed them out. He made coffee and waited for Niall to speak.

Niall summarised his thoughts while Errol sat in silence.

"So," Niall concluded, "I'm thinking the problem has to be in a very small part of Europol. I had a quiet chat with a mate of mine in Covert Policing in the Met during the week. He doesn't think anyone in the Met was aware that there was a Jamaican source, either CHIS or a U/C, in the job you were on. Someone on the Met could have compromised you, but not the Jamaican guy. That had to have come from somewhere else, and Europol is the only common denominator in your case and the others I'm concerned about."

"So what are you thinking?" Errol asked warily.

"Julia. Julia Kelso. She's Europol these days, and she's coordinating Joint Investigation Teams. It's possible that she's the leak, but we know her, don't we?"

"We do," Errol agreed, "but do we know her well enough?"

"That, as they say, is the million-dollar question," Niall replied. "I reckon there's only one way to find out if she's straight or bent. You up for it?"

"I'll get my coat," Errol sighed.

******

They drove in the rental car to The Hague, Errol concealing himself while they checked in for the Shuttle through the Channel Tunnel. There were no issues. On the outskirts of the city, Niall pulled over. He took out his mobile and scrolled through his contacts. He called a number.

"Kelso," he heard.

"Julia? It's me. Niall Morton. How are you?"

"Niall? Are you still here? I thought all you guys had gone home after the conference. I was surprised that you didn't call me."

"Sorry, Julia, you know how these things are, always a bit manic. Do you have time for a chat? Somewhere quiet, away from the office?"

"Are you still in The Hague, then?" she asked.

"Just for a while. Can we talk? It's important."

"Alright," she said, sensing his seriousness. "Come round to mine this evening. I'll be home around six. I'll text you the address."

"Thanks Julia, I appreciate it. See you later."

A few seconds later his phone beeped and an address appeared in his messages. They drove around and found her place, a non-descript house in a quiet residential street. They parked up and waited, keeping watch in silence. They didn't see anyone coming or going, except a tall, youngish woman wrapped up against the chill wind who turned up pushing a baby buggy. The woman let herself in with a key.

"Was that Mel Dunn?" Errol asked.

"Don't know mate. I haven't seen her in years. Maybe Julia only has a flat here."

Just before six they saw Julia Kelso. She was also well wrapped up but riding a sit-up-and-beg bicycle. She looked serious. They gave her a few minutes.

"Let me go first," Niall said, "if everything's cool I'll give you a wave, okay?"

Errol agreed.

Julia opened the door. She had changed and was now in jeans and slippers.

"It's been a long time Niall, how have you been?" she smiled at him.

"I'm fine, Julia. You're looking well, is this your place?"

"Just renting it while I'm here. Mel's here too, we sort of share it."

"So it was her, then."

"What?"

"We arrived a while ago, before you got home. We saw someone pushing a pram. That must have been Mel."

"We? Who's we, Niall? Have you been plotting me up?"

"Nothing like that, Julia. We just found it a bit quicker than we'd expected and we were waiting for you. I'll get him in."

Niall opened the door and waved. A moment later Errol appeared on the doorstep.

"Errol!" Julia looked taken aback. "I'd heard something terrible had happened to you. Thank God you're alright! Are Sasha and Steven okay?"

"That's what we want to talk to you about, Julia," Errol said, trying to stay calm.

Chapter 12

Julia Kelso sat very still while Niall Morton spoke. There was no way she could fully conceal the tension she felt as his words tumbled on logically and relentlessly. He finished speaking. Julia looked at him quizzically. She said nothing.

"You can see, can't you Julia," Morton said, "that the 'problem', for want of a better word, must be inside your organisation, inside Europol?"

"And that it could be me? Is that what you're not quite saying?"

He nodded.

"Well, if what you're saying is the correct interpretation of events, I'd say you're right. It could be me. I could be a traitor, selling out cops and informants with no regard to what happens to them. But if you really thought that was likely, you wouldn't be here, and you wouldn't have brought Errol with you, would you? So, what do you want me to do?" Julia had spoken calmly, but her fists were clenched.

Errol spoke for the first time.

"We want you to stop it. Find out what's happening and why, and then stop it. And make sure it can't happen again. Can you do that?"

She looked at him. She hadn't seen a man that angry for a very long time. She thought for a moment.

"Frankly, I don't know. If there is a way, and if I can do it, I will. Now, I'm going to call Mel in. I want you to start all over - tell me again with her listening too."

Julia called out; Mel emerged from a doorway off the kitchen where they were seated. She looked surprised to see them.

"We don't get many visitors, Errol," Mel said, "who's your friend?"

"He's Niall Morton, Mel," Julia interjected, "you'll remember the name but I don't think you've met before. Niall is currently the UK Liaison Officer in Budapest. You remember Errol, of course. Can you spare us some time?"

"As long as the little monster stays asleep, fine. I'll go and get the monitor."

Mel was back a minute or two later with a small wireless speaker. Sounds of a baby sleeping were barely audible. Mel placed it on the kitchen table and took a seat. Julia nodded at Morton, who started.

"I believe, and so does Errol, that there is a well-placed traitor in Europol who is giving criminal targets key information about covert investigations and covert sources, human sources, inside criminal organisations."

"Why would they do that?" Mel asked.

"In the past few weeks," Niall continued without answering her, "there have been at least three operations that have been compromised, resulting in the death of three informants or undercover officers. Errol here narrowly avoided becoming the fourth. That number doesn't include other criminals or innocent bystanders who have also died.

"What links the three jobs is that they were all Joint Investigation Team cases, multi-national operations coordinated by Europol."

"But that's your job, Jake," Mel said.

"I know. That's why the guys are here," Julia said.

"So, you're saying there's some sort of high-up corruption involving people who must be very senior in law-enforcement? Isn't this where we came in, Jake?"

"What do you mean, Mel?" Morton asked.

"It's a long story, and if I told you you wouldn't believe me anyway," Mel replied. "Carry on."

For the next hour Niall spoke evenly about the three cases, reciting what he had found out about each one. Mel listened intently, making occasional notes on a sheet of paper and asking questions from time to time. When Niall had finished, Julia turned to Mel.

"Well, what do you think?" she asked.

"Circumstantial, but not enough. Not enough to justify an analytical premise, I mean. We need more to go on," Mel said.

"You know what I think of coincidences," Julia responded.

"That doesn't mean they don't happen sometimes, though, does it?" Mel said. "I need to look at more Joint Investigation Team cases, at least half a dozen. Can that be done, Jake?" Mel asked.

"I don't know, but I doubt it. JITs are like the crown jewels. If you worked for me and had the correct clearances you could get to see what I can, and I can access just about everything, as far as I know."

"Who else can?" Mel asked bluntly.

"Not many. The boss, the chief legal rep for JITs, the governance board - but they'd have to ask specifically, case by case. JIT data is kept very securely on the Europol Information System, for obvious reasons. So either it *is* me or the boss or the lawyer, or something's gone wrong. How do we find out, Mel?"

"I'm glad you're not ruling yourself out, and I know what you're saying. You mean that you might have been nobbled in some way and you are leaking sensitive information unknowingly. We can talk that through later."

"I think we need a drink," Julia said.

******

Niall Morton and Errol Spelman left Julia Kelso's house before ten. Jake and Mel stayed up a while longer after checking on Freddie, who was sound asleep for a nice change.

"Penny for your thoughts, Jake," Mel said.

"I'm scared, Mel. I've been trying to think of some explanation, some way to say Niall's wrong. Short of some miraculously evil twist of fate, there isn't one that I can think of. We know that Errol was named by someone who knew both his cover identity and his real one, including his home address. That could conceivably have come from inside the Met. As for the other source, the Jamaican guy, I don't think the Met even knew about him, and if that's the case they couldn't have exposed him to Adda.

"There aren't any common links between the Austrian case and the Portuguese one, except Europol HQ. Each case on its own could have had a leak or the teams could have made a mistake. I don't think mistakes would have such extreme consequences. It's possible that there were corrupt leaks somewhere along the line in each one, but why would there be these extreme consequences? Professional criminals understand risks and they tend not to take unnecessary ones. Car bombings, arson and assassinations seem to me to be unnecessary risks, unless the professional criminals had been sold a tale that made the victims seem much more dangerous to them and their businesses than they really were. The Austrian and the Portuguese operations were both at an early stage, far too soon to present a major threat to the targets. I'm not sure about Errol's case, but my impression from the briefings I sat through was that it was going to be a long job, nowhere near ready to do any damage to Adda and his crew."

"So," Mel said, "if it does come down to coordinated corrupt leakage in Europol, the question has to be why, doesn't it?"

"It is, it really is. Will you help me, Mel?"

"You know I will, if I can," Mel said.

They sat in silence, sipping their drinks. The baby monitor started to squawk.

Chapter 13

Several hundred kilometres away from Julia's house, in a small and exclusive restaurant beside an Italian lake, two people, a couple, were sipping *digestifs* after a wonderful dinner. The man was speaking softly in a monotone, his facial expression blank.

"So, do you think the project is going well?" he asked.

"We've made a good start, Guido," the woman, Isabelle, said, "but it is too early to start celebrating. We have a lot to do, not just with Europol but with other bodies too."

"I agree, Isabelle," Guido concurred, "how is the media campaign looking?"

"It needs to be subtle," Isabelle responded, "I have found several journalists who have good reputations and who may be sympathetic to our aims. I will feed them snippets as and when I think fit, so the ridicule can start slowly. It will take time, undoubtedly, but it won't look like propaganda. Leave it to me."

"Good," Guido said. "What is next?"

"A few more Europol disasters," she said, "maybe not as spectacular as the ones we've engineered to date. More ridiculous than tragic, I think."

"I would prefer a few more tragedies," Guido interjected, "two or three more, just to establish a clear pattern of incompetence. Three could be excused as accidental or just bad luck, six or seven starts to look like systemic failure. Get the Frenchman working on it."

"I will, of course, I will see him again soon," she answered.

"When?"

"I'll be seeing Antoine in the next few days, by the weekend at the latest. I'll call him later; he always comes running."

"Don't get too attached to him," Guido warned.

"I won't."

"How much do you think he understands?" Guido asked.

"As much as he wishes to believe," Isabelle replied, "he is an idealist, a romantic, and when he is with me he is in heaven."

"We are pragmatists, are we not?" Guido said. "We have affairs to run, we need to minimise obstruction and interference."

"Scrutiny, you mean?" Isabelle asked.

"That too, of course. And when we are done, we can return to business as usual, with healthy competitors."

"To healthy competition," Isabelle raised her glass.

Guido did the same and they drank a toast. He signalled for the check; he would pay, as always.

******

In The Hague, Jeroen Faber made his way home after another evening at the office. He was still passionately excited about the project that Antoine had proposed. Holland, the Netherlands, should never have become so involved in the web of international bureaucracy that had undermined its independence so completely. His once proud nation reduced to a laughingstock with a comedy language and a reputation for laxity. He hated having to go to Amsterdam these days, having to see the stoned tourists and lecherous perverts prowling the *Nieuwmarkt*. He had said as much to Antoine when they happened to meet at a security conference in Paris, where he lived. Antoine was charming and he seemed to enjoy Jeroen's company. They had had a few drinks in the evening and Antoine had sought him out at coffee breaks during the conference then next day.

Antoine had asked him where he worked and why he was at the conference. Jeroen had told him. He was the deputy head of Europol's internal security department, responsible for physical security, access control and staff badging. He had explained that every member of staff had to have a unique badge which gave them access to parts of the Europol estate that they were allowed in, and also gave them access to computers on the Europol information system. All carefully controlled and segregated, to make sure there was no improper use and no unauthorised access to sensitive information.

Antoine and Jeroen had exchanged phone numbers at the end of the conference and they had gone their separate ways. Some weeks later, Antoine had called him. He was in The Hague on business; could they meet for a coffee? And so, over time, they had become friends. As their mutual confidence grew, Antoine started to share his own sentiments. Like Jeroen, he did not like what had been happening to his country. The erosion of independence, of sovereignty, was a humiliation. The ruling hand of Brussels was poking its fingers in places where they did not belong, stopping Frenchmen going about their business and enjoying their lives. The French should concern themselves with France; Europe should stick to its origins as a useful trade facilitator and preventer of conflict. Jeroen had to agree.

Some months later, Antoine had introduced Jeroen to Guido and Isabelle; he said they were involved in a special project but did not expand on it. Isabelle was French, like Antoine, but while he was Parisian through and through she was from Alsace in the east. She spoke both French and German as mother tongues, as well as fluent Italian and English. Guido was Italian, from the industrial north. The four of them had met over a brief lunch in The Hague, but he hadn't seen them since.

Even now, Jeroen was thrilled that Antoine had asked him to join the project. He was not used to being courted, or even included. Their aim was not to destroy the EU, but to undermine confidence in its institutions and capabilities so that, in due course, its burgeoning powers would be reduced. In short, they wanted to put Europe back in its subservient box. And he could help. In truth, Jeroen would have helped anyone who took the trouble to ask him, almost regardless of the task.

Antoine had even explained it. As any politician in a democracy knows, the most wounding assault is ridicule. No one could respect a person they always laughed at. No one could respect a person who had a reputation for incompetence. The project was aimed at making EU institutions seem incompetent and ridiculous. And although Jeroen relied on one such institution for his livelihood, he was more than happy to help where he could.

Jeroen let himself into the modest apartment where he lived alone. He prepared for bed and turned his thoughts to Julia Kelso, the senior Europol officer he had chosen to help him, not that she knew it of course. He had seen her a few times in the gym at the office. She was very attractive and, as far as he knew from surreptitiously accessing her personal file, single and unattached. He knew her address but had not yet summoned up the courage to go there or to approach her in any way. He had a feeling that she might be sympathetic to his cause. She was a Scot, after all, and everyone knew about the independent nature of the Scots. Also, she didn't seem to fit the Europol mould - she seemed to be a loner. Not that she was unfriendly or antisocial, she had a way with people. She just didn't seem to be like the other high-flyers who came and went, the senior law-enforcement officers from member states who revolved through the upper posts of Europe's FBI.

He went to sleep dreaming of Julia Kelso in her Lycra running shorts and loose polo shirt as she pounded a treadmill across the gym from him. Had she really smiled at him, or had he just imagined it?

Chapter 14

Jeroen spent the following evening at his desk again, working late into the night. He looked at Julia Kelso's diary to see when she would next be away somewhere, or when she was likely to be in the gym again. Then he went back to looking for her on the internet. He found lots of mentions of her in media reports, but next to nothing about her private life. One or two snippets from college friends' scant social media, but nothing substantial. She was a very private person.

Julia was due to travel to Brussels in two days for a meeting that required an overnight stay. Jeroen made the most of it. On the day, once he knew she had gone and having swiped her back into the building with the cloned badge he had made, he let himself into her room and closed the door behind him. Just to be safe, he locked it from the inside. Then he started her computer. He used the cloned badge to log on to the system as her. He spent an uninterrupted hour going through ongoing Joint Investigation Team operations, finding two that were suitable and which involved the use of undercover officers or informants. He copied the notes he needed onto a memory stick he had with him before closing her machine down and letting himself out of her room. He hadn't left a trace that anyone else could find. He swiped Julia Kelso back out of the building before retreating to his lair, buried deep at the back of the lower floor, not far from the boiler house and the janitors' rest room.

******

In Vienna, among the shabby market stalls and tired kebab shops south of the main train station, Efe Öztürk looked once more at the screen on his phone. There was a simple text message from a number he didn't know. He read it again, then went to see his uncle.

"This appeared on my phone, *amca*, I don't know where it came from or why it came to me. What does it mean?" he asked his uncle, a feared and fearsome man.

"It is a sign, Efe," his uncle said, "we should take it seriously. If it is correct, we have a spy in our camp - someone we thought we could trust. Bring Mehmet to me, take your brothers with you."

The message had said simply that Mehmet, a distant cousin and very much part of the family organisation, was working for the Austrian police and was providing information on the family operation running Afghan heroin up to Frankfurt and Berlin. The uncle considered this at length. There were indications in the short message that worried him. The mention of Frankfurt and Berlin was one such indicator - almost nobody in the organisation knew of the recently established German connection. The message had to mean that this connection was now known to the police. Mehmet had questions to answer.

******

Urgent calls had been made between the Joint Investigation Team leader in Vienna and his colleagues in Berlin, Frankfurt and The Hague. The team's main intelligence source, a Turk named Mehmet, had failed to make two meetings and could not be contacted. Mehmet had been turned by the Austrian police and had been promised protection and anonymity once the notorious and elusive Öztürk crime family had been put out of business. Mehmet's had been the first successful agent recruitment by any agency into the organisation, which had a justifiable reputation for both intolerance of betrayal and extreme violence. The Austrians were very concerned for Mehmet's welfare. Discreet observation was kept at his home, a flat he shared with other Öztürk family members or workers, but there had been no sightings. All seemed calm at the address.

Three days later, the battered and disfigured body of the informant Mehmet was pulled from the Danube. The Austrian police rounded up the usual Öztürk suspects but found they all had unshakeable alibis for every moment that Mehmet had been missing. They were all eventually released.

The Öztürk family regrouped and carried on as normal while the Joint Investigation Team pored over the files looking for anything that could have gone wrong and which could have compromised the late Mehmet. They found nothing and prepared a report for Europol HQ.

******

Inspector Henri Jeanson of the Police Judiciaire, the PJ, was enjoying his few days off. He had been in Italy for the past two weeks, committed all day every day to the case. The double life would have floored most people, but he was a natural. He inhabited his false identity like a second skin; he was at home being undercover.

It was warm and sunny on the Cote d'Azur, a perfect day. He had just dropped the twins off at the swimming club and was on his way now to the huge Auchan hypermarket near Toulon to do the monthly shop. All was well.

He pulled into the sprawling car park and found a shady space for his four-year-old Peugeot. After the shopping he paused for a coffee inside the supermarket, watching the world go by and just being normal for a while. He pushed the cart back to his car and in an unhurried fashion loaded his purchases. He retrieved his one Euro coin and sauntered back to the car. By force of habit he looked around and saw nothing to give him any cause for concern.

As he headed for the autoroute to make his way back towards his home above Le Ciotat he began to feel uneasy. A car, a BMW, had been behind him for two or three kilometres. He slowed to allow it to pass. It slowed as well and maintained its distance. Jeanson accelerated, so did the BMW. What Jeanson was less aware of was the dark Mercedes van in front of him. He was focussed entirely on the BMW. The traffic had thinned out. Suddenly the BMW braked and fell back. The rear doors of the Mercedes van opened and two machine guns sprayed Jeanson's car with dozens of rounds. He was hit several times in the chest and head, and he would have died almost instantly. His car veered off the autoroute and rolled over on the hard shoulder. The BMW and the Mercedes van both sped off.

The French police found both vehicles burned out an hour later. There had been no witnesses to the shooting. The murder investigation found out that both vehicles used to ambush Inspector Jeanson had been stolen some days earlier in Italy, in fact from a car park in Genoa. The investigators soon concluded that Inspector Jeanson, who had worked in the organised crime division of the PJ, had been assassinated in a professional hit.

The leader of the Joint Investigation Team that Jeanson had been working for launched an investigation into his own case, desperately trying to find out what had gone so badly wrong. He had been certain that Jeanson's cover had been sound, that there were no flaws or leaks in his team. How had this happened, assuming it was connected with Jeanson's role on the Joint Investigation Team as opposed to anything else he might have done in the past?

After a week of searching, the team leader could find no explanation, no reason. He started to prepare the report for Europol HQ.

Chapter 15

Julia Kelso groaned inwardly as she read her morning emails. Two conference calls had been set up for later that morning so that details of the latest Joint Investigation Team fatalities could be examined at length. In her short time at Europol she had found the JITs to be the slickest and safest operations carried out by law enforcement anywhere. They worked and worked well. Professional criminals who had slipped through the fingers of national police services were now languishing in often foreign jails, having been brought down by collaboration and use of the most applicable laws in whatever country they had been banged up in.

As far as she knew there had been no major compromises - occasional operational slips and bumps, naturally, but nothing like what had happened in the last few weeks. Five JIT operations had been aborted because agents - informants or undercover officers - had been exposed and killed. Julia was grateful that Errol Spelman, a man she liked and respected, had managed to survive. The implications of the five failures were not lost on her.

The calls had ended. They had been sombre and subdued, dwelling on the serial tragedies that were now impacting families and loved ones across Europe. They had the facts, what had happened, when and where. The 'why' and how' were missing. Especially the 'how'. Julia had an idea of the 'how', but she had no plans to share it at the moment, not until she had done some checking of her own. Back in her room, Julia made a call.

"Mel, it's Jake. I need you to come to the office, soon as you can," she said briskly.

"What about screaming Lord Such? He's having a bit of a meltdown - didn't like the lunch I gave him, apparently. Not that I blame him, it looked disgusting," Mel replied.

"Can you park him somewhere, just for the afternoon?"

"He's a baby, Jake, not a bicycle. I'll have to bring him with me - once he's settled a bit and stopped howling. Why do you need me, anyway?"

"I'll tell you when you get here, there's serious stuff going on," Jake said.

"Serious stuff, like we spoke about after Niall and Errol came to see you?"

"Yes, that stuff. There's more. Have the reception call me when you arrive, I'll have to sign you in."

"Okay. See you in a while." Mel cut the call.

She looked at little Freddie. Seemingly, the sound of his mother talking had calmed him to the point of sedation and he had nodded off in his highchair. She couldn't help smiling.

Mel pushed Freddie in his buggy and strolled to Europol HQ. She didn't like the building; underneath a few strokes of colour it was a dark place, grey stone, seemingly in perpetual shadow. Its history was dark and brooding too. At one time it had been a base for commanders of the occupying German forces and, reputedly, the Gestapo. Kelso had told her that Europol would be moving to a new building sometime soon. It had to be an improvement.

Julia came to the reception area to sign Mel in.

"There is a crèche, apparently, but it's for employees only," Jake said, "so you'd better come and work for me. At least you'd get some peace and quiet."

"Don't tempt me, Kelso," Mel said.

"Why not? I could really use your help here."

They rode up in the elevator. In her room there was just about enough space to put the buggy and Freddie in a corner while Jake and Mel sat at her small meeting table. Julia went through the latest two killings, sticking to the bare bones and suppressing her feelings of anger and frustration.

"So," Mel said when Jake had finished, "it looks like there are several small, coincidental leaks or cock ups, or one monumental one, probably here."

"I had worked that out, Mel," Jake said, "I need you to help me find out which it is. Where do we start?"

"I'll need to see all the case files, the electronic ones and any paper ones that are kept here."

"I'll have to sign you up as a consultant or something and get you access to the information system. There aren't any paper records here, not anymore, everything's digital. It might take a few days, but I can log in and let you make a start using my badge."

"Let's not, Jake," Mel said, "if we do that it could screw up any potential audit trail if there is a problem with the system."

"Of course, you're right. I was just a bit overkeen to make a start. Let's get the admin started."

Julia called HR and told them she needed to take on a consultant on a short-term contract. Easy, HR said. They took Mel's details and started filling in the form. They suggested that Julia speak to the director of personnel, who didn't like surprises but was usually very helpful if he had advance notice. Julia took the hint.

A short while later Julia, Mel and Freddie were in the office of the director of personnel. It was a tight fit, his room being no larger than Julia's. Julia explained that she needed some specialist analytical help and some advice to improve the security of Joint Investigation Teams. It wasn't something, in Julia's opinion, that existing Europol resources had time to take on. The director nodded approvingly and asked Mel some fairly banal questions.

"Thank you, Julia," he said, "for discussing this with me first. I am supportive and will sign it off as soon as the request to take on Ms Dunn as a short-term consultant arrives. You should ask Jeroen Faber in corporate security to start the badging and IT access process. It will save time."

Julia called Faber from her office and made an appointment for Mel to be processed and issued with a badge and a user identity the following morning.

Mel departed soon afterwards, saying she was taking Freddie to the park on the way home. She could stop and get something in if Jake wanted a meal at home, and a few drinks, just like old times.

Jake did. It would be good to have something at least a bit like old times.

Chapter 16

Jeroen Faber dealt with Mel's badge himself, taking her photograph and printing it onto the badge with its embedded chip. Mel didn't see what he was doing behind the printer, but it seemed to be taking quite a long time.

"Sorry," Jeroen said, "sometimes it's a bit slow if it hasn't had time to warm up properly. All done now."

Jeroen handed Mel the badge and a new lanyard.

"Wear it at all times while you're in the building, but not outside. You will need it to access the information system - you can use any terminal here or in one of the outstations. You'll need to enter your user i/d and your PIN, and the badge must be inserted in the reader. As soon as it's removed, your access will be cut off and you may lose anything you haven't saved on your own drive back here at HQ. I suggest you save anything you are doing frequently - until it's saved there is no back up. Any questions?"

"No, thank you. It's all very clear," Mel said.

"Good. I will take you to the crèche and then to Ms Kelso's room, then." Jeroen offered.

Mel thought it unnecessary but said nothing. Little Freddie, still asleep in his buggy, was deposited with the childminders while Mel gave them detailed instructions about his food, nappies, nap times and so on. They took her mobile number and Jake's extension and said they'd call if there were any issues. The crèche would close at five in the afternoon, so could she be sure to collect Freddie by then?

Jeroen watched her swipe in through the turnstile and he followed her through. He took her to the elevator and they rode up in silence. Jeroen knocked on Julia's door and waited. She called out. Inside the room he seemed nervous. He didn't take his eyes off Julia for a second. After a few moments of awkward conversation Jeroen left the room.

"He's a bit smitten, Jake," Mel commented, "is there something you're not telling me?"

"I don't know what you mean," Jake replied, "I've seen him around the building but I don't think I've ever actually spoken to him before now."

"You'd better keep an eye on him, in case he starts following you around. Does he do all the badges himself?"

"I don't know," Julia said, "I think he did mine but I don't really remember. Why?"

"Don't know, he did mine and it seemed to take a while. They had a similar set up at NCIS as was - it was a lot quicker. Faber said it was because the machine hadn't warmed up properly. Shall we make a start?"

Mel logged on to the machine on Julia's desk, while Julia herself made do with a laptop on a small table.

"I've got meetings for most of the morning," Julia said, "so make yourself comfortable. The cafeteria is on the fourth floor - avoid the coffee, it's cold and weak."

"Thanks for the warning."

Mel scanned the filing system - she had the same access rights as Julia - and for twenty minutes or so she asked questions about operation names, Europol acronyms, where to find the stuff about informants and so on. When she went quiet and started to concentrate Julia left and went about her business. By lunchtime, Mel had filled half her notebook with pages of diagrams and scribbles.

As the light began to fade Julia returned. Mel paused and stretched. She looked at her watch.

"Jesus, it's nearly five! Got to go," Mel said, "can we talk at home later?"

"I'll be in the gym for an hour, so see you around seven?"

Mel didn't answer as she rushed off for the lift. She had no idea what happened if one of the charges wasn't picked up from the crèche in time, and she didn't want to find out.

By the time Julia arrived home, Freddie had been fed, bathed, and put to bed. He had enjoyed his day with complete strangers, it seemed, which Mel found slightly disappointing.

"He didn't cry or miss me at all, Jake," Mel complained, "they said he's lovely and well-behaved, welcome any time. Mercenary little toad that he is."

"Stop being a mum and act like a grown-up, Dunn," Jake said. "Now, what did you find out?"

"Only the obvious, which is that there are no connections between the operations that have been compromised, apart from Europol HQ. I took a look at a few other JIT cases, ones that have been concluded, and on the face of it nothing has been done any differently to the ones that we're interested in. I can't look back at the records for cases before you came to Europol, so I don't know if anything went wrong before."

"I can find out tomorrow," Jake said, "what else?"

"There are three new operations lined up, ones that haven't been signed off yet but which seem about ready to go. All JITs with Covert Human Intelligence Sources. Have you seen them?"

"Yes, I'll be meeting with the team leaders in the next week or two for final briefings. I've been through them all and sent them back for additional information or processes. I'll be signing them off if everything's been done."

"I think you should treat these as high-risk, Jake. Can you put covert markers on all the case files?"

"How do you mean?"

"Find some way to get yourself a heads-up if someone looks at the files when they shouldn't, without making a noise about it."

"You think someone's been accessing the files without authority?"

"Not necessarily without authority, just for the wrong reasons or without taking the right care. I think that's a possible cause of the compromises."

"Not the only possible cause?"

"No," Mel said, "the other possible cause is a deliberate act. Someone purposefully telling the opposition about these cases, identifying the covert sources, people, to the enemy. I'd prefer it to be accidental or even negligent rather than deliberate, but for now I think it could go either way."

"Corporate Governance have a covert flagging system, only them. I'll speak to them tomorrow. Anything else?"

"Just one small thing," Mel said.

"What's that?"

"When I said the only connection between all of the compromised operations is Europol HQ, I meant something more specific. I meant you, Jake. You are the only connection between all the compromised jobs."

"You think I did it?" Jake started to protest.

"God, no!" Mel said, "I know you didn't do it; you're not bent or careless. I know you well enough to be sure of that. Besides, I can prove someone else has been in your files."

"How?"

"There's a keystroke out of place in one of the documents I looked at. I noticed it because there aren't that many typos. You can hardly see it, just a forward slash in the wrong place - easy to do if you're using buttons to scroll through a document. The programme Europol has for shared documents is the same as the old NCIS one. It logs all the changes made in every document, with date and time, and the user i/d of the person logged in at the time and what machine they were using. That way all changes can be tracked for audit purposes. This one keystroke was made while you were shown as being logged on as the user on your machine in your office. At the time, you were with me at the post-natal clinic, we took Freddie there when we thought he was getting sick that day. You drove us and came in with me. You can't have been logged in on your desktop in your office making typing errors while you were sitting with me in a clinic on the other side of town holding a baby that had just thrown up all over you, could you?"

"So someone was using my log-in. That's not supposed to be possible."

"Either that, or there are two of you. And I don't think that's very likely. There couldn't be two Jake Kelsos."

"What now?" Jake asked.

"First of all, I need to check all current and new operation files very carefully - I can do that tomorrow. I need to look for any signs of meddling. While I'm doing that, you need to go to the shops and get a couple of those miniature cameras that Alf was so fond of. Get your office videoed up. You can't take this through Europol channels, not yet. If there is someone interfering with your files, it has to be an insider. Until we know who that is, we can't talk to anyone about this."

"I'm with you, Mel," Jake said. "I'm just as interested in the why as the who. Why is this happening? What's behind it?"

"We can find out, Jake, we'll get there."

"I wish Alf was here," Jake said.

"Well he isn't," Mel said, but not harshly. "We have to do this ourselves. But we can use what we've learnt from him, the way he does things - did things. Now, I'm going to have a shower. I think Freddie's shoved some of his dinner in my ear."

Chapter 17

Two days later they sat in Jake's office watching the downloaded footage from the new miniature cameras that she had concealed to cover the door and her desk. The cameras were working but there was nothing to see.

"I've been looking at the files," Mel was speaking, "and I've found a few more anomalies. Can you open your appointments?"

Mel produced a list of dates and times. Jake compared them with her diary entries.

"I've been away or in meetings every time one of these 'anomalies' happened," Jake said, "so whoever it is has access to my appointments diary as well as my computer account!"

"Looks like it," Mel said.

"So let's put a few new dates in, shall we?"

Jake made up a few diary entries and saved them.

"What have you found in the pending operations, Mel?"

"Well, whoever it is, they've had a look at all of them. Going on your diary dates, every case has been accessed using your log-in while you've been somewhere else. I haven't found anything specific, but I'd suggest it's time to make a few changes."

"I assume you mean to source identities and specific dates, times and places. I'll do a printout of the real data first. Of course, there's no guarantee that whoever it is hasn't already got the data."

"True, but the log-in times suggest that they were just having a quick look. On the compromised operations, the access was for much longer periods."

"They were making notes, extracting detailed information, maybe even copying documents," Jake was thinking out loud.

"I'd say. There's quite a gap between the first three, including Errol's job, and the most recent two. It looks to me like whoever has access is under orders, they're told when to extract information. I think whoever gives the orders is the one in contact with the targets, the one who's passing information about sources."

"The person who knows the 'why'," Jake said, "that's who I want to talk to."

******

They took Freddie to the Madurodam theme park the next morning. Julia's diary showed that she was out of the office in meetings until the afternoon. Madurodam didn't interest Freddie at all - it was a compact version of the Netherlands, a model country, complete with towns and highways and airports. It showed the history of the country, outlining its heritage as a colonial power with far-reaching influence on the world stage. Freddie slept through most of it but liked the waffles.

That afternoon, having deposited Freddie in the crèche, Julia and Mel looked at the footage in her office. At lunchtime, when most offices were empty, Julia's door had opened. They weren't overly surprised to see Jeroen Faber enter and take a seat at Julia's desk. They saw him insert a badge in the reader and start the computer. He put a thumb drive in a USB port and started opening files. Faber spent a full hour at Julia's desk. When he was done, he withdrew the memory stick and closed down her machine. He tried to open the desk drawers, which Julia had made a point of locking. Faber stood, clearly frustrated. They watched him pick up Julia's gym bag and open it. They saw him fondling her running shorts, touching her polo shirt. Julia wanted to retch. They watched him leave the room, carefully closing the door behind him.

Mel let out a breath.

"So that's the first 'who', creepy sod," she said. "What now?"

"Leave that with me," Julia said. "See if you can find out what he was looking at precisely."

It took Mel just a few minutes to find out.

"He was looking at one of the future operations, the human trafficking one involving Greece, Italy and France. The Greeks have a source inside the target group - you changed the name and other details."

"That one is due for approval this week," Julia said, "I'll stall it for another week. We need some people, people we know and trust, and fast."

"Is Niall Morton around?" Mel asked.

"I'll call him."

Morton answered his mobile immediately.

"Niall, it's Julia, where are you?"

"Just about to head back to Budapest, I was held back to talk through some Balkan issues."

"You're still in Holland?"

"Just up the road, why?"

"Can you get Errol over? I need some back-up. I think we've got a lead on the people who tried to take him out. Call me back when you've spoken to him."

"Sure, give me ten minutes."

Thirty minutes later Julia, Mel and Niall Morton were sitting at the kitchen table in Julia's house.

"We've found that there's someone inside Europol who's been taking an undue interest in Joint Investigation Teams. It looks like he's extracting information about sources, undercovers as well as informants, and passing it to someone else. That information gets into the hands of the targets, the criminal organisations.

"The person, and I'll tell you about him in a minute," Julia said, "uses my log-on details and my computer while I'm out of the office. He was there this lunchtime looking at a JIT in the planning. We need to know what he's going to do with information he took away. It was on a memory stick."

"You can't go official with this?" Morton asked.

"Not until I'm sure there's no one else in the Europol chain of command involved."

"Okay, so you want me and Errol to follow this guy around, do some digging?"

"In one, Niall." Julia said.

"Okay, Errol's on his way, he'll be here by this evening. Who's the target?"

"His name is Jeroen Faber, he's deputy head of internal security here. It sounds grander than it is, he's in charge of physical security, access control and the badging office. He lives in an apartment a few blocks from the Centraal Station."

"How will I know him?" Niall asked.

"His shift finishes at five. He's just under six feet tall, medium build. Reddish hair, cut short but not too brutal, the beginnings of a beard. I'm going to linger in the reception area and as soon as I see him coming out I'll walk through the door in front of him. I'll talk to him briefly then walk away."

"Got it, all good. Can I leave some stuff here and get changed?"

"Of course. I've got your number; I'll call when we're about to go."

Julia gave Niall a spare key. She and Mel left and went back to the office, where they had left Freddie in the care of the baby-wranglers in the crèche.

Chapter 18

Julia saw Jeroen Faber walking towards the turnstile, jacket on, carrying a shoulder bag. She turned her back on him and timed her exit so that she was one or two people ahead of him as they left the building. She paused to look for something in her handbag before looking up at Faber.

"Hi Jeroen," she said, "thanks for your help with Mel Dunn the other day. Have a good evening."

She didn't look back, but across the street Niall Morton, now free of his smart business suit and dark blue tie, watched the target gazing longingly at Julia Kelso's retreating back. Niall almost heard him sigh as he walked towards the tram stop. In your dreams, Niall thought. Morton followed Faber to Den Haag Centraal Station. He had to close in so he didn't lose sight in the evening rush, but luckily Faber was wearing a distinctive light-blue jacket. A few blocks west of the station Niall watched Faber let himself into a block of flats, seemingly well-kept. He saw a light come on in a second-floor window, and moments later he watched as Jeroen Faber drew his curtains.

Niall scouted the area and worked out that the route Faber had taken to get to his flat was almost certainly the route he would take when leaving it. One road provided a convenient choke point, and there was a café-bar overlooking it. Niall went in and ordered a beer. He took a seat by a window and made a call to Errol.

"How are you doing, mate?" he asked.

"Just on the train from Schiphol, I'll be at Den Haag Centraal in about ten minutes."

"Great. I'm in a bar a few minutes' walk to the west of there. Call me when you leave the station and I'll talk you in. I'm watching for the man, so if I have to move out I'll let you know.

Twenty minutes later, Errol Spelman, beer in hand, took a seat beside Niall Morton. They chatted like old friends, and Morton brought Errol up to speed on what was happening.

"So we keep tabs on this Faber and see if he goes to meet anyone this evening?" Errol asked.

"That's it. Julia thinks that Faber is acting on orders. He took some information this morning and she thinks he'll try to hand it over quickly. She wants to know who he gives it to. We try to take him to any meeting and get a handle on anyone he sees. If he meets more than one person we'll try to take one each, if it's just one, life will be a bit easier."

"Fine," Errol said, "I'll take my lead from you. We've got no comms or transport, so we'll need to be lucky. I've only got my phone for any pictures. I'll turn the flash off."

"Here we go, Errol, that's our man!"

Morton had seen Jeroen Faber walking briskly towards the station and its many bus and tram stops and taxi ranks. He had changed and was now dressed in a smart tailored jacket and blue jeans. He wasn't carrying anything.

They followed, splitting up and walking on opposite sides of the street. Faber seemed preoccupied, not alert to any possibility of surveillance. Faber walked straight past the station heading toward the centre of town. After a kilometre or so he walked into a smart restaurant, looking around for someone. Errol was closest to him and was able to see Faber make eye contact with a lone man sitting at a table towards the back of the place. The man had a drink in front of him and he rose to greet Faber, smiling and shaking his hand warmly. Faber took a seat opposite him and both men studied the menu.

Errol and Niall took a chance and went in. They asked for a table and were shown to a vacant one near the door. It gave them a good view of Faber and his companion. Niall pretended to take a call while taking several shots of Faber's friend.

Niall had almost forgotten that Errol was a foodie. He was getting quite excited about the menu.

"Concentrate, mate," he said quietly.

They saw a bottle of wine arrive and orders were taken. Faber visibly relaxed and sat back in his chair, apparently enjoying the other man's company. They obviously planned to have a leisurely dinner. Niall and Errol decided to do the same.

During the evening, they were able to take several photos of Faber and his friend. The got a shot of Faber sliding a small item, maybe a thumb drive memory stick, across the table and saw the companion slip it into an inside jacket pocket.

Errol and Niall finished and settled up. They waited outside in the shadows. Faber and his companion rose soon afterwards, the companion having paid the bill in cash. They said goodnight in the doorway of the restaurant, again shaking hands - so clearly not a close relationship, however warm it first seemed.

The companion set off in the opposite direction to Faber. The detectives followed discreetly. Unlike Faber, the man seemed more wary, so Niall and Errol fell back and kept their distance. The man's destination was a boutique hotel in a side street near the Embassy Quarter. A well-dressed woman was waiting in the lobby and she rose to greet the man, embracing him and kissing him on the lips. They walked hand in hand towards the elevator. Niall and Errol stayed outside.

The hotel had a small parking lot. Errol and Niall were able to photograph all the number plates on parked cars, most of them being foreign, as one might expect.

Niall had booked two hotel rooms by phone from Julia's house earlier in the day. The hotel was central and low budget. They checked in and went to their rooms to rest and get a few hours' sleep.

The next day they were up and out by six and back at the boutique hotel shortly afterwards. They had to wait until after ten before the target, the man from the previous night, emerged. He came out at the same time as the woman. They kissed again, parted and got into separate cars. Errol got the registrations. Both cars were on French plates. Despite the fact that both the man and the woman were well and expensively dressed, his car was a relatively ordinary saloon, the sort that might be given to sales reps or civil servants as work cars. Hers was a high-end luxury SUV.

Errol and Niall watched them go. They called Julia and stopped for breakfast on their way to her house.

Chapter 19

Julia had gone to work. Mel waited in the house for Niall and Errol. She made them coffee while listening to their collective account of the previous evening's dinner and the morning hotel departure. She made a note of the car registrations and emailed herself copies of photographs taken of Faber, his dinner companion and the woman.

"What now?" Errol asked her.

"Well, I can run down the cars through the Europol system, and I'll have a look to see if there is any facial recognition database. Then we wait to see what Jake, Julia, wants to do next. How long can you two stick around?"

"I can probably stretch my absence without leave for another week," Errol said.

"I'm due back in Budapest, but I am my own boss and can stay on a few more days if it comes to it," Niall added.

"Good to know. I'm going to drop Freddie at the crèche and go to work. Make yourselves at home, guys," Mel said.

"Can I ask you something?" Niall asked.

"Like what?" Mel said.

"The set up here, you, Julia, the baby - are you….?"

"Am I what?"

"The two of you, are you, you know, together?"

"Does it matter?" Mel asked.

"No, not really. It's just that sometimes it helps to understand the dynamics of a team. I have some idea of how Julia works, and things might get rough."

"Nothing for you to worry about," Mel said coolly, "I'm off. See you later."

******

"Antoine Durand and Isabelle Meyer-Ricci," Mel announced, "Durand's car is registered to an address in a suburb to the east of Paris, quite a long way out by the look of it. Meyer-Ricci's car is registered to a business address in Strasbourg, but it's in her name. Neither of them are on the targets database. I'll do some more digging. What are you thinking?"

"My hunch," Julia said, "is that Faber isn't a big player. He just hasn't got it in him. The way he seems in the pictures, he's almost in awe of that guy, Antoine. I think we should give him a fright."

"So you're not going official with this, then?"

"Not until I know what 'this' is," Julia said. "If we go official now Faber will get fired, Europol will do some housekeeping on system access and that will be the end of it. There have been too many casualties to accept that as the end result. I want to know what's been going on and why it's been happening, then we can go official if it's the best thing to do. Are you okay with that?"

"I guess so," Mel said.

"What's up?" Jake asked, catching Mel's uncertainty.

"I don't know, I was kind of hoping all this was behind us, now that Alf's not here," Mel said quietly.

"It's never been about Alf, Mel, not *just* about Alf, I mean. It's always been about showing the untouchables that they can't keep getting away with it, that some form of justice will catch up with them and make them pay for what they've done. It's been about what we believe. Don't you believe, Mel?"

"I do, just having a bit of a wobble. Hormones, I expect."

"Keep the faith, Mel, just for a bit longer. Can you do that?"

"Yes," Mel said.

"Come here," Julia held her arms out. The women clung to each other in silence for a few moments before Julia broke the clinch.

"Let's get on with it," Julia said.

"What sort of fright do you have in mind?" Mel asked.

"Nothing physical - unless Faber starts it, of course. Something to make him really not want to do whatever it is he's doing with the information he's stealing, and something that makes him really want to tell us what he's up to. And why, naturally."

"And just how are you going to do that?" Mel asked.

"You'll see. Are Niall and Errol still around?"

"They said they could be for a few days."

"Good, I can use more of their help. Let's have a group chat at home this evening. Now, I've got my day job to do."

******

That evening, Julia opened a couple of bottles of wine and sent out for an Indonesian takeaway. The four of them sat round the kitchen table and talked. They talked about Budapest and how Niall found living there. They spoke about Errol's partner, Steven, and his sister,

Sasha. They spoke about little Freddie, but not about his father.

"Julia," Errol asked, "can you find out who was at the MPS Executive Leadership Team dinner, the one at The Dorchester on the night my cover was blown?"

"I should be able to, it's usually the same people, sometimes with a guest speaker. I've never been to one, you have to have the word 'commissioner' in your job title to be invited, that or be the head of finance and the civil staff. You think someone there gave your name to Adda?"

"I think it's a possibility."

"I'll see what I can find out. Mel, while you're digging around on the Europol system could you have a look for any reference to the Met Police leadership team?"

"I can have a go," Mel said, "not that I know where to start."

"You'll think of something," Julia said.

When they'd finished eating, Julia raised the subject of Jeroen Faber.

"I was saying to Mel earlier that I don't think Faber is a major player in whatever's going on. What do you two think?" she asked Errol and Niall.

Errol spoke first.

"I agree. His body language last night with Antoine what's his name was very subservient, sycophantic even. Like he felt honoured to be there. When he handed over the thumb drive or whatever it was he was almost begging for praise with his eyes."

"Absolutely," Niall agreed, "there's no way Faber's a leader."

"Okay, we're going to have a wee chat with him, then. It will be tomorrow evening, after work. I'm going to entice Faber to meet me out of the office. I don't think he'll need much persuading. I'm going to get him to meet me for a drink in the Piano Bar in Scheveningen. You two, Niall and Errol, need to be there too, but get there first, before six. Get one of the booths, the ones with the semi-circular bench seats. When I arrive I'll take the booth and you go and get a drink at the bar. When Faber arrives I'll make sure he's on the bench seat, then you two come over and pen him in. Follow my lead after that. Be prepared to look menacing, but unless we are grossly underestimating Faber, I don't think you'll need to use any force. Then we play it by ear. All okay?"

Both men nodded.

"Good. Who's for another drink?"

Chapter 20

Julia spent the following morning hearing applications from prospective Joint Investigation Teams. The ones she had chosen today did not involve covert sources or undercover officers, which made her decisions easier. Mel was in Julia's office, immersed in Europol's extensive information system and the internet. At lunchtime Julia brought sandwiches to her office while Mel made coffee.

"Nothing much on Isabelle Meyer-Ricci," Mel said, "nothing on Europol records anyway. Seems she's a partner in a PR and lobbying firm based in Strasbourg but with branches all over. Nothing about her personal life and very few images, just the odd photo at some high-profile do. Antoine Durand, though, is all over Europol records. That's because he's high up in the French police. He's number two or three in the CODF, that's the organised and financial crime sub-directorate of the Judicial Police. As far as I can make out, he's head of the financial crime bit, fraud, money laundering, stuff like that."

"Anything detrimental, Mel?"

"Not that I've seen. He's got quite a profile on the internet, lots of quotes from him, media interviews, and more pictures than you'd expect from someone in his position. He's married with kids, no address quoted publicly but it does say he lives 'just outside Paris'."

"So a senior French cop is meeting a Europol employee and taking sensitive information from him? Information which may directly compromise covert human sources and which appears to end up in the hands of criminals under active investigation?"

"That's a reasonable assumption at this stage," Mel agreed.

"Then the same cop seems to be having an affair with a woman who is a partner in a leading PR firm. Is that connected, do you think?"

"I can't say, can't even guess," Mel said. "I'm going to look at her business contacts, the ones that are visible, and at her client list. It doesn't seem a natural fit, Isabelle and Antoine."

"Okay, I'm going to the gym," Julia said.

"You'll get indigestion, you've just finished eating."

"I'll risk it. I saw Faber going in on my way up, I want to catch him while he's sweaty."

"That's repulsive!" Mel said.

******

Julia had changed into her sports kit and her entrance coincided with Jeroen Faber finishing off his circuits. He was red, hot and breathless.

"Had a good workout, Jeroen?" she asked, smiling.

"Jerry, you can call me Jerry," he panted, "yes, a good one. Why don't I warm down while you warm up?"

"Why not?" she said, walking towards two vacant treadmills.

They jogged alongside each other for a few minutes.

"I'm warm enough," Julia said, "I'm going to speed up in a minute. Look, Jerry, I don't know many people here in The Hague, it would be nice to have a drink with a friendly face. Are you doing anything this evening?"

From the corner of her eye she saw him almost fall off the treadmill.

"I suppose I could be free," he stammered slightly.

"Shall we say the Piano Bar on the seafront in Scheveningen at six thirty?" She flicked him another smile.

"Of course, I will look forward to it."

Julia turned up her throttle and started running hard.

"See you at six-thirty then," she said as she started to breathe more heavily.

******

Julia arrived at the bar just after six. She saw Niall and Errol seated casually in one of the booths. The place wasn't that busy. When they saw her, the two men rose and moved to the bar. Julia slid into their booth and ordered a gin and tonic from the waiter. At six-thirty exactly, Jeroen Faber walked in. Julia thought he had probably been waiting outside looking at his watch. She stood and waved to him, sitting down again on a chair. She shepherded him onto the bench seat.

"Hello, Jerry," she said, "what would you like?"

He asked for a beer initially, before changing his mind and asking for a white wine instead. Julia signalled for the waiter again and placed the order. She chatted inconsequentially until his drink arrived, then raised her glass.

Taking this as her signal, Niall and Errol strolled over and slid into the booth, one each side of the startled Jeroen. He looked at Julia, panic stricken.

"These gentlemen are friends of mine, Jerry, good friends. That's Niall, although you probably haven't heard of him. That one you may have heard of. He's Errol Spelman, sometimes known as Tallboy. Does that ring any bells?"

Julia watched the blood drain from Faber's face as his hands started to shake.

"I see it does mean something to you. Errol is very, very unhappy, as I'm sure you'll understand. Now, you don't have long to tell me what you are up to before Errol's unhappiness starts to make him more difficult to control. I'd say about two minutes. Start talking, Jerry."

Faber sat in stunned silence. Julia produced a couple of prints from her handbag and placed them on the table, directly in front of Faber. They were both of Faber's dinner with the man they were calling Antoine; one of them showed Faber passing over a thumb drive. She slid a third print across, showing Faber in her office at her computer screen.

"You had me followed?" Faber said. "I was just having dinner with a friend."

"No you weren't Jerry," Julia said, "you were meeting a contact to hand over stolen confidential Europol information. You were committing a crime."

Errol stirred menacingly, staring hard at Faber. He cracked his knuckles. Faber crumbled.

"I'm sorry!" Faber said, "I didn't know people were going to get hurt."

"You gave information that you had stolen from the Europol system to an unauthorised person, information giving away the identity of covert officers or informants, and you didn't think that someone might get hurt? Are you that much of an idiot, Jerry? You must be, either that or a criminal looking at a very long time in jail. Which is it?"

"I'm sorry! I really am sorry," Faber was on the verge of tears.

"From the beginning, Jerry," Julia said.

Chapter 21

A few hundred kilometres away in her suite at the Hotel Royal in Luxembourg, Isabelle Meyer-Ricci had finished showering and was about to call her husband. She slipped a bathrobe on and returned to the crumpled bed, which the Frenchman had vacated just half an hour ago.

"Guido," she purred when her husband answered, "how are you *mon cher*?"

"All the better for hearing your voice," he whispered back, "has he gone?"

"Yes, half an hour ago. He is very energetic, you know, but he lacks finesse."

"Does he still adore you, *cara*?"

"Of course he does, as do you. You wouldn't have asked me to do this if you didn't. Are you at the villa?"

"No, I'm in Rome this evening. I will be home tomorrow, I hope."

"I need to be in Strasbourg tomorrow, and I probably won't get back until Friday. I'm going to send you the material that Antoine gave me, I think it could be helpful. Look out for it in the other inbox."

"Of course. Now, I must go, someone is waiting," Guido said.

"I need some food and some sleep, I wish you were here," Isabelle said.

"It would be a little crowded, don't you think," he said drily. "*Ciao, bella.* Sleep well." Guido cut the call.

Isabelle smiled to herself while studying the room service menu. She didn't feel like dressing for dinner.

******

"I met Antoine, the man I had dinner with, in Paris," Jeroen started. "It was a security conference, IT security, internet stuff, and fraud prevention. It was quite interesting. I got talking to Antoine over coffee, and we got to know each other slowly. Just as professional colleagues at first, then more as friends."

"Do you know who Antoine is, what he does?" Julia asked.

"No, I've never asked. I know he lives near Paris and does something in security," Jeroen answered. "Antoine came to The Hague from time to time, and he always made a point of calling me to meet for a drink or some food. We got round to talking politics, and I said I didn't like the way our independence in The Netherlands was being eroded. He agreed and said it was the same in France. We discussed it several times over a few months.

"One day, he told me that he was working with other people on a project to try to encourage some checks and balances, ways to shore up national independence and reduce the influence of EU agencies and other bodies. To restore the equilibrium, he said. Antoine said that he and his friends had worked out that EU bodies were becoming too well-established, too well respected for their competence and professionalism. They wanted to change that. They wanted the bodies to become objects of ridicule, reputedly full of incompetent buffoons, always making mistakes and fouling up. Antoine said I could help."

"How?" Julia asked.

"I had told him I worked at Europol in the corporate security department. I had told him that I was in charge of badging and access control, and IT security. Antoine asked if it would be possible for two badges to be issued to the same person at the same time. I thought about it, and while it shouldn't happen, it is technically possible. I can print two identical badges as long as I do it at almost the same time. Same coding, same PIN, everything. I just have to do it before the first one is registered and stored on the system. It takes a minute or two, no longer than that. The system just looks at the badge, not the name on it. It thinks that one badge has been aborted, cancelled, not that two identical badges have been made. I told Antoine this."

"Then what?" Julia asked.

"Antoine said he had heard about Joint Investigation Teams; he said they were an example of Europol overreaching itself and taking on more than it had a right to. He said each country needs to set and enforce its own laws, not have someone from outside telling them what to do. I have to say I agreed with him.

"Antoine asked me to find out who knew all there was to know about JIT operations, who knew all the details. What targets, what crimes were being investigated, what resources being used, any covert sources like phone tapping or informants or undercover officers. I did what he asked, and I came up with you, Julia. You were due to start and hadn't yet been given a badge. When you arrived, I made a cloned badge when I printed yours out. That way I could get access to everything you could.

"Antoine was very happy when I told him. He got quite excited. He asked me to give him details of a current JIT. I did; he was pleased. Then he introduced me to his friends, Guido and Isabelle. He said they were involved in the project but he didn't say how. They invited me to lunch. Antoine never told me what they wanted the JIT information for, or what he was going to do with it. He just said that they, I think he meant Guido and Isabelle, wanted to make Europol look ridiculous."

"Have you ever contacted Guido or Isabelle yourself, or have they contacted you?" Julia asked.

"No, it's only ever Antoine."

"Carry on," Julia instructed.

"So I've kept doing it, I've been giving Antoine JIT details for a few months. He said he only wants ones with informants and especially undercover police involved at the moment. He said that they were the most useful, the most valuable."

"Do you know who Guido and Isabelle are?" Julia asked.

"No," Jeroen answered.

"Is this Isabelle?" Julia slid a fourth print across the table, the one showing Isabelle and Antoine in the hotel parking lot. They were holding hands. Jeroen seemed shocked.

"Yes, that's Isabelle," he said, "but I didn't think that she and Antoine were involved, not like that."

"Did you think she was involved with anyone, like that?" Julia asked.

"I didn't consider it much, but I had assumed she was with Guido. There was just that air about them."

"Okay, Jeroen," Julia said, dropping the Jerry, "I'll tell you what happens now. Listen carefully. You are to continue your meetings with Antoine, but you must tell me first and only meet him if I say you can, do you understand?"

He nodded.

"Good. You will *only* pass information to Antoine that *I* give you. You will not take any information from Europol to him unless *I* have approved it first. Do you understand?"

He nodded again.

"You will give me the cloned badge you made."

He reached into a pocket and produced an exact copy of Julia's Europol badge. He laid it on the table.

"Have you made any other cloned badges?"

He nodded.

"I made one for your assistant, Mel Dunn," he said.

"Where is it?"

"I don't have it with me. I haven't used it yet; it was just in case yours stopped working. I will give it to you tomorrow."

"When I'm done with you, one of two things will happen, Jeroen. Either you will be charged and found guilty of serious crimes and will go to jail, or you will resign from Europol and run away to hide in the dark under a rock somewhere. I will decide which will happen, and when it will happen. In the meantime, Errol knows where you live, and as I said he is very unhappy about what you did to him. If you disobey me, even in the slightest way, you will get a visit from Errol and some of his friends before you go to jail. Am I being clear enough for you?"

"Yes," Jeroen whispered.

"Give me the number you contact Antoine on, then go. Be in my office with Mel's badge at nine tomorrow morning. Then I'll tell you what will happen next."

Faber looked at his phone and wrote a number on a napkin. Niall Morton moved to allow him to get out of the booth. Faber slipped out and almost ran to the door, clearly broken.

"Will he comply, Julia?" Morton asked.

"I think so. I think he's more scared of me and Errol at the moment than he is of Antoine and the other two."

"What next?" Errol asked.

"I'll try to find out if there's a problem with the Met Police, and if it's all clear I think you need to go and make your peace with them. As for Antoine, Isabelle and Guido, Mel and I have some work to do. If I need you, can one or both of you help me out if it comes to it?"

"Of course, Julia," Niall said.

Errol nodded quietly, watching her face carefully. All he saw was cold anger. She was terrifying.

Chapter 22

In Rome, Guido Ricci was preparing himself for the ritual. His installation as the latest Grand Master of *l'ordine*, a secret society which was thought to have become extinct in the 19th century, was a spectacular moment in his already spectacular career, even if it was just for show. From humble beginnings in the shadow of the giant Fiat works in the south of Turin, where his father and uncles had worked shifts for their whole lives, to the majestic villa overlooking Lake Como and his black book full of the private numbers of the world's richest and most famous. His shrewd, and often unscrupulous, investments had made him a wealthy man, and his wealth had bought, or at least rented, him power. As the formally installed Grand Master, his access to unquestioned power had just multiplied exponentially.

That *l'ordine* still existed was a closely guarded secret. Initially it was true to its original belief; its aim was to create an independent, united Italy, freed from the clutches of feudal lords and parasitic priests. *l'ordine* had worked tirelessly in a twilight world, in secret cells, using whatever means were necessary. Their secret arms had reached out, taking *l'ordine* beyond Italy to other nascent states in Europe and the wider world. After breaking cover in the 1830s in a series of uprisings that did not work out as planned, it was assumed that *l'ordine* had faded away. In fact it had been in hibernation, and it stayed that way for more than a century. After the Second World War, the faithful members - many of them descendants of the original few - regrouped, still in secret, and started to build their influence, and wealth, once more.

Now, *l'ordine* had cells in every European country as well as the Americas. The members were drawn from selected professions and callings. *l'ordine* was open to carefully vetted people from skilled trades, the military and law-enforcement, medicine, commerce, finance and the media. Adamantly excluded were elected politicians, clerics and lawyers. Tonight, each regional cell would send one representative to witness the installation of the new Grand Master. It was an appointment for life, and the ritual was as much a vote of thanks for the life and work of the late incumbent as a celebration of the elevation of the new leader.

Guido was ready. He was taking it over.

******

The following morning, his skin still tingling in places from the initiation ceremony, Guido took breakfast alone in his suite. On a laptop he opened the email inbox that his wife used to send him confidential communications and he studied the latest contribution from Antoine. Antoine was a useful functionary. As well as having the ability to obtain good quality confidential information, he was also expendable and deniable, as in fact were most members of *l'ordine*. Guido and Isabelle had manufactured enough of a story around Antoine to sink him without trace if he became over-ambitious or was exposed.

The snippets he'd provided were useful. More of the infernal Joint Investigation Team operations trespassing across borders, one involving not one but two undercover police spies, another a treacherous turncoat informer. He would delve into his black book for names of contacts, preferably members, brothers, of *l'ordine*, who were most likely to be able to pass such information on to interested parties, namely the criminals being targeted.

There was also an account of another Europol operation, this one related to human trafficking. The target gang of people-smugglers had panicked and abandoned a truck load of migrants, all of whom had perished. Guido saw an opportunity to blame Europol for this dreadful incident, and he sent a message to his wife asking her to start preparing a plan to insert in the mainstream media some derogatory pieces condemning Europol's lack of competence. He wanted Europol to become known as a rogue agency with few constraints and poor leadership. They could build on this theme over time. He had learned over and over that the same lie repeated often enough soon becomes the truth.

Guido was no supporter of criminals, although he did have some respect for their raw and unfettered application of capitalist principles. When the time was right, he and others of a similar mind would bring them to heel and exploit their energies in a more productive manner. But for now, he would ignite their wrath and sit back as they meted out vengeance on the spies and traitors sent to hurt them.

More importantly, Isabelle had included her more general plan to start the media campaign against Europol. She had listed several contacts able to plant stories in newspapers pandering to both the Eurosceptic right and self-righteous left. She had already started to send tiny morsels to them, completely untraceable and unattributed, pointing to the fact that unelected bureaucrats in an ivory tower in The Hague were launching disastrous and unwarranted adventures across Europe, costing the lives of good and loyal public servants along the way. Europol was incompetent, out of control; it must be stopped!

When he was ready, he took a taxi to the station and boarded his first-class carriage on the express train to Como. He travelled light, just a briefcase. He kept the hotel suite in Rome on a permanent basis, a home from home. One of his cars, the new Quattroporte he hoped, would pick him up at his destination, and he would go home to wait for Isabelle. He was already anticipating hearing about her treatment at the hands of the lascivious Frenchman. The way she recounted what Antoine had done to her always thrilled and excited him.

Chapter 23

After Jeroen Faber left the Piano Bar Julia left Niall and Errol to it. She had booked rooms for them at one of the large business hotels dotted around The Hague. She decided to walk home. It took quite a while, and the streets near her house were dark and empty by the time she got there. Mel was still awake.

"How did it go?" she asked Julia, handing her a large gin and tonic.

"Faber rolled over almost immediately. Admitted everything and said he never knew anyone was going to be harmed. I was expecting more of a fight, but he doesn't seem to have it in him. I think he just wants to be loved, even liked a little bit. It's sad. He cloned your badge too, by the way, but he says he hasn't used it."

"I'll check tomorrow," Mel said, "what now?"

"He's coming to my office at nine tomorrow to return your cloned badge. Then I'm going to use him to introduce me to Antoine Durand."

"You're going to do what?"

"Get him to introduce me. I want to know what this is all about, who's behind it."

"Are you on something, Kelso? Why not just give Faber to Europol and the Dutch police, let them take it from here?"

"I can't do that yet. I've a feeling that there's something strange behind this. You haven't found anything on that Isabelle woman, have you?"

"No," Mel said, "nothing to speak of. Why?"

"Faber said that Isabelle, who we thought was with Antoine Durand, is more likely to be with someone called Guido. Faber implied that this Guido seems to be above Antoine in whatever hierarchy we're looking at. I was wondering if there is any link between Isabelle Meyer-Ricci and any Guido."

"Give me a moment," Mel said, opening her laptop.

A few minutes passed. Julia poured herself another drink.

"How about this?" Mel asked. "Pictures from a gala charity dinner in Monaco ages ago. Would you say that's Isabelle?"

Mel zoomed in on a figure on the screen. It was Isabelle, almost certainly. Beside her was a man, medium build but starting to run to fat, well groomed, but totally without expression, and wearing a black tuxedo. Julia scanned the caption.

"Signor and Signora Guido Ricci, honoured guests of His Highness Prince Albert, patron of blah blah blah," Julia read out. "So Faber was right, Guido and Isabelle are a couple. I'd like to know if he knows about Antoine and his wife. Look up Guido Ricci on the net and check him on the database tomorrow."

Mel was busy for another ten minutes.

"Very low internet profile, which is unusual given the circles he seems to move in. There are a few more mentions of him, and sometimes Isabelle, at various dinners and concerts, but nothing of any substance. No address, not even a hint of where they live, other than 'in Italy'. He's obviously pretty well-heeled. I'll do some research on Italian business sites tomorrow and do a dive on the dark web."

Mel stood and stretched. She went to the fridge and got herself another glass of wine.

"Jake," she said, "are you sure about this? You've not been at Europol that long and already you're going all unorthodox on them. If it all goes wrong you are toast, you do know that, don't you?"

"I guess so, but it won't go wrong, not unless I screw it up, or if it's meant to be."

"What do you mean, 'meant to be'? Are you saying it's fate, in the hands of the gods?"

"Isn't that true of just about everything? Good and bad luck, the breaks, fate? It's all the same. Why are you worried? You'll be fine."

"Not the point, Kelso. It's not about me being fine, it's about you *not* being fine. I don't want to be visiting you in jail or leaving you a bunch of flowers on your birthday and at Christmas."

"So you do actually care about me?" Jake asked.

"Of course I bloody do, and I care about me and Freddie too, especially Freddie. He needs you! He can't just have me! And I know you care about us, too. Can't we just try to be like normal people, at least for a while?"

"But we're not like normal people, not now, not anymore. We stopped being like normal people when we found out that Ferdinand had killed Vincent Carlton and that maniac mate of his, not to mention that evil bastard Roger Banbury. We stopped being like normal people when we knew what he was doing and we *didn't stop* him. We *helped* him. And all the while since, the things we've done, the difference we've made. We've done, I've done, some bad things, Mel, but more good ones. And the bad things have been done for good reasons.

"I tell you what, when we've got to the bottom of this we can go away, take a long break. I'll quit Europol and when I'm bored with you and Freddie I'll give in and accept a job from Hugh Cavendish. He still calls me once a month to ask me to go and work for him at Six. You can go there too, I'm sure."

"Look, Jake, I'm concerned about you and about us. I think a long break is a good idea, for all of us. Whatever you do afterwards is up to you. I won't be going to work for Hugh Cavendish, though. I spoke with Roisin in Dublin, Eugene Flynn's niece. She's finished winding up the trading company that Alf and I set up for the Nigeria job. It seems we were really quite good at legitimate oil trading and we made a decent amount of money. Roisin says that as the only traceable shareholder, now that Alf (as Piet Kuyper) can't be found, it all comes to me. There's enough to keep me in wine and sandwiches for a very long time."

"So you're going to retire?"

"No, I'm going to be a responsible mother to Freddie and I'm going to go back to something more academic than scary."

"Good for you, Mel, I'm happy for you. We'll go and see Roisin when we're done. She said that Alf had left instructions, whatever that means, then we'll have that break. I suspect we've a long day ahead tomorrow, I'm going to have another drink and take a nice long bath."

"Shall I do your back?" Mel asked.

"I thought you'd never ask," Jake said, smiling.

Chapter 24

At eight-forty-five the next morning, a forlorn Jeroen Faber was sitting on a hard chair in the corridor outside Julia's office. He hadn't slept at all and he looked awful. At nine precisely Julia called him in. Mel was there too.

"The badge, Jeroen," Julia held her hand out.

Faber handed her a plastic card, the cloned copy of Mel's badge.

"Thank you. Now, I want a list of every document you've seen, and every scrap of information you've given to Antoine, or to anyone else."

"There is no one else, just Antoine," Faber mumbled.

He thought for a while, then started to recite operation names. There were around ten of them. Mel made a list.

"Good," said Julia, "now what information did you hand over from each one?"

Again Faber thought for a moment.

"Apart from the Portugal operation, from the first eight I gave Antoine the operation name, the target identities, the type of criminality, what resources were being deployed, the names and nationalities of the team leaders, and the identities of any informants or undercover agents. The Portugal operation was different, with no specific targets, so I gave Antoine the names and nationalities of the team leaders and the addresses of properties acquired by the team in Portugal.

"For the last two, the most recent, Antoine had told me he was looking for something a bit different. He wanted me to give him details of any mistakes, failures, compromises, things like that."

"Why did he want those?" Julia asked.

"I don't know; he didn't say and I didn't ask," Faber replied.

"I might have an inkling," Mel said, "look at this."

Julia went over and looked at Mel's screen. She was reading an article in a Belgian daily. The headline translated as 'Another Europol Blunder' and the article concerned a recent tragic discovery of a truck full of migrants who had been abandoned by traffickers and had all suffocated. The newspaper claimed that Europol 'agents' had been monitoring the truck but had failed to take any action to protect the migrants, preferring to pursue the supposed smugglers in a surveillance operation covering at least three countries. The story wasn't entirely accurate, but there was enough actual verifiable detail to make it look very bad for Europol.

"Not true, but close enough," Mel said, "it's clever, Jake."

"Is Antoine behind this, Jeroen?" Julia asked.

"I don't know. It is one of the operational failures I passed to him, so he could be."

"Okay," Julia said, "when you get back to your office you'll see that you've been copied in on an exchange between me and your boss. All of my team are going to have their badges changed today. You will assign a team of your assistants to do the badging before the end of the day, but you will not operate the equipment or even be in the room. Is that clear?"

Faber nodded.

"Go back to work. I'm going to need you to do a few more things for me before I decide what to do with you. I'll call you when I need you. And Jeroen, I will be watching you. If Antoine contacts you, tell me at once -

before you respond to him. If he calls you, don't take his call or call him back before you've spoken to me. You got that?"

"Yes, ma'am," Faber said.

"Good. Leave now."

Jeroen Faber, now pale and frightened, rose and slunk out of the room.

Mel had started looking at all the operations Faber had compromised. Two of those where informant details had been handed over were still underway and did not seem to have been blown yet.

Julia picked up the phone and placed urgent calls to the respective team leaders telling them that there may be a security issue and their operations may have been compromised. Their covert human sources could be at risk. They were to withdraw the human sources and place them under protection, even if that meant aborting the operation. Julia would provide more information as soon as she was able to. The team leaders weren't exactly thrilled, but they did appreciate the urgency of the warning, especially since they were very well aware of the recent problems with other Joint Investigation Team operations. Rumours were already flying around European police services suggesting that Europol could not be trusted.

"What now?" Mel asked.

"First, we go and get our new badges, then I have to get ready for tomorrow's Management Committee. The main agenda item being guess what?"

"Could it be compromised Joint Investigations?"

"You've got it, Miss Dunn. We have to go through everything that Faber has given Antoine Durand. I need to be sure that there are no ticking time bombs before I go after him and the other two."

"What are you thinking, Kelso?"

"That they are about to get a new friend," Jake answered.

"You're going to pretend to be one of them?"

"I don't know what 'one of them' is, not yet. When I do find out, and if I think it's viable, I'm not going to pretend. I am going to *be* one of them. It's a lesson I learned from Ferdinand. If you go up against someone, a criminal - a target, and just pretend, you won't succeed. They can smell pretence. You have to be what you say you are, really *believe* it. If you don't believe it, neither will they. He used to say it saved his life more than once."

"And now he's dead, Jake!" Mel almost shouted.

"Only do this with me if you want to, Mel. I don't know if I can do it on my own, but I know I can't if you aren't fully with me. I'd rather give it a go on my own than take you with me as a reluctant partner."

"Are you saying you don't trust me?"

"Of course I trust you," Jake said, "but I can't be worrying about you if I'm out there doing whatever I might have to do. It's all or nothing, Mel, as far as this goes. It's up to you."

"And you want to do this your way, not the sensible way? Not just tell the police and let them do their job?"

"If this was just a thing between Faber and Durand, that's just what I'd do, but the other two? I'm smelling something sinister, something complicated. A full-on police investigation won't stop them, the Ricci's, it will just tip them off. They'll come back stronger and do whatever it is they're doing better."

"Jesus, Kelso! Okay, then, but let's make this one last time, like we said last night." Mel sighed and went back to her screen. At least she understood her screen.

Chapter 25

The Management Committee meeting room was fuller than usual - everyone had turned up. Julia took her seat at the long conference table. The head of Organised Crime Operations started by summarising the separate ongoing murder investigations in Budapest, the Algarve, Vienna and London. He had received updates from the respective Senior Investigating Officers overnight. In all cases, except Portugal, the notable gangsters being targeted and their henchmen had all been pulled in for questioning. The Austrians had enough forensic and communications evidence to lay charges, and the Hungarians were confident that they would be in the same position soon.

The Head of Analysis was up next. Her teams had been working round the clock, crunching the most minute data on each of the compromised cases. What they had come up with was the fact that there was no common factor linking any two of the operations, let alone all of them. They were reluctantly heading towards the conclusion that the compromises were unfortunate and separate examples of abysmal luck. Julia knew differently but kept her counsel for now.

Discussions and suggestions followed for the next half hour before the Director General interrupted.

"Thank you all," he said, "I appreciate your input and ideas. I must admit I find it hard to believe that all the unfortunate incidents have been the result of bad luck, and we must keep looking for connections. One thing that hasn't yet been mentioned is the possibility that the single common factor that we *are* all aware of is the source of the problem. That common factor is, of course, us. Europol is the only common link between all the compromised operations. I have asked Internal Affairs to look carefully at access to the files here at Headquarters and across the outstations. They have alerted me to one thing already.

"Julia," he said, "I understand that yesterday you informed two Joint Investigation Teams that their operations may also have been compromised, that the identity of covert human sources may have been leaked to the targets, and that operations should be suspended until we know more. Is that so?"

"It is," Julia replied.

"Why those two?" the Director General asked, looking straight at her.

"I looked at the timing of the compromises to date. There seems to be a sequence starting on a certain date with the Budapest incident. I had my analytical consultant do a quick sweep of earlier JITs and so far there have been no issues with them, so I acted on the assumption that operations which commenced after the Hungarian one were the most likely to be at risk. Those I contacted were the only two featuring covert human sources, so I thought it prudent to warn them that the possibility of a compromise existed. I was going to tell you after this meeting."

The DG looked at her for a moment, sizing her up.

"Thank you," he said eventually, "I don't doubt that you acted correctly, but it would have been helpful to have some advance notice. I've had a few irate calls from heads of national police services."

"This isn't the best forum for a detailed discussion, DG," Julia said, "can we talk about it afterwards?"

"Yes, Julia, but your colleagues need to be aware of events. Transparency is an important part of our collective confidence."

Julia bit her lip, suppressing the urge to say that, given the current circumstances, transparency was not at all helpful.

"My people will be studying all Joint Investigation Teams since their inception so we can be sure that there haven't been any other leaks, should it transpire that we have one now," Julia told the meeting. "I do share the DG's doubts about the likelihood of the compromises being serial bad luck. If, as seems at least likely, we do have a problem, I hope we can all work together to resolve it as quickly as possible."

Some other matters were discussed before the meeting broke up. Julia had noted that Jeroen Faber's boss had remained silent throughout.

Back in her room she closed the door and leant back on it. Mel looked up.

"How did it go?" she asked.

"I nearly tripped myself up with the warnings I gave the two JITs yesterday. The DG fronted me with them in the meeting. I think I covered it by saying that we figured the leaks started after the Budapest job and the two I tipped off were the only ones that had vulnerable human sources in play. I'm going to see him later, so I'll need lots of details to throw around. He's launched an Internal Affairs investigation to find out if there actually is a leak, by the way."

"Wouldn't it be a good idea to cooperate, then?" Mel asked.

"We've been through this. I'll give them everything when the time is right, when I've worked out what's going on and why."

"Well I wouldn't leave it too long then," Mel said, "if Internal Affairs get to Faber before you're ready to tell all, you'll have had it. He'll shop you in an instant, and I don't think you'll be able to talk your way out of it this time. Ask yourself, Jake, is it really worth it?"

"I think it is. I need to do this, one last time, like we said, to keep the faith. You're right about one thing, though."

"What's that?"

"I do need to get a move on. Get Faber in here will you? I need the loo."

Mel picked up her phone while Julia went down the corridor. She locked herself in the toilet and began to shake a little. When Ferdinand had been around she'd had more self-confidence. She realised it was because she trusted him, and he trusted her. Mel's was the voice of reason, as it always had been from the outset, but right now she didn't need reason. She needed someone to go into battle with, someone who had her back and who she could also fight for. She missed him. Julia splashed cold water on her face and dried herself. By the time she got back to her office, Faber was there, sitting still and looking terrified.

"Okay, Jeroen," she started, "we don't have much time. I want you to contact Antoine, tell him you need to see him urgently. Can you do that?"

He nodded.

"Do it, then," Julia insisted.

Faber took out a mobile phone and composed a text message. A few seconds later his phone buzzed.

"He says why?" Faber told her.

"Tell him that Europol thinks that someone has been leaking information. They don't suspect you, but you need to hand over the material you already have before you suspend things for a while."

Jeroen said alright and started typing on his phone.

"Brussels, this evening," Faber said when he'd read the reply. "Now what?"

"Tell him yes. Say you'll text him when you arrive and fix a place to meet."

He did. Antoine said okay.

"Good, Jeroen," Julia said. "Now tell your boss that you've been sick, say you think you have norovirus or something - it's very contagious - and you need to go home. You'll be off sick for at least a week. Then go home, pack an overnight bag and meet me at Centraal station at four this afternoon. We're going to Brussels. And if you're thinking of doing anything silly, just remember that Niall and Errol are still watching you. Understand?"

"Yes," he said quietly.

"Oh, and Jeroen," Julia added, "if you think that confessing to your boss or Internal Affairs will help you, it really won't. You *will* end up in jail. If you stick with me, you might just have a chance of avoiding that. Now, don't let me keep you."

Chapter 26

Before she left the office to go and pack her bag, Julia called Will Connaught, her former chief at Scotland Yard. Connaught had recently been appointed an Assistant Commissioner and as such he was now a regular member of the Met's Executive Leadership Team. When Julia had left the Met Connaught had not been sorry to see her go, but since then she had made peace with him and they were almost friends again.

"Connaught," he answered his mobile.

"Hi Will, Julia Kelso. How are things?"

"Good to hear from you," he said, "the Met's as busy as ever. I can't be laid back and easy anymore. How is Europol?"

"Different sort of animal, Will. I'll keep this brief, but I will buy you lunch next time I'm in London. I want to ask you about the most recent ELT dinner, the one at The Dorchester a few weeks back. Were you there?"

"I was, but you know I can't talk about what we discussed," he was wary.

"Of course not, Will, I wouldn't dream of asking. I just want to know if anything out of the ordinary happened, if there were any guests or visitors, anything like that?"

"It was all perfectly normal, quite dull actually. There were the usual dozen or so of us there; we had a private room and we had dinner while we talked. No guests this time, although sometimes we do have them. Why?"

"Nothing really, it's just that I heard that one of our investigation targets was in The Dorchester at the same time. I just want to make sure there's nothing we, or you, should be concerned about."

"All I can say is that no one apart from the servers came into the room, and no one left until we all did. It wasn't a long evening."

"What time did the meeting start and finish?"

"We were all seated by seven-thirty and we left together just before ten."

"That's a relief then," Julia said, "the target was there briefly between eight and eight-thirty. We had a report that he'd met someone in the lobby."

"I can ask if you like," Connaught volunteered, "we use The Dorchester because the head of group security for the outfit that owns it is ex-Met, he was second in command at Royalty and Diplomatic Protection, very well connected. He makes sure we aren't disturbed and we get a sensible rate for the room and dinner. He's Duncan Traynor. Do you know him?"

"I think so. Don't put yourself out, Will, I can have a chat with him myself if I need to. Look, I've got to dash but I'll call you when I'm next in London. It would be good to see you."

"Likewise," Connaught said, "I'll look forward to it."

Julia cut the call and then called Errol Spelman on his mobile. He answered immediately.

"Errol, Julia. I think it's safe for you to surface. I spoke to someone I know who was at the Executive Leadership Team dinner. I don't think that whoever did the dirty on you is one of them."

"Good to know, thanks," Errol said, "I'll make a call when we're done. I did see Adda talking to someone, though, a tall, well-dressed guy."

"Ever come across a Duncan Traynor, ex-Met and formerly high up in Royalty Protection?"

"Not really my social circle, Julia," Errol said. "Why?"

"He's head of security at The Dorchester. Look him up. If he's the guy you saw talking to Adda we'll need to have a good look at him, if not he may be able to get you CCTV of Adda's contact. Let me know how you get on."

Errol called back a few minutes later.

"I've googled his picture, Julia. He's the one, the one who was talking to Adda - and it didn't look like a hotel security man talking to a guest. What do you want me to do?"

"Do some digging, get Niall on it too. I want his background, reputation, anything dodgy that he's been connected with. I'm going to be busy for a couple of days but I'll come to London as soon as I can. We'll need a word with Mr Traynor."

"Cool, let me know when you're arriving," Errol cut the call.

Julia looked at the time and swore under her breath. She grabbed her coat, logged off the system and left the building. She swung by her house to grab her overnight bag and arrived at Centraal Station just after four p.m. and saw an anxious-looking Jeroen Faber pacing up and down. She paused at a ticket machine and bought two returns to Brussels.

"Let's go," she said unceremoniously, almost making Jeroen jump. "Our train leaves in five minutes."

The train took around an hour and forty-five minutes and they pulled in at Brussels Midi shortly before six.

"Where's the meeting?" she asked when Jeroen had exchanged messages with Antoine.

"Le Quinze, it's a hotel on the Grand Place," Jeroen said.

"He has expensive taste, then," Julia quipped.

"He likes it, it's his usual place in Brussels."

"You've met him here before, then?"

"Yes, a few times. Mostly on his own, but once or twice he was with Isabelle. She never stayed, though."

"Okay, this is how it's going to work. You go to meet him on your own. I'll be somewhere close by. You will know when it's time to take your leave. When you do, find yourself a budget hotel and get a train home in the morning. Don't go back tonight - I might need to talk to you. Is that clear?"

He nodded glumly. They queued for a taxi in silence.

At the hotel, which was more stylish than opulent, they parted company, Julia letting Faber go ahead of her. She melted into the crowd in the lobby and kept a close eye on the Dutchman. He went directly to the bar and walked over to Antoine Durand, who was seated at the counter with a tumbler of amber liquid in front of him. Julia watched the two men shake hands.

Satisfied that they were alone, she made her move. She walked over confidently, pulling her wheeled suitcase behind her.

"Who's your friend, Jeroen?" she interrupted their conversation. "Don't tell me, it's Antoine, isn't it? I'm Julia Kelso."

She smiled and extended her hand. Durand took it, shaking it gently and holding on to it for just a bit too long.

"Off you go, Jeroen, I need a wee chat with Antoine here."

Faber felt his cheeks start to burn as his humiliation sank in. The man he'd thought of as his friend had said nothing; he only had eyes for Kelso. Not a word or gesture that he should stay, that Antoine wanted him to be present. He turned on his heel and walked out as briskly as he could without running. Outside he gasped for breath, having to support himself by leaning on the hotel wall.

Julia Kelso could go fuck herself, he thought, and fuck her instructions too! He wasn't her lackey! He set off for the station, his face set in a ferocious scowl. A light rain began to fall; Faber's scowl dissolved with the raindrops and melted into a picture of tearful self-pity. He paused in a dark doorway. There was a basement area, littered with rubbish and dead leaves. He dropped his small overnight bag over the railings and walked on slowly, dejected.

Chapter 27

Antoine Durand's gaze took in the woman sitting next to him. She was certainly very attractive, blonde, nice figure. He sat a little straighter and returned her gaze.

"Let's get a booth, Antoine," she said, "it'll be more comfortable."

She slid off her bar stool and led him to a vacant booth at the other side of the room. She signalled for a waiter and ordered herself a gin and tonic. She didn't ask if he wanted a drink, so he added his order to hers himself.

"So," she started once the drinks had arrived, "what are you up to, Antoine?"

"I'm sorry," he said, "I don't know what you mean." He spoke in English.

"Shall I try again in French, then?" she asked, "it's a simple enough question."

"I know what you said, I meant I don't know what you are talking about."

"Yes you do, Commissaire Durand," she said.

He was shocked to hear her use his rank and surname.

"What are you up to with Jeroen Faber?" Julia asked again.

He didn't respond.

"Let me guess, then," Julia continued, "Faber has been passing you sensitive information about ongoing joint investigations being coordinated by Europol. That much I know. Some of that information has been supplied to the targets of those investigations, and people named in the information Faber gave to you have been killed, murdered. One of the people killed was an undercover officer from your own department, the Police Judiciaire. What I don't know is why. Care to enlighten me?"

Durand remained silent. Julia sipped her drink. She hadn't raised her voice and she looked completely calm. He was getting nervous.

"You won't be seeing Faber again, not unless you really like him, which I doubt. He's of no further use to you now. I don't think Faber gave you the information in return for money, so what was it?"

Durand still said nothing.

"I don't think it was sex, or am I wrong? If it wasn't money or sex, what was it? Why did Jeroen Faber jeopardise his job and his liberty by stealing Europol information and giving it to you? Why did you want it? Was it sex? Do you swing both ways, Antoine?"

Durand shook his head.

"Oscar Wilde once said that everything in life is about sex except sex, which is about power. Have you heard that before?" Julia asked. "Who has the power, Antoine?"

"I have no idea what you are talking about," Durand said eventually.

"Alright," Julia replied, "let me ask you something. Does Guido Ricci know you're fucking his wife? Or is she fucking you?" Julia watched his expression closely, saw a puzzled look cross his brow.

"Oh, is that it?" she asked. "Isabelle is letting you shag her and you can't quite believe it, can you? She's a good-looking woman, out of your league I'd say. Did she put you up to it? Tell you to exploit poor little Jeroen

Faber, the man with no friends, in return for a fumble with her in bed?"

"It's not like that!" Durand almost spat.

"Isn't it? Let me show you some pictures, Antoine," Julia reached into her bag to pull out a slim sheaf of prints. "This is you and her outside that hotel in The Hague, holding hands, kissing. This one is her in her car, driving away. See that expression? Her look? What does that tell you?"

"She says she loves me," Durand said.

"Well the look on her face in that picture tells me, as a woman, that she certainly does not, Antoine. That look tells me she thinks she dominates you; she thinks you are pathetic. How do you think she'll react when she finds out that your source inside Europol has gone, that you have no access to the information she wants? Will she still 'love' you then, Antoine, still want you to do all those wicked things to her that you think she likes?"

"What do you want?" Antoine asked her.

"I want to know why. I want to know what Isabelle does with the information."

"Why?" he asked.

"So I can make my mind up about what I'm going to do about it," Julia said.

"How do you mean?"

"Well, I can tell my boss what's been going on, show him the evidence I have, and sit back while he tells your boss and you get arrested, and then your boss will go after Isabelle and Guido."

"Or?"

"Or I don't."

"Why wouldn't you?"

"Don't be naïve, Antoine!"

"You want something?"

"Doesn't everyone? We aren't getting any younger, Antoine, either of us. You're doing this for some fun with someone else's wife, I'd rather have something longer lasting. Make me an offer."

"It's not up to me. I'll need to speak to Isabelle and Guido," he said.

"So it's them who have the power, Antoine. What does that tell you about where you stand in all this? If I were you, I'd look for something longer lasting too. Mark my words, when they're done with you, you'll be in jail or dead unless you look out for your own interests. If French jails are anything like the British ones I know, you'll be having a very different type of sex - not nearly as comfortable as you're used to with Isabelle. Now, it's time to come clean. What's this all about?"

Durand let out a sigh. He signalled for the waiter and ordered two more drinks.

"It's punishing, being in the PJ. A constant battle with criminals who are better equipped, more organised, less constrained by rules and procedures. You must know this too, from your own experience. I know who you are, Miss Kelso, where you're from. Sometimes it is necessary to seek something more rewarding, more satisfying, which is why many of us in the police seek out like-minded people to share our concerns and give each other some comfort. We have societies, clubs, informal gatherings where we can relax and be ourselves. Do you understand me, Julia?

"One society I belong to has links with a few others, other societies not associated with the police but which share some common goals and interests. I have been invited to meet with some of these from time to time.

One meeting was in Monaco. I went along with a friend, another member of my society, and the guest of honour was Guido Ricci. He is a wealthy Italian businessman, very well connected. After the formal meeting ended, Guido Ricci sought me out. He had heard that I was senior in the French police and he said he was interested in me. He invited me to dinner that evening. He can be very charming when he wants to be. We talked for hours; we have a lot in common.

"Over time, we got to know each other. He never asked me for anything at all, but to be honest if he had done I probably would have helped him if I could. We met from time to time when he was in Paris, and on one occasion he brought his wife, Isabelle, to dinner. She was friendly, warm. As you have seen, she is a very attractive woman. While Guido was in the men's room, we exchanged phone numbers.

"A week or two later Isabelle called me, asked if we could meet. An important matter had come up and she wanted my advice. I was flattered. The wife of such a rich and important person as Guido Ricci wanting the advice of a lowly policeman. We met at a hotel in Paris. We spoke in the bar, then she said she wanted to speak privately and could I go with her to her room. It was a suite, separate sitting room and bedroom. We spoke for a while, then she came to sit next to me and it started. She started it. The next morning I left - I had called my wife to say I had been detained in Paris on a case. Isabelle hadn't asked me to do anything, she said she just needed to be with a man who understood her.

"A few weeks later she made her first request. She was talking about the way Europe was becoming too overbearing, Brussels interfering too much in people's lives and businesses and privacy. She said it was overstepping its rightful boundaries, that people needed to assert their rights in their own countries and to do things the way that they had always done, according to their own traditions and values. I didn't disagree with her.

"She said that one institution that was making too many waves was Europol, with its new Joint Investigations operating freely across national borders and jurisdictions. Isabelle said Europol needed to be cut down to size, and a way to help it happen would be to sabotage a few of the Joint Investigations. A few failures would make Europol look incompetent, which would encourage national police forces to stop cooperating with them. She asked me to find someone who could provide information that she could pass to others, others who would be able to use it for this purpose.

"I had already met Faber a couple of times. I told Isabelle about him. She was very happy. And that is how it happened. I haven't taken a cent from Isabelle or anyone else, just expenses for hotels and travel to meet Faber or to see her. Isabelle always pays for the hotel when we stay together. I haven't seen Guido for a while."

He stopped. Julia had been listening intently. A few moments elapsed in silence.

"Thank you for telling me, Antoine. I'm a Scot, a minority in the UK. I can see the point Isabelle made. It applies to my country under English domination as much as any other country under European Union domination. I think I can help, but on my terms. Can you introduce me to Guido Ricci? I doubt Isabelle will be too interested in me, but then you never know."

"Isabelle will be here later this evening. It's why I came to Brussels. Faber calling me to arrange a meeting was just a coincidence."

"Good. I'll wait then. I can start with her. Where will you meet her?"

"Here, in the hotel. She has a suite reserved. She will be here within the hour."

"We'll have another drink then, shall we?" Julia said.

Chapter 28

For the next hour Julia Kelso probed and prodded Antoine Durand. In the end, she decided he really didn't know how the information he had obtained from Jeroen Faber ended up in the hands of murderous criminals. All he did, Durand had insisted, was pass it to Isabelle Meyer-Ricci during their trysts. Durand also didn't know whether Guido Ricci was aware of his love affair, as he called it, with Isabelle. Julia had no doubt at all. It was clear to her that Guido Ricci had to be using his own wife as bait, or a reward, for the lascivious French policeman, pimping her out.

Isabelle Meyer-Ricci entered the bar, her presence immediately apparent. It was the first time Julia had seen her in the flesh, and she was stunning. She moved with smouldering sinuosity, barely suppressing her sensuality. She was subtle, though. There was nothing brash or erotic about her dress or her manner, she was just naturally very, very sexy. Julia was impressed. Durand stood when he saw her.

Isabelle paused for a moment when she saw Julia in the booth, but her composure returned almost immediately.

"Are you going to introduce me, Antoine?" Isabelle asked in French.

Julia introduced herself, not waiting for Antoine. She also spoke in French.

"Julia Kelso, a new friend of Antoine's. I'm from The Hague, Europol in fact. I believe you know one of the security team there, Jeroen Faber?"

Isabelle switched to English.

"I have met Mr Faber on one or two occasions. Why do you ask?"

"Jeroen is no longer available, Madame Ricci, or may I call you Isabelle? You will be dealing with me from now on, if we can agree appropriate terms."

"You are very presumptuous, Ms Kelso," Isabelle said cooly.

"Julia, please. I don't think I'm presumptuous at all, merely pragmatic. Faber is of no further use to you, while I could be. Let's talk privately. I understand you have a room."

Isabelle had remained standing; Antoine hovered nervously.

"Very well," she said.

Isabelle turned and walked towards the exit. Durand started to follow.

"Wait here, Antoine," she said, "I don't think this will take long."

Durand was visibly deflated; he sat down again. Julia rose and followed Isabelle into the lobby.

******

While Antoine Durand waited and sipped another cocktail, across town in a sports bar Jeroen Faber was on his fifth Leffe beer. He was unused to its strength, and he was starting to feel dizzy. His resolve to avenge himself on Kelso was weakening as his brain fogged. He would think it through in the morning, but now, as soon as he finished this beer, he would head for the station and get a train home.

Jeroen staggered out of the bar. He tried to remember what had happened to his bag, which had his train ticket and his keys in it. He recalled dropping it in a basement area somewhere between the bar and the Grand Place, but he couldn't remember where. He started retracing his steps. Soon he was completely lost. The streets were dark, rain was falling. Every corner he turned seemed less and less familiar. He felt his anxiety rising; his head was still spinning and he was unsteady on his feet. He pulled his phone from his pocket and fumbled with the screen. His cold fingers couldn't compose the code to unlock the phone, which was getting slippery in his wet hands. It slipped from his grasp and crashed to the ground. He heard the crack as the screen broke. He bent to retrieve the damaged phone, but as he did so, he lost his balance and toppled forward.

It was all they needed, the three chancers who had been marking the drunk for some time. They pounced while Jeroen was trying to regain his feet. A flurry of fists and feet laid him low again. Rough hands tore through his pockets, taking anything they found. Passport, wallet, bank cards, even some small change. They pummelled him, shaking him and yelling at him to give them the PIN for the cards. He mumbled a number, terrified and confused. A final kick to the head from the ringleader and Jeroen passed out in the street, bleeding from his nose and ears.

******

In her suite, Isabelle opened the bottle of champagne that was chilling in an ice bucket. Without asking, she poured two flutes and handed one to Julia.

"*Prost*," she said, "or *santé* if you prefer."

"Cheers," Julia said.

Isabelle looked at her, watching her face for any sign of her intentions.

"What is it you want, Julia?" she said at last.

"For a start I want to know what you're doing and why you're doing it. I want to know what's in it for you, so I can decide if I'm in or out. And if I am in, I want to know what's in it for me too. Nothing complicated."

"And if you decide you are out?" Isabelle asked.

"Then the next time you see me I won't be on my own," Julia replied.

Two minutes passed in silence as Isabelle considered her response.

"Do you believe in choice, Julia," she said eventually, "in independence of action? Do you believe that the state, any state, should leave it to people to decide what they want and need, to do what is best for themselves and best for the state itself? Or do you believe that the state, the faceless bureaucrats and self-seeking politicians always know best? That they have a right to power, a right to dictate their will to the people, regardless of what is best for them or what they actually want?"

"That's quite a loaded question, Isabelle, and I can guess what your position is. Let me give you mine. I'm a Scot, a proud one. I believe that an independent Scotland is the best thing for Scotland and the Scots. I also believe that we should have cordial relations with the English, and also the Irish and the Welsh and with Europe, but as an equal partner. As for bureaucrats and politicians, I'd rather leave the ball-breaking admin to people like them. But the power, the real power, should rest with those best equipped and suited to use it well."

Isabelle refilled their glasses.

"We think alike, Julia. What we are doing, in our small way, is chipping away at the general acceptance that Europeans needs to abandon national identity and independence. We want to start to shake people's faith in European institutions so that their ever-expanding powers can be restrained. We want to start to dismantle the reputations of institutions, not just Europol but all the other interfering and intrusive ones that seem to think they can dominate the people. We think that showing their incompetence and exposing them to ridicule is one way to do this."

"And do people really need to die to make this happen?" Julia asked.

"A sad necessity, Julia, a few unfortunate deaths laid at the door of Europol, for example, are a potent demonstration of institutional incompetence. Besides, we don't think that many more will be necessary, not as far as Europol is concerned anyway."

"Okay, now what's in it for you? Why are you doing this?"

"We, and many others like us, are in business. We create wealth, opportunity and, of course, power. But our efforts are being progressively stifled. We need to clear the weeds. Please don't think there is some massive conspiracy, Julia, we are just part of a loose collection of like-minded people, business leaders, entrepreneurs and the like. There is no mastermind or central plan. We act independently, each trying to contribute to our collective goal, which is the restoration of free markets and free trade without bureaucratic and quasi-democratic hindrances."

"But you do intend to make money from it?" Julia asked.

"Inevitably we will, but it is also about shaping the future, making the world function in a better way, one that benefits those who deserve it. If you join us, it will be worth your while."

"Is it worth Antoine's while?"

"It is to him. He gets what he wants, as long as he remains useful."

"That being you, I take it."

"I wouldn't put it quite like that, but essentially yes."

"And your husband is okay with that?"

Isabelle threw her head back and laughed.

"Guido isn't some petit-bourgeois moralist, Julia, of course he's 'okay' with it. We have no secrets. I am a woman, Julia, and you are too. We have the advantage of being able to win more battles in one hour lying down than most men can in years of painful combat. Are you interested?"

"In lying down, or in joining you?"

"In joining us, of course. No disrespect, Julia, but you're not my type."

"You're not my type either, so I'm relieved. Am I interested in joining you? Maybe, I need to know more. What now?"

"I can arrange for you to meet Guido. You can talk. If he approves, we can discuss terms and expectations. Now, if you'll excuse me, I have to get ready. Could you send Antoine up? Don't tell him it's probably his last time, will you? If you are on our side, I don't think he'll be of use to me for much longer."

Julia wrote her personal mobile number on a pad on the sideboard. She controlled the urge to scream or vomit as she left Isabelle alone in the suite.

Chapter 29

Julia hailed a taxi and looked out of the window as it made its way towards the Midi station. She was distracted by flashing blue and red lights down a side street. Police vehicles and an ambulance were huddled in the rain and she saw paramedics crouched over a person lying on the wet pavement. She was sorry for whoever it was.

She caught the last train of the evening back to The Hague. She was practically alone in the carriage and she called Mel.

"How are you?" Julia asked when Mel picked up.

"Knackered as usual, why?" Mel was tetchy.

"I'm on my way back. I decided against a night in Brussels."

"Missing me too much?" Mel asked.

"Hardly. Listen, do you have access to that Dark Web thing - I mean from home? You don't need to be in the office or anything?"

"Are you calling from the Stone Age, Kelso? Of course I can access it, anyone can, from anywhere."

"Well, if you've nothing better to do until I get back, could you have a dig around? I had a long chat with Faber's friend Antoine - I'll tell you all about it later. One thing he mentioned was that he belongs to some sort of society, a bit secretive. He said lots of cops do."

"You mean like the Masons?"

"That sort of thing, but if it was the Masons I'm sure he would have just said so. Anyway, he said he met Guido Ricci through this society at some sort of meeting in Monaco. That's how he got to know Ricci and Isabelle.

He's been passing the information he got from Faber to them, and only them, he says."

"So you want me to have a rummage and see if I can find any connection between Ricci and some sort of secret-ish society?"

"Exactly, and if you can link Antoine Durand to it as well..." Julia left the sentence unfinished.

"I'll have a go. Hopefully a bit of splashing about in the sewers of the Dark Web will be the perfect antidote to an hour and a half of 'The Wheels on the Bus'."

"Thanks Mel. See you in a while."

Julia then called Jeroen Faber. There was no answer, so she tried Niall Morton.

"Morton," he said.

"Niall, Julia, how are you?"

"Fine, I'm at home. I took a week off - figured you had something up your sleeve for us. I'm with Errol, Sasha and Steven. It's cosy."

"It's Friday tomorrow, so I'm coming over for the weekend. Have you done anything on that security guy, Duncan Traynor?" She asked.

"We've done a bit, just discreet like. It's just the two of us so it's a bit superficial. We know where he lives, what he looks like, and we've been behind him for a while. He's very casual, easy to follow."

"Do you think we can get hold of him for a chat?"

"We being?"

"You, me and Errol. I want Errol to be there."

"Reckon so. We'll make sure he's tucked up safe and sound so we can take him tea and biscuits in the morning on Saturday."

"Sounds good. I'll call you when I get in. Say goodnight to everyone for me."

******

In the side street in Brussels, the paramedics were satisfied that the patient could be moved safely. They scooped him onto a stretcher and into the waiting ambulance. Although he was barely conscious and clearly concussed, the police officer riding in the back with the paramedic and the patient insisted on asking questions. The patient was not engaging at all.

"Officer, he has concussion and also a broken jaw. He will not be in the mood for a conversation. We don't even know if he speaks French. Let him be, please," the paramedic said.

The officer reluctantly complied. The patient had no identification, no phone, wallet, nothing. He couldn't talk, even if he wanted to, assuming he could speak French or Flemish Dutch. He'd seen the man's hands, both looked pretty bad. It was likely he had broken bones, so when he was up to communicating he wouldn't even be able to write his name. At least the officer would be out of the rain for the next couple of hours.

******

Julia had taken another taxi from Centraal Station in The Hague to her house. It wasn't that far, but the rain hadn't let up since she left Brussels. Mel was at the kitchen table, laptop open, when she walked in. Julia hung her coat up and poured herself a drink. Mel was engrossed and hadn't spoken yet. In fact she'd held a hand up to stop Julia speaking while she concentrated on her screen. Julia saw that Mel's wine glass was empty, so she filled it up and waited until Mel looked up.

"Hi Jake, cheers," she took a drink, "how did you get on?"

"Later. You seem grabbed by something. What have you found?"

"Ever heard of *carbonari*?" Mel asked.

"Like in spaghetti?"

"That's *carbonara*. The *carbonari* was a loose association of secret societies back in the eighteen-hundreds, quite an eclectic bunch by all accounts. The name means charcoal burners, but I don't think there were too many of them involved. In a nutshell, and as far as I can make out, the *carbonari* had various revolutionary tendencies, but mostly they were rebelling against any form of absolutism or repressive government. They were anti-feudal, and they wanted a unified Italy with any sort of government that didn't involve regional autocrats.

"While they were around, they spread out into loads of other countries, mostly in Europe and Russia, but also in Central and South America."

"You said 'while they were around'?" Jake asked.

"Yes, they're supposed to have disappeared more than a hundred years ago. They've popped up in various novels and films over the years, mostly as romanticised versions of themselves."

"If they've disappeared, why are we talking about them?"

"Because," Mel said, "there are a sprinkling of clues on the Dark Web suggesting they've come back."

"Have they now? Tell me more."

"So, they are supposed to have disappeared, become redundant, in the mid-nineteenth century. Italy and Germany had each unified as new countries, feudalism was on the wane, a form of democracy was taking hold, so their job was done. Bearing in mind that the sort of democracies around in the nineteenth century were very much the sort of thing that the wealthy entrepreneurs and property owners liked - no involvement of poor people, a rigid class structure, tame parliaments and governments mostly comprising landed gentry and a few industrialists. The poor people were just there to do the work, grow the food and provide the soldiers to fight the wars.

"Anyway, what I've been finding are a few - not that many - mentions of secretive groups that hark back to the *carbonari*, or more precisely, the sort of regimes that made the *carbonari* redundant. Come the twentieth century with socialism and broader electorate-based democracies emerging, the throwbacks seem to have started revolting again. They are especially grumpy about inter-governmental cooperation, in fact any international cooperation on anything other than free trade; they hate cross-border political parties and organisations - even though that's what the original *carbonari* were - and anything that places regulatory obstacles in the way of business. If you ever meet any of them, please don't mention the European Union!"

"You're telling me that these *carbonari* have come back?" Jake asked.

"Not exactly. They don't use the name. In fact they don't use any particular name. The references I've found just mention '*l'ordine*', it means 'The Order' in Italian."

"And am I right in guessing that this *l'ordine* has something to do with Ricci?"

"Correct, Kelso, at least I think so. I found a private exchange of messages - it was hacked and put on the Dark Web for anyone to look at, it happens all the time - between two people, one in France, the other in the US. They were saying how good it was to have met again at the induction of the new Grand Master in Rome. The person in France comments on how the new Grand Master, only he used the initials G.R., had endured the initiation rituals with great dignity and courage. There are other snippets in the message exchanges, which aren't actually between groups or organisations but rather between two individuals at any one time. These are people who seem to share a secret, but most of them don't know each other. I saw a remark that only one representative from each country was allowed to attend the induction ceremony. It's just lucky that the two I found already knew each other and decided to chat about it."

"Just individuals? No groups, no one copied in, nothing like that?" Jake asked.

"No, always one on one, only one on one. It's pretty good security."

"So how do they know what they're supposed to be doing?"

"Don't know, at least not yet. But now we've found them we can keep an eye on them, can't we?" Mel said. "By the way, is this on the books yet?"

"Not yet, no. I need to keep digging a bit more. Which means…"

"No warrants, no investigators, no help," Mel completed the sentence.

"Not quite no help - we've got Niall and Errol, and you, of course," Jake said.

"But no one else."

"No, no one else, Mel, and I miss him too."

Jake stood and stretched. She looked down at Mel, still seated.

"Coming to bed?" Jake asked.

Mel smiled up at her.

"I'll just do my teeth and get the squawk box, I'll be up in a minute."

"I'll wait," Jake said.

Mel emerged a few minutes later, wearing one of her long tee shirts and holding a baby monitor. Jake stood and held out her hand. She led Mel up the stairs to her room, her sanctuary.

Later, they lay beside each other, holding hands and talking quietly.

"You've taught me so much, Mel, about this."

"About what?"

"This, being with someone, sex, everything. This is the bit when you really need someone else, isn't it? The time afterwards, when your heartbeat is back to normal, when you just need to touch someone, to talk."

She wrapped her arms around Mel, who snuggled into her.

"I think you've gone soppy, Kelso," she said, but lifting her head to kiss Jake softly. "I need sleep. Sweet dreams."

Jake lay awake for a while, listening to Mel's deep, even breathing. After a while her eyes closed. Dreams did come, but they weren't sweet.

Chapter 30

They sat in Niall Morton's rented car in a residential street outside a respectable looking semi. The curtains were still drawn, but then it was still only seven in the morning. They waited until the upstairs curtains opened. They saw a woman in a dressing gown tidying them and opening a window. Ten minutes later they walked up to the front door. Niall knocked loudly.

A man opened the door, wearing neat trousers, a cardigan over a pale shirt, with a Paisley cravat knotted loosely at his throat. His slippers were highly polished. He looked enquiringly at the three people on his doorstep. Niall flashed his police i/d.

"Can we come in?" he asked.

Duncan Traynor stood aside and ushered them in.

"Tea?" he asked.

"No thanks," Julia said. "I'm Commander Kelso, this is DI Morton and DS Spelman. Are you Duncan Traynor, formerly Chief Superintendent in Royalty and Diplomatic Protection, currently head of security at The Dorchester Hotel?"

"Not just The Dorchester, but yes. How can I help you?"

"You met and spoke to a man, a black man, at the Dorchester," Errol gave him the date, "I saw you speaking to him."

"I really don't remember, I speak to a lot of people," Traynor said, unruffled. "Why?"

"Because after you spoke to that man, who goes by the name of Adda, he sent some thugs to burn my house down," Errol said calmly. "His aim was to kill me, but I got a head start. Adda was wearing a sharp suit; he's not a big guy but he has a scary presence. He's about five-six, close cut hair, wears a lot of after-shave. Remember him now?"

"He had your house burnt down?"

"Flat, actually, in Streatham. You might have seen it in the papers. Two of my neighbours died, several more hospitalised, including firefighters. Just minutes after he spoke to you."

"Well, I'm sorry, but it had nothing to do with me," Traynor said.

"Just tell us what happened, Mr Traynor," Julia interjected.

"I remember it now. I had been asked to give an envelope, a letter, to someone. I was told that the recipient would ask for me at the hotel, and then say a certain phrase. If the phrase was correct, I was to hand him the letter, that's all. I wasn't told who it would be or what was in the letter. The man did what he was supposed to do, I gave him the envelope and he went away. That's all I know." Traynor was starting to look uneasy.

"So, who told you to do this?" Julia asked.

"I really can't say," Traynor replied.

"And why is that?"

"It's a private matter, confidential."

"Just so you know," Julia said, "this Adda character isn't just some sharp-dressed hotel guest. He's a cold-blooded murderer, a prominent Jamaican gangster. He's a major drug dealer, as well as a vicious piece of shit. After he left you and had Errol's flat torched, he tortured and killed an informant and then turned on his own lieutenant here in London. He was found, also tortured and killed, tied to a tree in Epping Forest. Whatever was in that envelope you gave him brought about this string of events. I think you'll find that trumps your confidentiality. Now, who told you to give him the envelope?"

Traynor had paled. He sat down heavily and took a deep breath.

"I'd like to help, I really would," he said, "but I honestly don't know."

"Do me a favour!" Niall spoke for the first time.

"Look, you don't understand!" Traynor said, urgently. "It's the way things work in the…"

"How things work in the what?" Errol demanded.

"I need a glass of water," Traynor gasped.

He stood and walked unsteadily towards the kitchen. Errol followed, but Julia gestured for Niall to stay where he was. In the kitchen Errol turned and leant casually against a counter. He watched Traynor carefully. The man took a drink of water and refilled his glass from the tap. Errol saw that he was deeply worried.

"Look, Duncan," Errol said very quietly, "whatever it is you're trying to hide isn't worth it. What you did that night, knowingly or not, has hurt me and my family, hurt us badly. I'm very angry about that. The families of the people killed and injured that night are also very angry. You've got one chance."

"Are you threatening me?"

"Nowhere near, not yet," Errol said calmly, "but I can. Or we can just bring your nice house and nice life down around your ears, just so you know how it feels. You see, what you passed to that evil bastard Adda was secret information, information naming an undercover police officer, that's me by the way, and a Jamaican police informer. Not just my cover name, Duncan, but my real one, and my address. Now that could only come from someone who could get hold of that information.

"Now, you're a former senior police officer. You could probably access that sort of information if you wanted to and were prepared to try hard enough. Probably using some of your old mates to help you. All of that can and will come out, I can make sure of that, when you're arrested for corruption and conspiracy to murder - that's what it looks like to me, and I do know about these things. That's not going to go down too well at the golf club or with the people who are topping up your pension fund, is it? What will your wife do? Where will she go when the reporters are camped out in the front garden, banging on your neighbours' doors? Not to mention when you're remanded in custody. Those Brixton boys will have some fun with you, I expect."

Traynor was sweating, shaking.

"It was a favour, a favour for a friend, a brother. I had no idea what was in the envelope, I swear!" Traynor blurted.

"A brother? Is that what I think it means? The Square?"

"No, not the Square. I am a Freemason, but I have other brothers too. It was for one of them," Traynor was on the verge of tears.

"Best you tell Miss Kelso all about it, Duncan," Errol said, "Let's go."

Errol led Traynor back into his sitting room. He nodded at Julia.

"He's ready," Errol said.

"Alright Duncan, tell me," Julia demanded.

Traynor was shaking, his eyes watery.

"When I went to Royalty Protection it wasn't long before I started to get invitations. Invitations to dinners, lunches, sporting events. People thought I might have some influence, be able to make introductions or just engineer situations in which someone or other might be able to have a few words with my Principal. I never compromised security, of course, but from time to time I was able to help people. I was invited to join the Lodge. It was explained to me that Freemasonry was and is a worthy charitable fellowship, and that it is now free of all the secrecy and intrigue that surrounded it for so long. As Freemasons, we pledge to serve our communities and each other, to give generously, to be good citizens."

Niall Morton barely supressed a laugh.

"You may mock, DI Morton," Traynor said, "but it is true and it is what I believe."

Morton said nothing.

"I served my Lodge faithfully throughout the rest of my police service, and I am certain I never compromised my oath or my loyalty to either; it is possible to serve two masters equally well. When I retired, the Lodge was very keen that I stay on; I had gained some seniority and I was happy to do so. I moved into the commercial world and I got to meet many other members of the Fellowship in many walks of life. It was and is a rich, rewarding experience.

"Recently, in the last couple of years, I was introduced to some members of another similar, but unrelated, brotherhood. It shares the same altruistic beliefs and practices, but it does have an activist edge to it. The guiding principle is that of individual freedom, for people and nations, countering political globalisation and cultural homogeny."

"And what is this brotherhood called?" Julia asked.

"I don't know," Traynor replied.

"You don't know?" Julia asked, incredulous.

"No, I don't. We don't use a name. If we did, it would inevitably lead to ridicule and slander; we would be labelled cranks."

"And you fear ridicule?" Julia asked.

"It isn't possible to be influential if you are a laughingstock, is it? Especially when you become one due to unwarranted mockery by ignorant enemies."

"Was it one of these brothers who gave you the envelope and the instructions?" Morton asked.

"It was, but before you ask, I don't know who it was. We operate in a very tight cell structure. I know only two other members, only the Masters know the identities of more than that. There are regional and national Masters, and one Grand Master. From time to time, we get to attend a gathering of maybe a dozen others, but we are always masked and we are prohibited from making or seeking introductions to one another. But there is an identifying recognition signal that we have.

"A few days before the incident we are talking about, a person I do not know contacted me at the hotel. We met outside, away from the CCTV cameras. He gave me the signal and instructed me to hand the envelope to a person who would ask for me by name at the hotel on a given day. The person would arrive in the evening, so I was to be sure that I was there after six p.m. I was told that the person would use a particular phrase and I was to hand him or her the envelope. That is all, and that is what happened. The person you call Adda asked for me, used the phrase and I gave him the envelope."

"And what was the phrase?" Julia asked.

"I can't see why it matters," Traynor said.

"Just tell me."

"If you insist. The phrase was 'I've seen a rat in the kitchen'. Just that."

"OK, Duncan," Julia said, "we'll leave it there. Keep this visit to yourself for now. If it's going any further, you'll be the first to know."

Outside in the car Errol was fuming.

"Do you believe all that crap?" he asked generally.

"I'm afraid I do," Julia said. "Errol, are you ready to go back to work?"

"I reckon so. I've spoken to them, welfare are sorting us out a place to stay while the insurance is settled, and now I know it wasn't someone in the command chain who did me in I'm happy to go back."

"Good. When you are back, see if you can do some financial digging on Mr Traynor. I didn't see anything inconsistent at his house, but it would be nice to know if he's on the take."

"Will do, Julia," he said.

"Great, thanks guys. If you drop me at a tube station I'll get out of your hair."

Chapter 31

Julia asked Mel to go into the office on Monday morning. Her task was to go through all the files relating to the Adda case to try and find out who had passed on the phrase 'I've seen a rat in the kitchen'.

"I think it must have been passed to Adda verbally, probably by phone," Julia explained. "Use Errol to help you find contacts in the Met who might have seen any intercept on his phone in the UK, and maybe get Abigail at Six to see what GCHQ can do."

Mel set to with enthusiasm. This was what she used to do for a living, before fate and Ferdinand intervened. It took her nearly all day.

"I think I've got it," Mel said when she called Julia.

"Tell me," Jake urged.

"So, Errol mentioned that he'd bought two phones on Adda's instructions. Adda threw the SIM cards away and used his own, but he called Errol once so he could have the number. Errol never had time to record it, and he threw the phone away on the fateful night. But, and this is lucky, he did make one call to Steven and another to the 999 operator. No joy on tracing that 999 call, but we pulled Steven's billing and got the number that Errol used.

"Then I traced back and found the only number that had called into Errol's temporary phone, which of course was Adda's UK one. Long story short, Adda made a brief call to a Jamaican mobile just as he was going into The Dorchester. Abigail got the Cheltenham guys to have a look, and the Jamaican number that Adda called is quite a busy one. Mostly used for local calls, but there are a few international ones logged.

"I've been through the Europol system and the number Adda called isn't known, except in the context of calling Adda, which it did twice in Jamaica. It called Adda's regular phone, not the temporary UK one. So, we need to find out who this phone belongs to." Mel paused and took a slurp of coffee.

"Unusually," Mel continued, "this particular phone is properly registered. The UK liaison guy in Jamaica was able to get a subscriber in no time. It turns out that the phone belongs to a pillar of the community, a senior figure in the Jamaican Exporters Society - I've got his name. A bit of internet and Dark Web digging shows that this chap is also a past master of a Masonic Lodge in Jamaica."

"This is getting to sound familiar," Julia said, "any calls to or from Europe?"

"A few yes, with Italy specifically," Mel confirmed, "one on the morning of Errol's incident and another a few days before. Both originating in Italy. I'm waiting on details."

"Great, let me know. Have you seen Jeroen Faber today?" Julia asked. Mel hadn't.

Julia called his office. It seemed that Faber hadn't reported sick after all, but he hadn't turned up for work that day either. He wasn't answering his phone. Someone had been sent to his flat but hadn't been able to get an answer. Julia expressed appropriate concern and asked his office to let her know as and when Faber was located.

"Mel, can you check the dates that Faber accessed my computer, specifically around the time that the Italy - Jamaica calls were made?"

"Already done that. He accessed Errol's case three days before the first call from Italy to the Jamaican number. And just to confirm what you're thinking, he did look at the files with Errol's personal details, and the ones with the Jamaican CHIS's as well. I'm thinking the Italian number probably has something to do with your man Guido Ricci. I'm working on it."

"Just so I'm clear," Julia said, "what it looks like is this: Faber finds information on ongoing operations that he thinks his friend Antoine might find interesting. He gives it to Antoine, who gives it to his supposed lover, Isabelle. She in turn gives it to her husband, Guido Ricci, then he decides what to do with it and who to involve. Does that fit with your thinking, Mel?"

"Pretty much," Mel said. "It's quite a job, but I'd like to have a look at the other compromises with that scenario in mind. If we can find any links from the Italian end to all or any of the compromises, then we have a workable theory to be getting on with. Ready to go official yet, Jake?"

"Not yet," Julia replied.

"I was afraid you'd say that. Why not?"

"One, because we don't know enough about Ricci and his connections. If his arms are long enough to reach Duncan Traynor in London and this guy in Jamaica, and if he *was* behind the other compromises in Hungary, Portugal, Austria *et al*, it's fair to assume he'll be well protected on his home turf. We don't know who by.

"Two, we still have no real idea *why* he's doing it. What interest can a wealthy, a very wealthy, businessman have in getting undercover agents and informers killed? Why would he go to such lengths? If he wants to discredit transnational agencies, surely there are more effective and less messy ways to go about it. What's in it for him?"

"Both fair points, Jake," Mel agreed, "but I still think it might be time to use the rest of the police, not just you and Errol and Niall. And me, of course."

"You know how it works, Mel. When an investigation starts it needs to have rules, aims, objectives, legal points to prove and disprove. An investigation won't get to the bottom of this. We've both seen it a thousand times. The top tier always get away unscathed, unless the investigation is prepared to take about a hundred years

"We might take out Ricci, but I doubt we'll be able to prove enough against him, and even if we did, is he the one we should be going for? Is there someone above him? If Ricci is top dog, I bet we'd only get as far as Antoine Durand, who would be set up to take the rap for all of it. Let's plough on a bit longer. I want to meet Ricci. After my talk with Isabelle, I think it might happen quite soon."

"Well," Mel said, "I hope you know what you're doing, and I also hope you'll be careful."

Julia stood and went across the room to her. She took Mel's hand in hers.

"I do, and I will. Promise. Now, get me those other connections. I'm going to see if I can find Jeroen Faber. I've a horrible feeling he's still in Brussels."

Chapter 32

Duncan Traynor was rattled. The early-morning visit from Kelso and her two attack dogs had unsettled him, more than that, it had terrified him. He'd had no idea what was in the envelope he handed to the agitated Jamaican at The Dorchester, he was only doing a service for the society. If the society was involved in the sort of thing that Kelso and Spelman were talking about, he wanted no part of it.

His only contact with the other British member he knew of was by text. They each had a phone that wasn't used for anything else. On reflection, Traynor thought, that was strange too. He took the phone from his desk drawer and, ignoring instructions to use specific prescribed phrases he wrote 'I need to see you!'. He pressed send and waited.

******

Julia Kelso put in a call to Jeroen Faber's line manager.

"Is Jeroen in yet?" she asked, "He was putting some statistics together for me and I'd like a quick word with him."

"Sorry, Julia," Faber's manager said, "he hasn't come in today. He may be sick or something; he said he wasn't feeling well yesterday and he went home early."

"Could he be on leave?" Julia asked. "I saw him on the train to Brussels yesterday afternoon, come to think of it. He had a case with him."

"It's possible, I suppose, but he hasn't registered any leave request. You said Brussels?"

"I went down to see a friend for dinner; Jeroen was on the same train. We said hello but didn't talk much. Let me know when he's in next, could you?"

"Of course, thank you, Julia."

As Julia expected, Faber's boss got in touch with someone he knew in the Brussels police and it wasn't long before he heard news that Faber's small suitcase had been found in a street near the city centre. It had Faber's name and address on the outside label. Of more concern was the fact that a known street gang member had been arrested and was found to be in possession of Faber's passport. He was saying nothing, of course. A trawl of all the reports of robberies was underway; unfortunately there were a lot to go through.

By early afternoon, the contact in Brussels reported that an unidentified robbery victim, matching Jeroen's description, was in a serious condition in the St Pierre hospital in central Brussels. The patient had no means of identification, and due to his injuries was unable to communicate at all. In fact, he was under sedation and would remain that way for a good while yet. This news was relayed by the line manager to Julia, who expressed her concern. The line manager was on his way to Brussels to see if the unfortunate victim was in fact his absent colleague, Jeroen Faber.

"So what happened to him?" Mel asked. She was in Jake's office and had been listening.

"I don't know," Julia replied, "he was fine the last time I saw him, even if he did look a bit pissed off. Now, what have you come up with?"

"I did what you asked, I've been looking for anything and everything on Guido Ricci," Mel said, "open source,

Europol and Dark Web. I've also had a peep at some Italian government records."

"How did you do that?" Jake asked.

"I've learnt a few tricks along the way, mostly from Nisha Chakrabarti. I'm not bad at it now, the hacking stuff. Don't worry, it won't come back to you or this place."

"Have you found anything to suggest a reason for why he's doing whatever it is he's doing? Why he's been sabotaging Europol operations and getting people killed?"

"If it is him who's doing it - we don't know that for sure yet, Jake. But the short answer is no."

"What do you have on him, then?"

"Born in Turin into a working-class family, all with jobs at Fiat. He did only so-so at school, no formal qualifications and no higher education. He got arrested a couple of times as a teenager for minor theft, unlicensed street trading, once for assault, but all small stuff. No suggestion that he joined the mafia or got into more serious criminal activities."

"So how did he get to be seriously rich?"

"When he was around twenty or so he got a job, not in the Fiat factory but as an office boy for a local accountant. He stayed two or three years, and when he left he started his first business - providing short-term finance for small businesses, ones with cash-flow problems. I don't know what his USP was, but he seemed to do well, made a decent living. Then he started taking over some of his clients' businesses. He'd made a packet by the time he was thirty, seemingly all legit. But...."

"But what?" Julia asked.

"But it looks like he had picked up a few tips at the accountants. None of the businesses he'd acquired continued making profits, at least on paper, so no tax was paid. Also, all employees were reclassified as self-employed, so no taxes there either. Sales tax was left unpaid, and when any payments were made it was always just enough to delay prosecution. A pattern started to emerge; he'd buy out a business, always for next to nothing, cream off any money set aside for tax and when the time was right the business would collapse with no assets and loads of debt, mostly to the Italian government."

"Why wasn't Ricci prosecuted?" Julia asked.

"Because he was never the actual owner or director of the company concerned, and because he'd made such a cat's cradle of the accounts and paperwork it always took the tax people years to untangle it all. For the sums concerned on each business it wasn't worth the effort, but Ricci was doing it multiple times in different regions, so collectively it amounted to very big bucks.

"Then he went international, cross-border, and started doing the same all over Europe. To explain his growing wealth, he did set up one or two legitimate concerns and hired proper management teams to run them. They do well enough and give Ricci a dividend and consultancy fee income that does the job and explains his lifestyle for anti-money-laundering purposes. It's only the tip of his iceberg, though. As far as I can make out, he's still making much more through tax fiddles and fraud than he's declaring."

"So Ricci is just a straightforward fraudster then," Julia said. "Is any of this evidential?"

"Not evidential, no. A lot of it comes from Dark Web chatter, other bits from curiously dormant Guardia di Finanza files. There's hardly anything in Europol records. It's not beyond belief that Ricci's paying people off, I mean in Italy, to be left alone. He can afford it."

"It doesn't explain why he's having undercover police and informants murdered. If he's cheating the taxman and bunging a few people he's dishonest, certainly, and a criminal, but it's a big jump from fraud to murder. Why's he doing it, Mel? And what's with these *carbonari* types? Any thoughts?"

"One possibility is that international law-enforcement cooperation, in the form of Joint Investigation Teams, is a direct threat to him. He may have Italy sewn up, but by the time you get a multi-national team working together with the aim of taking criminals down in whatever jurisdiction can do it, his ability to buy off the heat is reduced. But I think there's more to it; I think that Europol is just a start. He wants to sabotage anything the EU does that will make it harder for him to make his frauds work. Closer alignment of tax authorities and regulations, data sharing, cooperation between states on tax fraud, frauds against national or international institutions and funds, it all makes Ricci's empire less stable. It could bring it all crashing down.

"Derailing international cooperation is an existential quest for Ricci, and many others like him. He can't be the only one doing this. They like the freedom that the EU and its principles give them to make their dirty millions, but they want it kept harmless, impotent. I think that's what the new *carbonari* are all about, I doubt that every member knows that, though. So, that's a theory. Means, motive, opportunity. Just got to prove it now - over to you."

Julia thought for a while.

"It makes sense," she said eventually. "We need more, we need something solid that we can act on. The open-source material is too circumstantial, the stuff you've nicked is unusable. If we can't get evidence to start a proper and thorough investigation, we need to get a source inside Ricci's operation."

"Could you ask Hugh and Abigail at MI6 if they can get anything?" Mel suggested.

"Good idea, I'll go and see them, and I'll have another chat with Duncan Traynor too while I'm at it. I also want to speak to Antoine Durand again. They're the only two probable *carbonari* associates we have."

"I expect you'll find they're just foot-soldiers, Jake," Mel said, "we'll need someone much closer to Guido or Isabelle to find out what's really going on - and work out how to stop it."

"You're right, Mel, I think we will," she paused reflectively.

"No, Jake, don't do it! Please don't."

Chapter 33

Two days later Julia met Hugh Cavendish and Abigail Ukebe for dinner at The Travellers' Club in London. It was one of Hugh's favourite haunts and good for discreet conversations. Julia set out her stall in respect of Guido Ricci and the new *carbonari* while they listened intently.

Abigail, now effectively Hugh's principal helper, was first to respond.

"I've seen something about a revival of an extinct secret society, although I don't recall it having a name like *carbonari*. It was referred to only as *l'ordine,* the Order, and it came from US liaison. They wanted to know if we'd heard of it, their interest being about a high-profile figure in the States with an aversion to compliance who may have joined it. I'll get back to them tomorrow to see if there is anything else and ask if they know Guido Ricci."

"Thanks, Abigail, I appreciate it," Julia said. "There's Ricci's wife as well, Isabelle Meyer-Ricci. She's involved in whatever it is he's up to. It's too early to say exactly what that is or how she's part of it, but I do know she's been having it off on Guido's orders with a bent French cop who's been feeding them Europol information. My theory is that the stolen information she's received has led directly to the murder of several undercover officers and informants."

A short while later Abigail excused herself and Julia was left alone with Cavendish.

"Tell me to sod off if I'm prying, Jake," he said, "but should you be doing this all by yourself? You're on your own over there in The Hague; when you went off the books here you had some support, resources and above all a warrant card to help you out if things got sticky. Now you haven't got any of those, you haven't even got your secret weapon, Ferdinand. You know I'm no stickler for rules and regulations, but is it worth the risk?"

"All good points, Hugh," she replied, "and if I was being sensible I'd agree with you and say no. I'm only planning to go it alone until I've got enough to hand it on to a properly sanctioned investigation team, assuming there is anything to hand on and to investigate. It still might amount to nothing."

"You have good instincts, Jake, so do I. We both know there's something in this, and it's probably very close to what you think it is. Ricci sounds dangerous. Think carefully, for me if not your mum and dad. If you crave skulduggery, why don't you take me up on my offer? Come and work for us. Europol isn't for you, nor is the Met now. And going back to mainstream policing in Scotland would bore you rigid in minutes."

"You're probably right. Let me get this one out of my system, one last time, then I'll come and talk to you. Now, let's get a night cap downstairs, shall we?"

The next morning, a Friday, Julia ordered a rental car and spent a couple of hours in the gym and pool at Dolphin Square, where she still had use of her father's flat. She treated herself to a leisurely lunch at Tate Britain and browsed the gallery for a gorgeous hour or two, just enjoying the freedom to do nothing if that's what she wanted.

Early on Saturday she was outside Duncan Traynor's suburban house. She waited for any sign of movement. Just after eight, the front door opened and Traynor emerged. He looked anxious. He opened the gate to his drive and carefully backed his car out onto the road. It was a newish SUV, a distinctive bright silver-grey colour. It would be an easy follow. Julia had taken the trouble to cover her blonde hair with the hood of a running top and she was wearing leggings and training shoes, like any number of suburban women on a Saturday morning.

Traynor drove surprisingly swiftly and he was soon on the M40 heading out of town towards Oxford. Julia kept pace, keeping a steady two or three cars behind him. Traynor pulled off at a motorway service station and parked as far from any other vehicles as he could. The place wasn't busy and Julia found a spot far enough away from Traynor to avoid him noticing her, but close enough to see what was going on. She watched as Traynor walked purposefully into the building. He went directly to a coffee outlet, ordered a drink and went to sit at an unoccupied table for two. Julia went to the washroom, and when she returned she saw that Traynor had been joined by a second man, this one a bit younger and informally dressed, even for a Saturday. They were engaged in an earnest and apparently tetchy conversation. The younger man looked decidedly annoyed. Julia took a seat outside the building and waited. After ten minutes Traynor emerged, walking fast and clearly unhappy. She let him go. The second man came out a few minutes later. Julia managed to get a quick shot of him on her phone camera as he passed, then she walked after him. He looked familiar, but Julia couldn't place him.

He went to a car, a low-slung Porsche convertible, got in and lowered the roof. He looked even more unhappy than Traynor. He gunned the motor aggressively and pulled away with a screech of tyres. She took another picture with her phone. Julia hurried back to her own rented car but by the time she got to it, Traynor's associate was gone. She followed as quickly as she could, and just caught sight of the convertible as it pulled off at the next junction. She lost him soon after that as he approached the city of Oxford and its mad traffic system. He clearly knew his way around the place.

Julia pulled over. She looked at the photos she had taken and emailed them to Errol Spelman. She added a few words asking him to 'do the necessary'. By the time she got back to Traynor's street she had the name and address of the owner of the convertible. He did live in Oxford, as she had guessed. She searched the name on the internet with her phone and quickly found out where she knew him from. He was Maurice Berwick, a well-known and publicity-hungry entrepreneur who appeared regularly on TV as a financial pundit and tormentor of left-of-centre economists. Although ostensibly not a member of any party, his published views did tend to chime with those of the most sceptical of Eurosceptics, who were found at either end of the political spectrum. Could he be another member of the strange secret society, Julia wondered?

She found that she had beaten Traynor back to his house. The driveway was empty and there was no sign of anyone moving inside. She decided to wait a while, at least until she started to feel conspicuous. As she waited, she called Errol.

"Thanks for the quick turnround on that vehicle, Errol," she started. "When you get a chance can you see if anything's known about the owner? He's got quite a high media profile, but it would be helpful to know if there's anything that's not public knowledge."

"I'll have a look, but it won't be until Monday. We're moving into our new house today and tomorrow; the Met's given us a new place in Bromley. A bit further out, but it's good. Why are you interested in Berwick, Julia?"

"It seems he's an associate of Traynor, possibly one of his secret squirrel club friends. They just had a quick and rather tense meet near Oxford. Neither looked happy. I'm waiting for Traynor now, outside his place."

"Call me later, okay? Just to let me know you're alright. If you need any help I can drop everything and come, but Stevie won't speak to me for a month. Niall's had to go back to Budapest, otherwise he could have helped if you need it."

"Thanks, Errol, I'll be fine. I just want another quick word with Traynor, that's all. Speak later."

She called Mel.

"Morning," she said brightly, "how are things?"

"Why are you so chirpy?" Mel asked.

"Why are you so grumpy?"

"It's easier. What do you want?"

"Maurice Berwick, the business and finance guy who's always on TV, can you find anything on the Dark Web about him, and any connection between him and Guido Ricci?"

"I'll have a look when Freddie's finished his tantrum, it shouldn't be too long now. Why are you interested?"

"He had a rushed meet with Traynor earlier this morning. Neither looked happy about it, and they don't look like old friends or natural allies. I'm thinking he could be another one of those *carbonari*."

"Call you in a while," Mel said.

"See you soon," she ended the call and waited some more.

Chapter 34

Guido and Isabelle had enjoyed a light lunch on the terrace overlooking the lake in Italy. Isabelle had taken a swim and was wearing a robe as she flicked through a magazine. Guido was reading the financial pages of *La Stampa* and he sighed loudly when his phone chirruped at him. It was not his usual phone, and it didn't often ring.

"*Pronto,*" he barked.

His face darkened as he listened to the caller, then he rose from the table and went inside the mansion.

"Tell me again," he said in English.

"One of the brothers in England used the emergency signal this morning. I contacted him, as the procedure states, and he told me that another brother, the only one he knows of, is in a state of panic. The brother he was speaking of was the former policeman. The policeman claims that he was used to convey a message from the Order to a criminal that resulted in acts of violence, including burning down the home of another policeman. Some people were killed or injured."

"And what did you tell him?" Guido demanded.

"That the brother must be having delusions, that the Order would do no such thing."

"Quite so," Guido assured the caller. "What is the former policeman going to do?"

"The brother who called me said he was extremely upset. He had been visited at home by detectives; they were quite threatening, apparently. One of them claimed to be the one whose home was destroyed. The brother wants reassurance 'from the top' or he will tell the police and the newspapers all he knows about the

Order. He wants to speak to you personally, Grand Master."

"Thank you," Guido said calmly, "you did well to contact me. Now, you must destroy the phone you are using. You can leave the matter with me. Do not respond to the brother who contacted you. Is that clear?"

"Yes, Grand Master, good day."

Guido went to the safe in his office and retrieved a small black book. It listed all the members of the Order globally - the number was not huge, not yet - as well as the names and contact details of people who could provide 'services' of varying descriptions. Some of these services could rightly be regarded as highly illegal. He found the name he was looking for and went to his desktop computer. Contact with the service provider was only by encrypted email on the Dark Web. Guido logged in.

Isabelle was back in the pool by the time Guido returned. He sat and watched her sleek body, encased in a one-piece swimsuit that accentuated her curves and shapes rather than protected her modesty. He was becoming aroused. Isabelle excited him in a way no other woman could. The thought of her beneath another man, or astride him in ecstasy, was incredibly erotic. He couldn't wait.

"Let's go inside, my sweet. I don't want you to catch a chill; I will warm you up."

She looked up at him, knowing exactly what he meant. She turned on her smile while sighing inwardly. Luxury and comfort did come at a cost.

******

Julia had stayed near Traynor's house longer than she wanted and she was starting to feel conspicuous. She started her car and pulled away, only to see Traynor's SUV coming from the opposite direction. He was alone, a look of fixed concentration on his face. Julia went around the block and passed the house again just as Traynor was unloading bags of groceries from the vehicle. Whatever he had discussed with Maurice Berwick earlier in the day had not placated him, or so it seemed.

Forty minutes later Julia knocked on his door. He opened it, and on seeing her he scowled.

"What do you want?" he demanded.

"That's not very polite, Duncan," she responded, "I just need another chat with you. A follow-up, if you like. Can I come in?"

He stood aside and indicated that Julia should go into a side-room, obviously his study.

"What can I do for you, Ms Kelso?" he asked coldly.

"A bit of clarification, Duncan, and do please call me Julia," she said.

"Clarification about what?"

"This secret club that you belong to, you and Maurice Berwick?"

"I don't know what you mean, and I don't know any Maurice Berwick," he responded.

"He's the man you met this morning at Oxford Services on the M40, the one you had coffee and a cosy chat with. He wasn't happy, was he? Is he your next link in the chain?"

"Why are you so interested? Why are you having me followed?"

"I'm just curious, and why do you think?"

"I have no idea. What is it you want from me?" he asked.

"Time's marching on, Duncan, it waits for no one, man or woman. Sometimes it's best to look after one's own interests, don't you think? I followed you myself, this is all off the books. I can't speak for the others, though, Errol and Niall, they're straight as you like, and Errol for one wants to hang you out to dry. He's really angry with you. If you want a crack of light, a hint that all this might somehow go away, you'd better talk to me, Duncan. Do you understand what I'm saying?"

"I'm not a rich man Kelso, you'll not get much from me," he protested.

"Duncan, please don't insult me or make yourself look stupid. I'm not interested in the bottom-feeders, there's no future in them. I want you to tell me all you know about the organisation, the society you belong to, let's just call it the Order, shall we, or *l'ordine* in its original Italian."

Traynor's face fell and his resolve melted. He went to a cupboard and pulled out a bottle of whisky. With shaking hands he poured some into a tumbler, splashing drops on the carpet.

"Too early for me, Duncan," Julia said pre-emptively, "but you feel free. I haven't got much time, so start talking."

He took a draught and coughed, refilling the tumbler as he organised his thoughts.

"Like I told you, the Order has a cell structure. The only other person I actually know by name is Berwick. We have a phone, we were each given one, that we can only use to communicate with one another. In due course, I will be given the name of another member, a brother - even female members are called brothers - so I will become a link in a chain."

"That's how terrorists work, Duncan, and organised crime groups," she said.

"We are neither! We are honourable people!"

"Really. How did you get involved?"

"Berwick invited me to dinner; we knew each other slightly from my time at the Palace and I'd seen him at Lodge meetings - though he wasn't in my Lodge. There were six of us, and we met at one of the clubs on Pall Mall, it doesn't matter which one. It was a good evening, mostly convivial, and afterwards we adjourned for drinks. The conversation became quite political, and although we weren't all British, there did seem to be a sense that a spirit of cooperative nationalism was something we all appreciated. Separate countries working together, but each remaining separate and acting in its own interests."

"Who wasn't British, Duncan?" Julia asked.

"Well, there was an Irishman, I think, and an Italian - he didn't say much. Another was a Scot, but he preferred to be known as Scottish rather than British. Me, Berwick and the sixth man there were English."

"What next?" she asked.

"I excused myself and went to the bathroom. When I returned, the others were in deep conversation. They stopped talking as soon as I came back, and everyone except Berwick left soon afterwards. Then Berwick asked me if I wanted to take our conversation further, to do something about what we had spoken of rather than just talk about it. I said of course, and he told me about the Order. He said he had been a member for a while, and he was excited that the brothers were working quietly and influentially behind the scenes to shape events and laws the way we wanted them. He said it was immensely satisfying. He never mentioned arson or murder, obviously!"

"So he invited you to join?"

"Not immediately. He said there was a vetting process and an initiation, but these should be a formality. He called me a few weeks later and said everything was ready. We needed to go to Italy for my initiation, which we did. The ceremony was arcane and quite uncomfortable, but in a way it was a spiritual experience. I felt cleansed. I was given my special phone and my ceremonial robes for use as and when invited to meet other brothers - we must always conceal our identities to avoid discovery and ridicule. Now I'm in my second year."

"And what have you actually done to shape the world, Duncan?"

"Well, not much yet. It takes time, one has to wait for the right opportunities, and to be called. I've been a conduit for messages; I've provided practical support to brothers, getting hire cars, booking hotels, that sort of thing, to protect identities."

"What a hero, Duncan. You're being taken for a ride, aren't you? You're what the Bolsheviks used to call a 'useful idiot'. Well, I think you've just resigned from your secret nationalistic boys' brigade. I want your phone and I want to see you in your dressing-up outfit. By the way, would you recognise the Italian you had dinner with?"

"I would, why?"

"I'm going to send Errol round with a photograph. I'd like you to tell him if it's the Italian you had dinner with that night."

"As you wish," Traynor sighed.

She left the house twenty minutes later, his secret phone in her pocket and with a photo of him in his ceremonial robes on her phone. She was tempted to gatecrash Maurice Berwick's weekend but decided to wait a while. She needed Mel's magic to squeeze out any unseen leads from the information she had obtained.

Chapter 35

It didn't take Mel Dunn long to identify Maurice Berwick's secret 'brotherhood' phone and check its call history. Apart from Traynor, the phone had been in contact with one other number, only one. It was in the UK and she put in a billing request for that one too. When it came back it showed that it had been used to contact Berwick and only one other phone. It was going to be a long slog, Mel thought.

She turned to the phone itself and checked its serial number and IMEI, which identified the specific device to any network it was trying to connect to. There are databases that have records of that sort of thing, and Mel knew where to find them. While the phone had a British pay-as-you-go SIM card, it had actually been sold originally in Italy as part of a bulk order around three years ago. Mel was trying to track the order down and find out who had bought a batch of rather basic mobile phones.

"Jake," she said, "it looks like Berwick's phone is part of a chain. It's in touch with two others, one of those being Traynor's. If there is a chain, it could take ages to identify all the links doing it one at a time. It would help if we could map the whole chain quickly, then concentrate on the phones that look like they're important."

"How can we do that?" Jake asked.

"We can give Abigail a call and get her to ask Cheltenham, GCHQ. They hoover up all sorts of phone traffic and have clever gadgets that can make sense of it in no time. Let's say that the Order uses these phones to communicate with its members around the world, and that in each country there are senior members who are at the top of the chain and can reach out to the centre, the top dog. My theory is that if we look at the usage of Traynor and Berwick's phones from last Saturday morning we could see the whole chain in Britain, and possibly get a connection between the British senior bod and the centre, or at least the next level up. It's worth a try, don't you think?"

"It is, can you give her a call?"

The following afternoon Mel had a call from Abigail.

"I've called in favours, Mel," she said, "and I've got a list of numbers for you."

Abigail read out a list of seven numbers, the last one being an Italian one.

"Brilliant," Mel said, "now can you call in more favours and get me anything they have on the last two numbers, the final UK one and the Italian one? I'd like call records, any speech they've got and any traces they or you have on any of the numbers."

"You don't want much, do you?" Abigail sounded exasperated. "What's this about, Mel?"

"Jake's in bloodhound mode."

"Again?" said Abigail.

"Again," Mel confirmed.

"I'll call you when I get anything," Abigail ended the call.

Jake had been out of the office. When she returned Mel filled her in on the call with Abigail.

"It looks like we're on the right lines, Jake. I'm running all those numbers through our system here; can you get Errol to do the same in the UK?"

"I'll be speaking to him later," Jake said.

Two days later they had made a lot of progress. Duncan Traynor had seen a press picture of Guido Ricci and confirmed it was him at the dinner in London. Abigail had provided a lot of data about the two numbers Mel was interested in. It was clear that both were part of a network that spanned several countries, and the Italian number seemed to be at the centre of a global one. Mel did some clever Dark Web stuff and got into the Italian service provider's billing systems. She discovered that the Italian phone was used from one location only, that being in the vicinity of Bellagio on Lake Como. It would take a lot of time and effort to trace its call usage, and without some serious justification and a lot of official paperwork, it wasn't going to happen.

"Can we go official now, Jake?" Mel asked.

"Soon," Jake replied.

******

In his villa overlooking Lake Como, Guido was mulling over his communication with the unsavoury service provider he'd been in touch with. The malcontent brother in England needed to be dealt with, but discreetly. The whole essence of the Order and its usefulness to him was blind, unquestioning obedience. A network of clean-skins, upstanding citizens with no criminal records, to do his bidding was essential to his continued success. Without a network to protect him, he could be vulnerable to intrusive and inquisitive interest from meddling authorities, be they police or tax officials. Guido knew that he, and his type, were the ones that kept the world turning, not governments or lawyers who only slowed things down.

What he had learnt from his unsavoury contact, who was far from a clean-skin, was that it would be possible to eliminate the unhappy brother and make it look like natural causes, but it came with risks and a very large price ticket. As a businessman, Guido understood cost-benefit analysis. Was it worth the trouble and expense of disguising the fate of the brother, or should he just have the man shot in the street like a rabid dog? He would decide after lunch. He went to watch Isabelle swim; it would give him an appetite.

In fact Guido made his decision much later. He was in a mellow mood, having spent an exciting and satisfying afternoon with Isabelle, who had talked him through her last encounter with the French detective in minute and graphic detail. He had decided on simplicity. There was less to go wrong, and it was cheaper. It made good business sense.

In his study, he contacted another of his unsavoury service providers and issued instructions. There were not one but two targets, both middle-aged men, photographs attached. He told his provider that they would be at a given place at exactly ten a.m. next Saturday morning. The method was up to the provider, but it had to be quick and clean. He transferred a large sum of money from one of his secret accounts to another one belonging to his service provider, with the promise of another, equal transaction to be made on successful completion. Then he used his special phone to send a message to the Regional Master for Great Britain.

In The Hague, Mel and Jake stared at the phone, Traynor's secret phone, on Mel's desk. It had just beeped. A message.

"It's from Berwick," Mel said, reading it. "He wants Traynor to meet him at the same place at ten on Saturday morning. Berwick has an answer to his question. What place, Jake, and what question?"

"The place is Oxford Services on the M40, and I should imagine that the question is one that Traynor posed. It could be an arrangement to meet the head of the Order," Jake said.

"Or it could be a set-up," Mel suggested.

"That too," Jake agreed. "Could you see what activity there was on the Italian phone and the one we think is at the top of the tree in the UK? Just to see if the chain theory works."

"Sure. What shall we do about Saturday? Shall we tell Traynor?"

"Let's not. I can go and see what Berwick wants, what his message from on high is. I'll take Errol with me."

"Here we go," Mel said.

Chapter 36

They sat in Julia's rented car, a different one this time, and watched the traffic flowing into the Oxford Services parking area. Errol had bought them take-out coffees and they waited. There was a steady stream of cars and vans, and from their chosen parking space they could keep track of them all. They had arrived well ahead of the appointed time. Julia took quick photos of all vehicles that had only one or two occupants, just in case. She made sure that she captured all their registration plates.

They saw Maurice Berwick's distinctive Porsche convertible arrive and they watched it park at the far end of the car lot. Berwick sat in the Porsche, his window open. A large white van, one of the ones that carry freight to and from Poland and Lithuania and Latvia, pulled out of its space and drove slowly towards the Porsche. Julia snapped its number as it passed.

"I don't like the look of this, Julia," Errol said, "I'm going to check it out."

He got out of the car and started walking briskly towards the parked Porsche, which was now obscured by the van. Julia followed him. As before, she wore a hoody and leggings with trainers on her feet. Errol broke into a run; Julia sprinted after him, covering ground quickly and closing the gap. They reached the van together, in time to see two large men attacking the Porsche with hammers and slashing at its soft top with large knives. Berwick was inside, terrified. The men were yelling in a foreign language. Julia and Errol took one each.

Julia launched a flying kick at the leg of her chosen target and he went down. His startled companion reacted, but not quickly enough to avoid Errol's first punch, which sent him flying. Then the knives appeared, long, serrated blades and savage sharp points. Each man had one. Julia's man struggled to stand; her kick had taken his knee out. As he tumbled, Julia went on the attack. She stamped on the hand holding the knife, grinding her heel on his wrist. He screamed. She twisted and twirled, aiming yet another kick - this time at the man's nose. It exploded in a mess of gore. One final blow and he was done. Julia turned to help Errol, who was doing just fine on his own. His man was now subdued, face down, no longer struggling. Errol had cuffed him. He passed Julia a spare set and she handcuffed her victim too.

They turned to Berwick, who was still in his car, the windscreen now crazed, frozen with fear.

"You're safe now, Mr Berwick," Julia said, "can we have a word, please?"

"I've called the police!" Berwick shouted, still terrified.

"Good," Julia said, "we can let them take care of these two. I'm from Europol, my colleague is from Scotland Yard, and we're not here by accident. We were expecting something to happen, something concerning you, but we didn't know what. Now, when the police get here I suggest you tell them that you were attacked by two thugs for no apparent reason. Passers-by came to your aid and subdued the attackers. You have no idea why your attackers did what they did. All this is true, of course, but you don't have to tell the police it was us who intervened. When you're done with them, we can give you a lift home and we can talk in the car. Is that clear?"

Berwick just nodded. Errol removed the handcuffs from the fallen villains and had a quick look at their van. He examined the registration plates, which were Polish, and pulled at the front one. It came off easily, revealing another plate underneath, this one Lithuanian. He snapped the Lithuanian plate with his phone. A siren was approaching.

"We're going now, Mr Berwick. Please do as I asked, and we'll pick you up when the police are done with you."

Julia left and walked briskly back towards the rented car, taking care to conceal her face from the CCTV cameras. She knew that the attack and their intervention would have been captured on film, but both she and Errol had studied enough hours of grainy footage to know that the chances of their being recognised were very slight.

They watched as a police patrol car on blue lights pulled up by the battered Porsche. A few minutes later a second one arrived. The officers gathered around Berwick, who was by now quite animated. The two fallen assailants were handcuffed again and pulled to their feet. Each was bundled into a separate police car while notes were taken and radios spoken into. After a while a third police vehicle arrived, this one manned by officers to examine the assailants' van and eventually take it away. After a while they all left, and Julia started her car.

They picked Berwick up near the petrol station.

"Are you alright?" Julia asked.

"Yes, thank you," Berwick said, "just a bit shaken. The police said that they were probably after the car. There's a big market for them in eastern Europe, apparently. They said it's quite unusual to have an attack like this in broad daylight, opportunist, they said."

"If that's what they want to think, that's fine," Julia said. "Truth is, it's all to do with the text you sent to brother Traynor earlier in the week. The one you sent after you got a message from the Regional Master, which was after the one he got from the Grand Master. I'm guessing the last bit; I can't prove it just yet. But the rest of it is fact, isn't it Maurice?"

"I don't know what you mean," Berwick said indignantly.

"Yes you do, Maurice," Julia responded, "You were Traynor's link with the Order, there's one person - your other contact - between you and the Regional Master, and he's in contact with the centre. You took Traynor to a dinner before you recruited him as a brother. The person I think is the Grand Master, the man behind the Order, was there. I know who he is. What I want to know from you is why you're involved? What's in it for you?"

Berwick thought for a moment.

"I did recruit Traynor, that much is true. The Order isn't illegal, it's not a crime to be a member. We are an association committed to helping one another, and we work together to bring about a safer, more just society, one in which reason rather than foolish politics sets the agenda. We believe there is a natural order of things, society too, and that there are those who are best suited to make decisions and make things work in the interests of everyone. Traynor agrees, which is why he was invited to join us. It's why I joined too. What's it got to do with Europol or Scotland Yard?"

"It all sounds very commendable, Maurice, if a bit daft," Julia said. "I don't want to get into theories of government and society, but I want to ask you one thing. Would you have joined if you knew that the Order was merely a vehicle to make one man's corrupt tax evasion and fraudulent businesses safer? That it is there to help deflect attention, to stop investigations? Would you join if you knew that the man behind it, the Grand Master, will stop at nothing to achieve his goals? That he will gladly kill, have people killed, to suit his own ends? That he would set up an attack on a brother, like the one on you today? Because that is what he did. This attack was meant for you and Traynor, only Traynor never got the message to meet you at Oxford Services at ten this morning. I got it instead."

"You don't understand!" Berwick said, "It's not like that!"

"But it is, Maurice. Think about it. I'll drop you at the end of your road. Sleep on it. We'll be in touch."

Julia slowed the car, and Berwick got out. They drove off with him staring after them, trying to make sense of it all.

Chapter 37

Guido Ricci was very angry, but you would have to know him extremely well to notice. His face was expressionless, his breathing calm and controlled. He was alone in his study. He re-read the message from his unsavoury service provider. The simple option, just having the targets killed in the street, had failed spectacularly. The money he had already spent was wasted, and the fact that the second instalment would not now be paid was scant consolation.

The unsavoury service provider had sub-contracted the task to a pair of Lithuanian clowns whose main job was smuggling goods, mostly tobacco and alcohol with a few synthetic drugs thrown in, across Europe. The UK was a regular stopping-off point. They had seen the photographs and said they were confident that the task could be completed without fuss. According to Guido's contact, only one of the targets had appeared, and the Lithuanians decided in their wisdom, or otherwise, that one target was better than no targets, so they attacked. The target in question had screamed and locked himself in his car, which the Lithuanians then attacked with hammers and knives to get at their man.

What happened next remained unclear to Guido, but the outcome wasn't. Both Lithuanians were now in police custody, one under guard in a hospital. The whole thing had been a failure, and now he had not one but two unhappy brothers, not that either was supposed to be alive anymore.

It was Saturday evening, and he was alone in the villa, apart from a few servants. Isabelle had gone to Milan to see an opera and would be back on Sunday, adding to his sense of disgruntlement. He decided to abandon Britain. His network there was small anyway, and effectively even smaller now after the day's debacle. He would simply cut the rest of them off.

His decision made, he logged on to his computer, found the correct lists and deleted all the British brothers, seven in total. One he would miss, the others less so. He then blocked all their numbers on his special phone, in which he had contact details for every member of his global network. It was for this reason that the phone never left his office, and unless he was actually using it, it remained locked in his safe.

Guido ate dinner alone, spent an hour sitting in silence with a glass of whisky and retired to bed. Isabelle would be back tomorrow.

In Milan, Isabelle sat through the first half of a tedious performance of something or other in German before leaving during the interlude. She made her way to the reputedly discreet hotel where Antoine Durand was waiting patiently. She hadn't abandoned him after all, despite telling Guido that she had. He did have a certain energy, and he was the right sort of age and build for her; she quite enjoyed him. It wasn't love, obviously, but he was something more than just a bizarre transaction on behalf of her husband. She enjoyed the deception too, although she had no idea how Guido would react if he discovered that she was seeing a lover of her own volition rather than at his command.

During the next intimate interlude, as Antoine was getting his breath back, she called Guido to say goodnight. He sounded distracted and she knew that his day had not gone well. Guido would need some consoling on Sunday. She let Antoine do his enthusiastic worst, just so she would have more lurid material for Guido after her swim tomorrow. She knew him so well.

The following day, back at the villa, things went pretty much as Isabelle had expected. Guido was calm now and satisfied. Her storytelling had been on top form. They were still in bed.

"I have closed down the British operation," Guido told her, "it has become too much trouble, more trouble than it's worth."

"Never mind, Guido," Isabelle was speaking quietly, "London is no fun anymore anyway. Britain is a troublesome little nation; it thinks it still rules the waves."

"It may think it does, but we know who actually does rule them, don't we?"

"Of course, Guido, you do. You are so clever."

"I am short-handed now, though," he said, "there are things planned in northern Europe and I need some more foot soldiers, maybe more than mere foot soldiers. I have let my lieutenant in Britain go, I will need someone reliable with a calm head in the next few months.

"I may have someone for you, Guido. Do you remember that pushy woman I told you about, the one from Europol who gate-crashed my last encounter with Antoine? Her name is Kelso, she's Scottish. She has dishonest ambitions and is curious about you. Maybe she will make a good recruit?"

"I do remember. I wasn't keen at first, which is why I didn't ask you to contact her again. She might be a good choice, a break from tradition, but it also might be hard to keep her in check."

"She has her price, Guido, she as good as told me. Once she has taken her pieces of silver she will be yours, won't she? You will have her for as long as you want. Shall I call her?"

"Tomorrow, my sweet. Now, tell me that story again, the one you told me just after lunch."

******

Julia travelled back to The Hague on Sunday. The incident at Oxford Services hadn't been quite what she'd expected, but it did make Guido Ricci's style and capability a little clearer. He was clearly unscrupulous, but his judgement and competence were now in question.

Mel was pleased to see her and handed Freddie over for a couple of hours while she went to the gym. Jake prepared a light supper for them and put a bottle of white in the fridge. She was looking forward to a nice normal evening.

The following day, Monday, was mostly taken up with meetings. At lunchtime Julia checked her phone and saw a message.

"Well," she said to Mel, "it's from Isabelle. She wants to meet for a chat. We're having lunch in Brussels on Wednesday."

"Will you go?" Mel asked.

"I think I will," Julia replied.

"Are you sure? After what Guido tried to do on Saturday? I tracked all the messaging, and it fits with him given the order to initiate the text from Berwick to Traynor."

"Read it yourself," Julia showed Mel her phone, "that's a different tone altogether. I think she, maybe they, want to talk to me about joining their mad band."

"Well, if you're determined to go, at least give me Isabelle's number so I can keep an eye on it. Keep your phone on too, so I can keep track of you."

"Yes, mother," Jake said.

Chapter 38

Julia took the train to Brussels on Tuesday evening and checked into the same hotel where she had met Isabelle before. She wanted to be rested and ready for the encounter. On Wednesday morning she was up early and she installed herself in a comfortable corner of the lobby. Isabelle arrived around eleven, accompanied by an older and only slightly taller man. He had thinning hair, just turning grey, and he wore an elegant, well-tailored dark blue suit. He was starting to develop a paunch but still looked to be in fairly good shape. But the thing that Julia noticed first about him was his face. It was completely devoid of any expression, almost reptilian.

He stood to one side as Isabelle spoke with the desk clerk. Julia saw a banknote pass between them, and the clerk nodded. She handed Isabelle two key cards. Julia saw Isabelle and the man she recognised from photographs as Guido Ricci go to the lift and ride up to the fourth floor. Julia ordered coffee and waited.

Shortly after midday, Isabelle reappeared, this time alone. Julia had changed position and rose to meet her. She extended a hand and smiled.

"Isabelle, so nice to see you again, I'd been expecting to hear from you."

"Julia," Isabelle said, her smile a little forced, "how have you been?"

"Fine, quite busy. I had matters to attend to in the UK, near London, closer to Oxford in fact. Do you know it?" She was looking for any sign that Isabelle had knowledge of the Oxford attack.

Isabelle shook her head. Nothing.

"You should visit, it's quite lovely. I went to university there," Julia said.

"Shall we go in? I've booked a table," Isabelle said.

Isabelle ordered champagne; it seemed to be all she drank. They ordered and as they waited for the food to arrive, Isabelle started.

"Have you seen Antoine since we last met? He hasn't mentioned it, but I need to ask you" she said.

"No," Julia replied, "I've no great interest in him, to be honest."

"Even though he's a corrupt policeman and you're a senior Europol officer?"

"Corruption has many definitions, Isabelle. What Durand did was unconscionable, certainly unwise, but the motivation behind it remains a mystery to me. If it was just for money or sex it would be corruption, but if there was some other, higher, reason, well, it might not be. Why did he do it, Isabelle, what did you have over him?"

"You overestimate me, Julia," Isabelle said, "I was just an additional reward for him, something to keep him interested and enthusiastic. His motivation is his belief, belief in what we are doing."

"And what is that, exactly?"

"We are fighting for our independence, like I told you. There is a society, like a brotherhood or family, from many countries. We all share the same belief, the same faith. We believe that each nation is sovereign with its own identity and its own laws and customs. Collaboration between states is to be encouraged for the greater good, but only with strict constraints. Trade agreements, easy movement of money and goods, that sort of thing. But no more blurring of borders, no more intrusive international bureaucracy, no dilution of personal privacy. The Italian members believe in a free Italy, the French in a free France, Americans in a free America."

"So no more EU, no more Europol, no more Customs Unions?" Julia asked.

"Precisely," Isabelle agreed, "they are intrusions, usurpers of national liberty. They interfere with individual liberty."

"What about the will of the people? What about the people who want their countries to remain part of larger unions?"

"Sometimes what the people want is not what the people need. Democracy is an admirable concept but a deeply flawed practice; too many idiots can vote. Equality does not exist in biological nature, and not all men, or women, are equal either. Most are not equipped to make wise decisions about the future for themselves or their country, or even decide who should lead it. So we just encourage the continuation of a practice that has been in place since emancipation became a general right, that being decision-making by a select, unpublicised few. The powers behind thrones and presidents and premiers. Many of our members are just those people, the ones who really make the world turn."

"Radical," Julia commented. "Does democratic government have a place in your brave new world, Isabelle?"

"If a semblance of it keeps people distracted, and if it is not allowed to disrupt the correct order of things, there is no harm in it. Let the masses think they have control, as long as they don't."

"Why now?" Julia asked.

"There was once a movement that had very similar goals. It had some success in removing inbred tyrants and incompetent leaders, but it made errors. It was highjacked by political revolutionaries with their own agendas and it fell into disrepute. It disappeared from sight for many years, but it never really went away. It has been responsible for the rise in global wealth for more than a century. We are just its modern incarnation."

"So you are the modern *carbonari*?" Julia asked.

"You have heard of them?" Isabelle seemed surprised.

"Vaguely; I thought they died out years ago."

"Well they didn't. They just disappeared from view. We are back now, in force, but we no longer use the old name. It is time to reactivate the movement, to stop the destructive changes taking place, the changes that are destroying individual and national rights and identities."

"By any means necessary?" Julia asked.

"That is an unnecessary question, Julia. If the means are necessary, they are necessary and they will be used."

"Why are you telling me this?" Julia asked.

"You are a clever woman, Julia, I'm sure you don't need me to spell it out. You are Scottish; you've been dominated by the English for hundreds of years. Now you're British and you're dominated by Brussels, a dull city in a dull country. Your freedoms have been eroded; as a nation you cannot do what you should be entitled to do without permission. You can help us change that, Julia. By any means necessary. I can see in your eyes that the idea appeals to you."

"I need to know more, but yes, it does appeal," Julia said. "When I was a child I dreamed of an independent Scotland, and I still do. I work for Europol because it's a job, that's all."

Their food had not been touched.

"Come upstairs with me, Julia," Isabelle said. "Guido is waiting for you."

Chapter 39

Julia followed Isabelle to the elevator. They rode up in silence; Julia almost felt nervous. Guido was sitting in an armchair in the suite, his back to the door, looking out of the window.

"Welcome, Ms Kelso," he said without turning or standing.

Julia said nothing. Isabelle went to the window and drew the curtains.

"We have a guest, Guido," she said, pointedly. He still didn't move. He merely glanced at the other armchair, diagonal to the one he occupied.

"Julia, please take a seat," Isabelle indicated the empty armchair, "I will stand."

Julia went to the armchair and sat. She looked at the man to her left with a mixture of curiosity and revulsion. The reptilian image stuck with her. He turned his head to look at her, still expressionless. After a moment he turned away again. Julia could see traces of spittle on his lips, as if he was salivating. She waited. Minutes passed.

"Ms Kelso," he said finally, "Isabelle has told you a little about us, has she not?"

Julia did not respond.

"She thinks you might be one of us, a fellow believer. Is she right?"

"I don't know what you believe, not yet," Julia said, "but on the basis of the discussion we've just had, I am interested in knowing more."

"You are a law enforcement officer, Ms Kelso," he continued, "I'm sure you will understand that I need to be sure that our conversation will go no further. I understand how these things work. Someone like you will feign interest in someone like me, then you will turn it against me and falsely represent my words to my detriment. Some would call that spying, I call it distasteful and insulting."

"If I was here in my official capacity you wouldn't be in any doubt about it, Mr Ricci, it would be abundantly clear. I am here in good faith."

"Then you won't mind if Isabelle takes some sensible precautions." His English was precise, but heavily accented.

"This way please, Julia," Isabelle said.

She led Julia to the bathroom.

"Your phone, please, and remove your clothing," Isabelle said, having closed the bathroom door.

Julia hesitated for a moment. She took her phone from her jacket pocket, grateful that she'd had the presence of mind to cut the call to Mel that had been running throughout her conversation with Isabelle. Julia made a show of turning it off before handing it to Isabelle. Then she started unbuttoning her shirt. A few moments later, Julia stood in her underwear and stared at a spot on the wall as Isabelle inspected her. She wasn't normally shy about her body, but she was struggling to control her anger and humiliation under Isabelle's scrutiny.

Isabelle examined the scar on Julia's abdomen and reached out to feel it. Julia grabbed her hand.

"Look if you must, but don't touch!" she hissed.

Isabelle withdrew her hand and unhurriedly carried on with her inspection.

"Thank you," Isabelle said eventually, "please get dressed now. I am sorry we had to do that, but we know there are people who do not understand us and would like to stop what we are doing."

Julia just nodded and briskly replaced her clothing. They returned to the sitting room of the suite. Julia sat down again and turned to Guido.

"Now that the paranoid nonsense is over, can we get on with it!" She was still trying to control her anger.

"I see you are spirited, Ms Kelso, I do like that. I will tell you what we do, if you tell me how you think you might be able to help us. Firstly, tell me what you think we are and what we do, and I will correct you if necessary. Agreed?"

"I think you are at the centre of a discreet organisation, a movement, that wants to restrict or reverse the erosion of the independence of nations and their domination by bureaucratic international bodies. I think you are trying to do this by bringing those international bodies into disrepute, demonstrating that they are incompetent and self-important. That's it, in a nutshell."

"You are correct, Ms Kelso, but it is not as easy as you make it sound."

"I'm sure it's not easy, Mr Ricci, if it was, you wouldn't need to do it."

"Quite right, Ms Kelso," he agreed.

"So, by way of detail," Julia continued, "I will speculate about your involvement with my own employer, Europol. You used your members, your 'brothers' Jeroen Faber and Antoine Durand to collect information about cross-border operations, investigations concerning two or more countries acting in concert. You then used that information to disrupt the operations by leaking it to target criminals and leaving the rest to them. You suspected that the outcomes would be spectacular and newsworthy, thus reinforcing the messaging you were simultaneously placing in the media about Europol incompetence. Am I correct?"

"You are, Ms Kelso, mostly. Antoine is a brother, Faber is not. He is merely a sad and lonely man who would do anything for a little praise. The principle here is that no one can fear something that is ridiculous, that is laughably inept. If Europol is not feared and respected, it is pointless and it will eventually be starved of funds and support and it will die. This is fundamental in nature, and economics."

"And why Europol, specifically?" Julia asked.

"It is not specifically Europol, Ms Kelso, we are doing the same with the European Central Bank, the European Commission, most of the EU decentralised agencies, including Europol of course, all of which interfere actively in the rights and freedoms of individuals in individual states. As a result of what we are doing there are growing signs of dissent within the European Union, which is encouraging.

"But also, it is not just Europe, although it is closest to my heart. We have members, brothers, working as hard against the Federal Government in America, against NATO, most of the global free-trade collectives and others. It is a global issue, a global task."

Guido's reptilian face had not changed in expression, nor had his voice become animated in any way. Julia found herself wondering how Isabelle could bear to be in the same room as this man, let alone in his bed.

"What's in it for you, Mr Ricci?" she asked.

"Belief, Ms Kelso," he replied, "I believe that we are doing what is necessary to protect individual freedom."

"And if I were to join you, what would be in it for me, and I mean something other than belief?"

"You are forthright, Ms Kelso," he said.

"It's a Scottish thing, Mr Ricci," she replied, "forthrightness is a freedom we Scots take very seriously."

"I see. I do take some compensation for my efforts; it is only right to do so. You would be compensated too. When and how this happens depends largely on your contribution, and on what compensation you value most. It is safe to say that none of the brothers feels undervalued or unsatisfied."

"I'm with you so far," Julia said, "but I want to make one thing clear: I'm not accustomed to playing second fiddle to anyone. I'll accept a framework, but I make my own decisions - for me that's an important individual freedom."

For the first time she detected a slight change in his facial expression, albeit fleeting. She was starting to get to him.

"You work in a disciplined occupation, Ms Kelso. If you choose to work with us, we too require discipline. We deplore intrusive governments, but we also deplore anarchy. We do not welcome those who might term themselves disruptors. We find them to be selfish and ignorant of consequences they do not understand. We need measured wisdom, Ms Kelso."

"*Your* measured wisdom?" she asked.

"For the time being, yes," he said.

"I understand what you're doing, Mr Ricci, and I am starting to understand you. I think we are travelling on the same road, so we may as well travel together. I can bring you inside knowledge from many fields that may be of interest or use to you, and I am persuasive. I have a strategic gene; I know how to get things done and make things change. I've been doing it most of my life. I have one condition, though. I want to understand your structure and your aims, so I need to be close to you, for a while at least. I am a fast learner. If you agree to that, I will commit myself to you and your cause."

Guido Ricci looked at her for a good while. She was aware of Isabelle in her peripheral vision; she looked anxious and apprehensive.

"Very well, Ms Kelso, I agree. It makes sense that you come to the villa in Italy initially. You will need a little time to arrange your affairs, I'm sure. Isabelle will make the arrangements for you to join us. You may go."

Julia stood, suppressing the urge to spit in his face. She turned on her heel and walked calmly out of the room. Isabelle came after her.

"Do not take it personally," she said, "Guido has many good traits. He can be very charming when he wants to be, but he can also be brusque and boorish. You unsettled him. He will relax as he gets to know you, I'm sure."

"I'll give him the benefit of the doubt, Isabelle, for now. You have my number, so call me in a couple of days with your address in Italy. I can make my own way there, I'm sure."

The elevator arrived and Julia rode down alone, wondering what on earth she was doing.

Chapter 40

"You do realise they're barking, don't you?" Mel said when Jake got back to the house in The Hague later that afternoon.

"Of course they are, if it's true - but I think it's all bollocks," Jake replied.

"What do you mean?" Mel asked.

"All that guff about independence and belief," Jake said, "I don't believe a word of it. He's just building a covert network to do his bidding, but on the cheap. My theory is that Guido and Isabelle are using the mystique of the Order to cover their own squalid money-making scams, creating such a monumental tangle of deceit that it will take years to unravel it all. We just need to prove it and get him banged up as the chiselling cheat he really is. Which is why I'm going to stay with them in Italy."

"You're doing what?" Mel said.

"Next week, when I've tidied up a few things, I'm going to their villa in Italy to stay. Just long enough to get what we need to break him. And her, of course. Have you listened to the conversation I had with Isabelle yet?"

"Yes, that's why I asked if you knew they were mad. I'm just wondering how mad the 'brothers' must be to go along with it, believe it even."

"I'm not agreeing with her at all, but you do have to admit that you don't need to be smart or rational to have the vote, and all you need is a convincing liar to make big changes happen. And as you know, fraudsters and conmen always do best with the gullible, which is what I think the 'brothers' are. More gullible than mad, maybe."

"So, what do you want me to do then?" Mel asked.

"I want you to pull together everything we have to date - the leaks, Faber accessing my files, Faber meeting Durand, Durand meeting Isabelle, all the phone and call data. When you've done that, I want you to tell me where the holes are, what needs to be found to complete the story. From the Italian end, I'll try to get anything I can about the Order and Ricci's financials."

"Then you'll go official?" Mel asked hopefully.

"I want a package to hand on; I think my time here will be done when this is over. If I'm still around when it all comes out, I'm sure I won't be welcome in the Europol bar. I'll take some leave to cover Italy, then put in my resignation. Hugh Cavendish wants me to go over to SIS - he says he's got something suitably sneaky lined up for me."

"And what about me, us?" Mel asked.

"What do you want to do, Mel? Do you want to come back to London, stay here, what?" Jake asked. "You're a free agent, Mel, so am I, you've always made that clear."

"True. I guess I'll stay here for a bit, until it's time to make a change for Freddie. We're settled; he's got his routine. I'll be bored rigid without something to worry about, so I'll miss you," Mel said.

"I'll miss you too, but let's not think about that right now, shall we? I'm going to get a drink; you want one?"

******

The following Monday morning Jake took a flight from Amsterdam to Milan and rented a car at the airport. She had decided to have her own transport available to her once she got to the villa. Isabelle had sent the address, it was near Bellagio, overlooking the confluence of lakes Como and Lecco. She had told Isabelle that she would arrive on Wednesday, so she drove north from Milan towards the lakes. She found a quiet *albergo* in the hills above the lake, well away from the glitzy tourists, and spent the rest of that day and all of the next exploring the terrain.

The villa was at the narrow end of a mountainous peninsula. There were only two roads, both hugging the shoreline - one to the east, one to the west. The roads were small, congested and very twisting. She was looking for an escape route, just in case, and the roads did not look like a good option. There were ferries operating from Bellagio to Menaggio or Cadenabbia, which also did not look like good options. She did find a few likely lads with speedboats near the Lido. Chatting to one of them while she sipped a coffee she learned that she could rent a boat at almost any time, day or night, to go wherever she wanted. Julia flirted a lot with one of the young men and walked away with his phone number, just in case.

She explored the other side, the western shore of lake Como to the south of the tourist hotspots. She ended up in Como town, a busy and bustling place, not without charm but also with a fair degree of commerce and industry. The town was also just a short drive from the Swiss border. In a dusty side street she found a small boarding house. The landlady was an elderly Italian woman wearing the dark clothing of a widow. The family home had been turned into a boarding house when her husband, a railwayman, had died a few years ago, she explained to Julia in Italian. There were two rooms available for rent, the third being already occupied.

Julia concocted a story and explained to the woman that she would be in the area for a few weeks researching a book. She wanted a base in which to leave a few things, and to return to from time to time to rest and write. A deal was struck, and Julia had a room of her own for the next month, paid for in advance. The landlady showed her the room; it was on the first floor, pleasant and airy with a small balcony and a handbasin in the corner. A bathroom was across the landing. The front door key was always kept in the same place, in a key safe with a four-digit code to unlock it.

Julia bought a second suitcase in town and decanted some of her possessions into it. She left the new case in the room and drove back to the *albergo* for the night.

After breakfast the next day, she set off. She found the villa easily. It was imposing in its anonymity, hidden behind large steel gates and tall walls. She pressed the intercom and waited. A disembodied voice asked what she wanted. She gave her name and said *signor* and *signora* Ricci were expecting her. A camera swivelled towards her. Moments later, the gates opened silently and she drove in. The gates closed behind her.

Chapter 41

Mel Dunn was alone in Julia's office in The Hague, focused on the task she had been set. Her concentration was interrupted when the door flew open. Jeroen Faber's line-manager, the head of Europol security, was clearly angry.

"Where is Ms Kelso?" he demanded abruptly.

"Not here, obviously!" Mel replied indignantly. "What do you want?"

"Jeroen Faber has regained consciousness in the hospital in Brussels," he said. "He cannot talk much, but he was able to say that Kelso had ordered him to accompany her to Brussels. She must explain herself!"

"I think Jeroen needs to explain himself first. Why would she do that? Anyway, she's on leave so you'll have to make an appointment to see her when she's back. Now excuse me, I have things to do," Mel said.

The man left, still angry. He closed the door loudly behind him, not quite slamming it but almost. Mel was concerned. She called Jake's mobile. There was no answer.

******

In the villa near Bellagio, Julia was left waiting alone in a huge salon. She sat for a while, then started to walk around. The views over the lake and to the distant mountains were spectacular. The villa's gardens were immaculate, the sloping lawns manicured and the shrubs and bushes meticulously pruned. The salon itself was sparsely furnished for its size. A handful of armchairs, a large sofa, a grand piano in a corner.

Everything in the room looked more expensive than tasteful, each piece a statement of wealth rather than an item to be comfortably enjoyed. There were no books on the shelves, just the day's newspapers on an occasional table.

After half an hour, a servant arrived with a tray of coffee. Signora Ricci would join her shortly, the maid said. In due course Isabelle arrived, her hair tidy but damp.

"I'm sorry to keep you waiting, Julia," Isabelle said, "Guido has certain needs in the morning that I must attend to. How was your journey?"

"It was fine," Julia said, "Guido is here then?"

"Oh yes, he will join us at lunch. Coffee?"

"How did you meet him?" Julia asked.

"Guido? It's a long story," Isabelle said. "We met by accident; some of our separate business dealings happened to overlap and we found we had similar interests and ambitions. He suggested that rather than be competitors we should unite, and that is what we have done. The arrangement works well."

"So a partnership of equals?" Julia asked.

"Each of us brings their own specific skills and capabilities, Julia. I did say to you that equality does not exist in nature, didn't I? The lion and the lioness are not equal, but the pride needs them both to succeed. Now, when you have finished your coffee I will show you to your quarters."

Isabelle led her up a grand staircase to the first floor. She was shown to a corner suite with its own sitting room, bedroom and bathroom. It was comfortably furnished and looked out over the grounds and the swimming pool beyond a large terrace. Julia was left alone again to unpack her things and get settled. She checked her phone and saw that there was no signal. She checked for wi-fi but no networks appeared on her screen. There was no telephone in the room, nor could she see a TV or radio. She was completely disconnected from the outside world.

She made her way back downstairs to the salon she had been in. Isabelle was still there, reading a newspaper.

"My phone isn't getting a signal, Isabelle," Julia said. "Do you have internet here?"

"Phone signals are blocked throughout the villa, apart from in Guido's study. There is internet in there too, but nowhere else. Guido can turn on mobile phone access on the terrace when he wants to, but it is off most of the time. We don't like people prying into our business, so we don't give them the means to do it, Julia."

"There is no TV or radio either," Julia said.

"Why would anyone want such distractions in a place as beautiful and serene as this? You should try to enjoy the peace, Julia."

"I'm not used to being out of contact," Julia stated.

"Then you may leave if you want to. It was you who wanted to come here."

"I would like to make some calls; I have a matter to attend to in the office. I'm going to drive down to the village and make the calls there."

"As you wish," Isabelle shrugged.

Julia went to the front door and opened it. Her car had gone, even though she still had the key in her pocket.

"Where's my car?" she asked Isabelle.

"Guido does not like vehicles outside the villa. They spoil the aesthetic, and sometimes drip oil on the gravel. It will have been moved."

"Where to?" Julia asked.

"Somewhere on the estate, I don't know where. You can ask Guido at lunch."

"Can't I ask him now?"

"No, he is resting, then he will work before lunch. You will have to wait."

"Then I'm going to take a walk," Julia said.

"Of course, you are free to do so," Isabelle said. "But you will find that your phone won't work in the grounds either, and you should be aware that we have a sophisticated and sensitive security system. Do not be alarmed if you see men in uniform with weapons as you walk around. They have been instructed not to talk to you, but they are there to ensure your safety and security. They will be monitoring your movements. You may prefer to use the pool instead - I have several swimsuits if you did not bring your own."

"The walk will be fine," Julia said.

"Lunch is at one on the terrace, Julia," Isabelle said, "don't be late."

With that, Isabelle stood and left the room. Julia remained outwardly calm, but inside she was beginning to worry. She was as good as imprisoned, albeit in some luxury, without any way of communicating with Mel or anyone else. After a moment or two, she went upstairs to her rooms and donned her running gear. She went out and set off at a steady jog. She needed to test the perimeter and find a way out, a means of escape, now that she was convinced she would need one sooner or later. She passed the terrace which overlooked the large and very inviting pool. A little way below it the slope of the garden had been levelled and there was a flat area, circular, about fifty metres across. Julia noticed two large, wheeled devices; each one draped in a canvas cover with the word '*Fuoco*' stencilled on it. The flat area must be a helicopter pad, the wheeled devices large fire extinguishers.

It took a good forty minutes to run the perimeter. She saw tripwires, cameras, microphones and infrared sensors all around the inside of the boundary. The boundary itself was a mixture of solid timber fencing and masonry walls, with a ten-metre gap between it and the nearest trees or foliage. The boundary fences and walls were all topped off with razor wire, painted to be less conspicuous. The main gate, where she had entered that morning, was covered by a discreet manned security post and several cameras. She found a second, larger gate well away from the main one, that was used as a service entrance for deliveries and tradesmen. That too had a manned security post and several cameras. She didn't see her car anywhere.

There were only two possible weak points that she identified, neither of them particularly encouraging. One was a small stream that ran through a wooded part of the grounds. It flowed under the boundary fence, although she didn't know where it went after that or if it had obstructions built in. The other was something that looked like a hole dug by a fox or badger right alongside a wooden part of the boundary fence. She stopped to retie her shoelace and have a brief closer look. The hole was sizeable, just big enough for her to get into. It went down at an angle of around thirty degrees, right under the fence. She stood and continued her run.

Behind the villa, and well out of sight, she came across a collection of outbuildings. Some were as old as the villa itself, but most were more modern. She kept running but noted that all of them seemed locked shut, with cameras and movement sensors in abundance. She saw tyre tracks near a few of the outbuildings, and she assumed that the estate vehicles, including her own rented car, were tucked away in them.

Julia returned to the villa in time to shower and change for lunch. By the time she got to the terrace Guido and Isabelle were already seated. He was wearing a cotton shirt with a silk cravat, she was in a wrap, her hair wet again. Presumably she had been in the pool. Guido looked at her with his reptilian eyes.

"Ms Kelso, or should I call you Julia?" he said. "Welcome to our villa. Did you enjoy your run? You seemed to; I was watching. All the security cameras can be monitored from my study. You have a very fluid running style, very pleasing to the eye."

She felt her skin crawl.

Chapter 42

Julia spent some of the afternoon in her rooms, which she searched thoroughly. She found miniature cameras in the bedroom and sitting room, but not in the bathroom. While she didn't find any, she assumed that there would be listening devices too. Conversation over lunch had been stilted at best; Guido hardly spoke at all and pointedly refused to answer any questions that Julia posed. Isabelle had tried her best, but eventually all three of them fell silent. As they rose to leave the table, Guido uttered a few words.

"Julia, come to my office at ten tomorrow morning. I want you to tell me what you can do for me in exchange for me telling you about my business." That was all he said before walking from the terrace.

Julia looked at Isabelle.

"He will come to like you, I'm sure," Isabelle said. "I won't be here tomorrow as I have to go to Strasbourg; I have my own business matters to attend to. Bear with him, Julia, and we may all get what we are after. Dinner will be at seven."

Julia reflected on Isabelle's enigmatic comments and wondered what she meant by 'getting what we are after'. She would give Guido Ricci the benefit of the doubt tomorrow morning, but she was already questioning the value of her being at the villa at all.

Dinner was no more lively or entertaining than lunch had been, and by nine Julia had retired to her rooms. She positioned items as casually as she could to shield herself from the hidden cameras and moved an armchair to the only point in the sitting room that could not be spied on. She read a book but soon became restless. She felt a sudden need to speak to Mel but knew she could not. Instead, she wrote to her.

In a small notebook she described the villa in detail and went over the security precautions. She wrote about the furnishings, her room, the hidden cameras. She wrote about Isabelle, about her strange relationship with Guido and wondered why a seemingly independent-minded, intelligent woman would pander to such a boring oaf. When she was done, she closed the notebook and placed it on the table next to her.

It was a long night. Julia didn't sleep until the small hours. Soon she was awoken by loud clattering and the roar of an engine. She opened the curtain and looked out at a helicopter landing on the pad below the swimming pool. Two people stood beside the fire extinguishers, ready to deal with an emergency or help load the luggage. Isabelle had been seated at the table on the terrace, and as the rotors slowed she stood and walked towards the aircraft. She carried a briefcase and nothing else. A few moments later the rotors accelerated again and with another loud roar the helicopter lifted off. It turned and climbed rapidly before disappearing over the treetops in the morning sunlight. Silence returned almost immediately.

Julia changed into her swimsuit in the bathroom and put on a bathrobe and flipflops. She swam thirty or forty lengths of the pool before towelling herself dry and donning the robe. Coffee and croissants had appeared on the table and she helped herself, suddenly quite hungry.

"You seem to take care of yourself, Julia," Guido emerged from a doorway, clad in a dressing gown and leather slippers. "I envy your physique. I myself never had the time for much exercise."

He sat at the table, at the opposite end to Julia, and helped himself to coffee.

"Good morning," she said to him, "I see Isabelle has left already."

"She has a long day ahead of her," was all he said before lapsing into silence once more. He was looking, staring, at Julia, his eyelids drooping like hoods.

"Shall we start our discussion now," she asked him.

"At ten, not before."

"Very well," Julia said, pouring more coffee, "I will see you then."

She took her coffee with her and went into the salon, pleased to see that she left a trail of water droplets behind her on the parquet flooring. In a leather armchair she glanced at yesterday's newspapers before heading upstairs to shower and change.

A few seconds before ten she stood in front of his study door, feeling like a pupil summoned to see the headmaster. He opened it at ten exactly and stood aside to let her enter. He closed the door behind her; she heard it lock shut. A large desk dominated the room. It was completely clear. On a side table there were two computer screens and a telephone. Guido Ricci moved to a large swivel chair behind the desk and sat down. He gestured towards a second chair opposite him, a few feet away from the desk. Julia sat down and waited, aware that Ricci could see her from head to toe.

"So, Julia Kelso, you have worked your way into my home. You are obviously interested in what I do, but you have no idea what it is. You have implied that you are available for hire, but your past reputation - I have done my research - suggests that you are not. You have made a very public and well-publicised habit of bringing down people you deemed to be corrupt. Which are you, Julia, a crusader or an infidel?"

"That's a very ambiguous analogy, Guido; the crusaders were arguably the infidels in the eyes of their Muslim opponents," she responded.

"I never wasted time on history books, Julia."

"I don't blame you," she said, "as well as being infidels, the crusaders were the most corrupt band of bigoted mercenaries you could imagine. They were in it for themselves, while voicing a belief that they were fighting God's battle against the enemies of Christendom. It wasn't uncommon then, and it isn't now. But to answer your question, Guido, I've spent my entire working life fighting God's battle against corruption and criminality, trying to defend the innocent, the victims, and what have I achieved? The enemies are still winning, and they always will. There are more of them now than when I started, they have more and better resources, their hands aren't tied behind their back.

"In the old days, and the not so old days, people who kept fighting no matter what the odds against them were, became heroes and saints and martyrs. But we know they were just foolish, don't we Guido? We know that you can do more good by winning than by losing. So I want to win, Guido. No more pointless acts of faith, no more throwing myself in front of trains and bullets, no more fighting for hopeless causes."

"Very eloquent, Julia; I wish I knew whether you are being sincere," Guido said.

"You need me to show you that I'm serious, I understand that. You need proof that I mean what I say."

"Precisely, Julia."

"And I will give you proof, once I believe that you are the right person for me. So we have a stand-off, I think," Julia said.

"But you must blink first," Guido said, "if you want to work with me. I share your sentiments, or the sentiments you expressed, but I already have my path and my direction of travel. I think you need me more than I need you, Julia."

"Fair enough, Guido," she said. "As you know, I am a senior officer at Europol. Europol has a huge amount of data about a huge number of people, not all of them major criminals, not outwardly at least. I have access to all that data, and if we are working together, so do you. In addition, I have a network of contacts across several agencies in the UK and Europe, agencies which make decisions and award contracts and spend public money. I also have contacts in other agencies, the ones that collect revenues and taxes and keep records about people who pay and those who don't. I'm persuasive, Guido, I can get almost anyone to do almost anything for me. I persuaded the head of Europol that he needed to hire me, while in fact I just wanted to get inside, to get at all the data. Could you do that, Guido?"

"You got yourself into Europol to exploit it for your own ends?" Guido asked.

"Of course," she said, "I planned it well. I'm not impulsive, Guido. Impulse is a foolish trait. Your turn."

"Very well, Julia," he said, "more eloquent talk, but still no hard proof."

"Fine, here's some," she replied. "Isabelle has told you she's stopped all contact with Antoine Durand, the French policeman, because Durand can no longer access Europol information about joint investigations. She lied; she is still seeing Durand, and he is still passing information to her. He has obtained a lot more than he passed on to you already - he's holding back because he likes his 'rewards' with your wife. His source within Europol has been removed - I did that - but he still has some juicy titbits up his sleeve for you.

"I have copies of everything that Durand has taken, not with me, of course. I know how his source operated and I've tracked everything he did for Antoine. I expect that Isabelle will tell you that Antoine found her and got in touch to hand over more Europol information, and she will give it to you. When that happens, I will give you my copy of the same information. Will that be enough for you, Guido?"

"It will, Julia, it will, but for now you will have to wait. I will not tell you about my business until that happens. You may go now - I mean leave the villa. I will have your car brought round. Come back in ten days. Isabelle will be back by then, and we can have this conversation again with her in the room."

Chapter 43

Julia watched from the bedroom window as her rented car was lowered from a tow-truck. The operator, a non-descript man in overalls, unhooked the slings from the car wheels and was soon gone. She finished packing her belongings, and a few minutes later she too was gone. Guido hadn't reappeared and she had let herself out.

She was surprised at how hot the car was. Wherever it had been was either exposed to sunlight or some other heat source, a boiler maybe. She opened all the windows and drove away.

She was back in The Hague that evening, having stopped briefly at the boarding house in Como to retrieve her passport. She had called Mel from the airport and she was waiting when Julia walked in, gin at the ready.

"That Guido Ricci is slimy," Julia started, "he makes my skin crawl. I'm going back in ten days, but we've a lot to do between now and then."

"It's 'we' again, is it?" Mel asked dryly.

"Always," Julia said, ignoring Mel's tone. "I want you in the office tomorrow; I'm not going in as I'm still on leave and I don't want to get into a fight with Faber's boss, not yet. I want you to go through a recently concluded Joint Investigation - that one involving laundering dirty Russian money in Liechtenstein via Hungary and Italy, remember?"

"I wasn't involved in it, but I know the one you mean. What are you looking for?" Mel asked.

"I'm looking for a credible but fictitious script, one that I can feed to Ricci, something that points to an infiltrator - someone who Ricci would like to arrange to have taken out."

"And what are you going to do?" Mel asked.

"First, I'm going to see Niall Morton in Budapest; it would help to have another player on the ground and I want to see if he's up for it. Then I'm going to track down Antoine Durand and have a quiet word with him too. He's got a job to do, but he doesn't know it yet. I'll be back in a few days, a week at most. Now, how have you and Freddie been?"

******

Julia made a quick call to Errol Spelman from the departure lounge at Schiphol to check that he was alright and to establish that Niall was actually in Budapest. Errol confirmed that he was, having been given a stern talking to by the ambassador about his sudden and repeated absences. Niall had been assiduously rebuilding his credit with the British Embassy, staying in town and schmoozing the locals. He would be there, and probably pleased to see her if she was passing.

The KLM flight to Budapest was uneventful and soon after landing she was in a taxi bowling through the drab Soviet-era suburbs of crumbling tower blocks and industrial estates on her way to the more attractive city centre. She had chosen the Intercontinental, situated conveniently centrally and overlooking the Danube, right in the heart of Budapest. Her room wasn't ready, so she dropped her bag with the porter and strolled round to Gerbeaud's, the elaborate Viennese-style coffee house in Vörösmarty Tér, just round the corner from the

British Embassy. She sat at an outside table and called Niall Morton.

"I'm at Gerbeaud's," she said when he picked up, "fancy a coffee? They do nice cakes too."

He was there ten minutes later.

"Unexpected surprise," he said once they had gone through the ritual greetings, "what brings you to this end of the universe?"

"A few things to attend to, and I thought we could have a catch up. We didn't get much of a chance for a talk while you were helping Errol out."

They chatted for a while about Niall's job as the UK's Police Liaison Officer in Hungary, which, he complained, changed its title every few weeks. He asked how she was finding Europol, how Mel was, and when they ran out of small talk, she started on her real reason for wanting to see him.

"I need your help, Niall," she said. "It's a delicate matter and not that straightforward. I'm trying to expose the person behind the attacks on Joint Investigations, the person who burnt out Errol and who blew up that Austrian undercover police officer right here in Budapest. I know who it is, and I think I know why he did it, but I need something concrete to take him. I need some convincing theatre, and I'd like you to help."

He watched her face as she spoke.

"You are one strange senior officer, Julia," he said after a pause, "I've not come across one like you before. Is this legit? All official and above board?"

"Yes and no, Niall," she replied, "it is legit, in that the person I'm after is behind several killings, but it's not so official, not just yet. The person I'm after is cunning, makes sure that anything nasty can't be traced back - everything is done through third parties with cut-outs and dead ends. It would take twelve lifetimes to get the evidence to destroy him in a courtroom. His main business is making himself incredibly rich, and I don't doubt he's bought as much protection as he needs to keep the cops at arm's length forever. Official and above board won't touch him, Niall, but I think I can take him down."

"I need to get back, Julia," Niall said, "the Ambo wants to see me at two. I'm only here for another couple of months, but I still need a good rating from him. Are you staying over?"

"Round the corner at the Intercontinental, just for tonight," she replied.

"I'll see you in the bar at six then, we can talk some more. I'm not saying no, but I can't say yes either, not until I know the ins and outs."

Morton rose and walked away towards the British Embassy. Julia wondered if she had gone too far with him, if she had presumed too much.

******

Julia smiled when she saw him enter the bar; she waved and he came over to her table.

"Everything alright? With the Ambassador, I mean?" she asked.

"Everything's fine, Julia," Niall said, "he just likes to remind us non-diplomats that he's in charge and that we're just numpties who have no idea about international relations. I try to keep a straight face and say 'yes sir' periodically. He's leaving post soon, or so I've heard."

"Shall we have dinner?" she asked.

"Sure, where do you fancy?"

"I've heard that Gundel's is going strong again," she said. "I've booked a table, but I could only get one at seven. We'd better go."

The taxi took nearly thirty minutes in the heavy evening traffic, but they arrived at Gundel's, the iconic establishment that had been through many ups and downs, but which had remained Budapest's finest restaurant for around a hundred years. Niall guided her through the Hungarian menu, helping her steer clear of the heavy dishes guaranteed to bring on heart attacks. The meal was excellent, the service efficient and seemingly unhurried. Throughout the evening, Niall and Julia chatted, getting to know each other a little better.

"Night cap?" she suggested in the cab back to the Intercontinental.

Over drinks in the bar, Niall momentarily took her hand before letting go again almost immediately. She waited.

"Julia," he said, "I do want to help you. I like you; I think I trust you, and I want to help if I can. Tell me what it is you want me to do?"

"Thank you, I appreciate it, she said. "I want you to pretend to be murdered."

He looked at her, his eyebrows raised in astonishment.

Chapter 44

Julia and Niall Morton were still deep in conversation when the bartender pulled the shutters down. She had outlined her thoughts about his 'murder', and he had asked a lot of sensible questions. He was still undecided. Julia had seen the way he had been looking at her throughout the evening, and for a fleeting moment she was tempted to ask him to stay. She knew he would have accepted in a flash, but her common sense prevailed. She didn't need any more complications.

"I can't decide, Julia," he said as they stood in the hotel lobby, "not yet. I'm going to Vienna in the morning; why don't I pick you up and we can drive up together and talk it through again? I do want to help you, but I need to sleep on it."

"Alright," she agreed.

"See you at eight," he said, "sleep well, Julia."

She didn't, of course. She lay awake in the unfamiliar bedroom listening to the unfamiliar muffled sounds of an unfamiliar city. She went over her plan, if she could call it that, time and time again with varying degrees of confidence. In a nutshell, she planned to present a story to Guido Ricci, the same one that Mel was currently preparing, about an infiltrated undercover investigation that was closing in on one or more of Ricci's enterprises. The story would name Niall Morton as an undercover infiltrator who was getting close to the truth about Ricci's operation. She would present an offer to Ricci to fix the problem and then arrange an elaborate hoax in which Niall Morton would be seen to be 'killed'. This, Julia felt, would give her enough leverage to get inside

Ricci's circle of trust for as long as she needed. What could go wrong?

She was ready and waiting in the hotel lobby at eight. Niall appeared, driving a standard-issue saloon car. She tossed her bag in the back and took the front passenger seat. He leant over to kiss her cheek. She let him.

The drive from Budapest to Vienna is not exciting once the hilly sprawl of the Buda side of the city is behind you. Niall had stayed on the Pest side and took the Erszebet bridge and headed west through the old city. Once on the M1 autoroute he engaged his cruise control.

"I've thought about it, Julia," he started, "and I think it's a mad idea, properly mad. I've made my mind up, but I have one question for you before I tell you what it is."

"Go on," she said.

"Why? Why are you doing this? Why does Guido Ricci matter to you so much?"

"That's two questions, to be pedantic," she said, "but I'll tell you. Firstly, it's not just about Ricci. It didn't take me too long once I'd joined the police to learn that the phrase 'criminal justice system' is a cruel irony. It doesn't deter criminals; it doesn't give victims the sort of justice they want and deserve, and it's more a lottery than a system. Criminal law is written by people with well-meaning remote ideas, or others - less well-meaning - with vested interests. Sure, high-profile killers and terrorists will be seen to have the full weight of the law come down on them, but people who have lost almost everything to thieves, cheats and liars, or who have been beaten up by bigots or their partners or complete strangers mostly won't get to see anything like that.

"Then there are the big-time crooks, the big dealers, fraudsters, gangsters, who buy or rent enough protection from bent cops or lawyers or politicians, or all three, to make sure they never see the inside of a police cell, let alone a courtroom. The criminal justice system can't get near them.

"So, some years ago, not long after I came to London, I saw something one night. A kid, a gay kid, on his way to a club for a night out, was getting beaten up by two louts. Just another queer-bashing. I knew what I should do, but I also knew it would be pointless. If I intervened and had the thugs arrested they would spend a few hours at West End Central, and so would the victim. The kid would have to relive his fear over and over again, and the thugs would be bailed. The whole thing would drag on for months or years, assuming it ever got to court at all. In the meantime, the thugs would get the name and address of the kid from the case papers and he would possibly get a visit to dissuade him from giving evidence.

"I had a moment of madness. I took down the thugs, little old me against two male monsters. I left them lying in their own blood and snot on the pavement and I sent the kid on his way. I didn't report it, nor did the kid or, as far as I know, the thugs. And you know what, Niall? It felt great, really good!

"Fast forward a little. A good and principled officer recruited an informant inside a major criminal organisation. It was the first time that anyone had managed it, but the officer didn't know that the criminal gang was run by a corrupt cop. The bent cop found out about the informant and told the organisation's enforcer, and the informant was brutally killed. The good and principled officer was incensed, but his moment of madness was more considered than mine. He took down the criminal organisation single-handedly, destroyed it completely; he killed three of the gang's enforcers and the bent cop. Then he vanished.

"And I helped him, Niall. The system couldn't or wouldn't. Taking out two thugs feels good; taking down a whole criminal organisation in a way that really stops it dead in its tracks feels a whole lot better. It doesn't change the whole world, but it changes the world of someone who likes to think they're invincible, untouchable. Guido Ricci is one of those, Niall. I want to change his world, permanently. Then I'll have to stop; I know that. That's why, Niall. Now, your decision?"

Niall Morton pulled the car over on the shoulder and looked at her.

"What you've just said could put you away, Julia," he said.

"I know," she looked at him, unblinking. "What are you going to do about it?"

"Exactly what you tell me to," he said. "I still think it's mad, but I'll do it, as you said last night. I've worked out some details and I know some people who would be happy to play along - I'm going to dress it up as a training exercise."

Julia smiled at him and leant across to kiss his cheek.

"Thank you, Niall," she said sincerely, "I'd like to say you won't regret it, but you almost certainly will. I hope you find it was worth it; I know I have. Welcome to my world."

Niall engaged gear and pulled back into the traffic flow. They drove in silence until they reached the redundant border crossing into Austria at Hegyeshalom. Thirty minutes later they pulled in at Schwechat, Vienna's international airport. Julia changed her ticket and boarded the next KLM flight back to Amsterdam. She needed to give Mel a nudge with the story.

Chapter 45

Julia gazed out of her window during the flight to Amsterdam, deep in thought. She thought about her time in the villa and started planning for her return to it, whenever that might be. She knew she needed to have a strategy to get out of the place, possibly in a hurry and pursued by Ricci's security people, so dramatic would be good. She also knew that she would probably only get one chance to find out exactly what Ricci was doing. She wanted to come away with enough information to close him down once and for all, which would probably be her last act as a law-enforcement officer. It was the least they deserved, the dead officers and informants - not to mention her friend Errol Spelman and those closest to him. She also needed to motivate the lustful French detective, Antoine Durand, and she weighed up her range of options. Some were repulsive.

She tried to put all this to one side and enjoy Mel's company for the evening. Mel seemed on good form, in an increasingly rare carefree mood. It was almost like old times; they drank too much, argued about things that didn't matter and threw affectionate insults at each other. Freddie went to bed at his usual time and had stayed asleep most of the night. Mel suggested that Jake must have put gin in his gripe water.

In the morning Mel brought them coffee and slipped back into bed.

"Thanks for last night, Jake," she said, "I needed it. I think you did too."

"Fishing for compliments at this time of day?" Jake asked, smiling.

"You know what I mean Kelso," Mel responded. "You said you wanted to talk to me about the story?"

"I do," Jake replied, "nice coffee."

She then went through her conversations with Niall Morton and her experience at the villa. She even read aloud the letter that she had written to Mel that afternoon when she was completely cut off from the outside world.

"So what I want is a credible story. You've downloaded all the files from that money laundering case and I want you to start editing your copies. Change the dates and some of the names, we can go through it together and decide which names to keep, add or get rid of, and insert Niall's identity as an undercover source who's infiltrated the laundering operation."

"How long have I got?" Mel asked.

"Not long at all, a day or two at most. I've a few things to do and I need to go and see Durand - hopefully before he has his next workout with Isabelle. I need to take the story with me."

"I thought you said that Isabelle told you she wouldn't be needing him anymore," Mel said.

"She let something slip - she asked me if I'd seen him since Brussels, then she said he hadn't mentioned it. That means they are still in contact, and the only reason Isabelle would want to do that is if she was still seeing him, in a lying down way I mean."

"I'd best get on with it then. I'll be in your office - where will you be?"

"Not so fast, I also want you to get a name for me, as a matter of urgency."

"What name?"

"A good drug dealer, ideally a crooked pharmacist and also ideally in Amsterdam," Jake replied. "Have a look on the system when you get in and let me have the name and a contact number or address later."

"I won't ask why," Mel said.

"Good," Jake said, "let me know if there's a team on whoever you choose as well; I need to speak to him or her without setting off fireworks or being rudely interrupted. I'll be in Antwerp for the rest of the day."

"Antwerp? You mean that dodgy bar that Ferdinand was so fond of?"

"The very one; I need some equipment," Jake said.

Mel groaned.

******

Julia drove down to Antwerp and by lunchtime she was seated at the counter of a bar waiting for Leo, the owner. Ferdinand had found Leo, who could get hold of just about anything illegal or unusual that anyone might need, for a price. He was busy at the other end of the bar, sizing Julia up while he was at it. Eventually he came over.

"You've been in here before, miss," he started in English, "you have a strange friend with strange requirements. Where is he?"

"He's dead, Leo," Julia replied, "killed in Africa."

"With him it was always inevitable," Leo said, nodding sagely. "What can I do for you?"

Julia told him. When she had finished he seemed relieved.

"Apart from two items, nothing is illegal. You want me to get everything?" he asked.

"Yes please," Julia confirmed, "ideally packed for concealment under the rear seat of a car. The gun and ammunition in one case, the crossbow, darts and bolts in another. How long?"

They settled on the day after next and agreed an inflated price. Julia hoped that Mel still had some of Ferdinand's illicit funds available.

Deal done, she returned to The Hague and waited for Mel.

"How are we off for Ferdinand's cash?" she asked as soon as Mel walked in.

"And how was your day?" Mel asked sarcastically. "Mine was quite fraught actually. Freddie had a meltdown in the crèche and is on a final warning; Faber's boss is stalking me and asking questions about you whenever I can't get away quickly enough. The DG wants to see you as soon as you get back from leave, and unless you start being nice to me I'm going to quit."

"Sorry, Mel," Jake said, sincerely. "Are you alright?"

"Fine. I've got the name of your drug dealer, and I've printed off three copies of the story you wanted."

"Thank you, Mel," Jake said, "can I get you a drink?"

"As soon as I've fed and hosed down Demon Boy you can get me several. Here," Mel tossed Jake a thick envelope, "read that; I'll be half an hour."

Jake read the folded pages. Each sheet looked like a direct print straight from the Europol information system. Mel's edits were undetectable and fitted seamlessly with the genuine text. Jake studied the story carefully, making her own notes on a separate sheet of paper. It all seemed to work.

Mel reappeared with a clean and quiet Freddie. She set about preparing his food as Jake poured the wine.

"Great story, Mel," she said, "it all fits, makes sense."

"Are you sure Niall's alright with this? I mean, if it falls into the wrong hands he'll have some explaining to do, at the very least."

"As long as I can do my bit, he'll be fine. It won't be getting anywhere near the targets, not this time. I'm just hoping that Guido Ricci finds it irresistible. Now, have we got any of his cash?"

"Of course we have," Mel said, "how much do you want?"

******

The next day Julia Kelso took the train to Amsterdam. She consulted the sheet of paper Mel had given her and studied the small photograph. The person she was looking for certainly didn't look like your average drug dealer. This one specialised in manufacturing her own cocktails, bespoke for very picky clients. A pharmaceutical chemist by training and a ruthless money-making machine by inclination, Ursula Klein ostensibly worked in a medium-sized laboratory hidden away in the University Quarter.

Julia found the building and took a seat at a sidewalk table outside a café. She watched the flow of people coming and going from the building, a surprising number. She guessed most were students but realised that a few people did not fit the stereotypical image. As the lunch hour neared she ordered and paid for another coffee and watched carefully.

Ursula Klein lived up to her name; she was a small stocky woman, probably in her thirties. She looked like she lived alone. Julia stood and followed her. Ursula clearly had a favourite lunch-spot and was soon seated with a modest meal in front of her. She looked startled, almost affronted, when Julia took the seat opposite her at her small table. She started to protest but Julia silenced her with a raised hand.

"Business, Ursula," she said quietly, "just keep eating while I tell you what I want."

Julia spoke swiftly and clearly. When she had finished, it was Ursula's turn.

"I have no idea who you are or what you are talking about. Please leave me alone or I will call the police!"

"Go ahead," Julia passed her mobile phone across the table and waited. "No, I thought not. I know who you are, Ursula, and what you do. You make up whatever drugs your clients want, and if they aren't sure you invent special cocktails for them, give them what you think they might like. It sounds pretty harmless to me, consenting adults and all that, but not everyone sees it my way. Now, can you give me what I asked for?"

"Why do you want it?" Ursula asked.

"That's my business, Ursula," Julia replied.

"I mean how do you plan to administer it? Orally, intravenously? It makes a difference to the composition and dosage."

"I see," Julia said, "most probably by skin penetration, direct into the body but not necessarily into a vein."

"And how big is the 'patient' in weight?" Ursula asked.

"I'd say around a hundred to a hundred and ten kilos, one-hundred and seventy-five centimetres or so."

"A man then. Is he fit, athletic?"

"No," Julia said.

"I can prepare what you need. It is very powerful and dangerous if too big a dose is given - it will be your responsibility."

"Fine. I want two doses for a person the size of the 'patient' I described, another two for a female - this one fit and healthy, sixty to seventy kilos, my height, and another five for someone taller and fitter than the 'patient' but around ninety kilos. Can you do it?"

"Yes," Ursula replied.

"Can you also get me some white phosphorous? I don't need much, just a small sample, like you'd use in a school chemistry lab."

"Yes, I can do that too, the phosphorous comes in pieces in a small, sealed plastic tub, filled with water. It is important that it is not exposed to air."

"I understand," Julia said.

"This is the price," Ursula wrote a figure on a napkin. "Come again in two days. You found me this time. Do it again but I will lead you somewhere different. Bring cash - I will not have the goods with me but will tell you where you can collect it."

"How do I know I can trust you?" Julia asked.

"You don't," Ursula said, "any more than I know I can trust you, but that is how this business works, isn't it?"

Chapter 46

Julia hadn't quite finished in Amsterdam. She took the train to Schiphol and rented a car for three days. She navigated her way out of the complicated airport and drove around the city's ring road. She found what she wanted after nearly an hour. It was a used car dealership, not too showy or shiny but with a good selection of tidy looking cars lined up on the forecourt. As a bonus, the salesperson she spoke to was a woman, an older woman in her fifties or early sixties, and she said she was the site owner.

Julia spun the story she had been rehearsing as she drove. Her useless husband had run off with some tart and had taken the car, their only car, with him, leaving her high and dry. She needed an inexpensive reliable car urgently as she had work to go to. It would be a cash purchase - she had cleared out the joint bank account that morning to stop him getting hold of her money as well as her car. What was available?

The saleswoman was sympathetic and showed Julia a selection of small- to medium-sized cars, all at reasonable prices. Julia selected a decent looking Volkswagen, haggled briefly and handed over a cash deposit. The saleswoman said she would service the car and it would be ready for collection in two days. Julia gave a made-up name and an address on the outskirts of The Hague that she had looked up to get the post code. Everything was in order, the saleswoman had said.

Julia made her way back to The Hague, stopping on the way at a large and busy service station. She filled the rental car with fuel and bought a plastic five-litre petrol container, which she also filled. In the shop she bought a pack of cable ties, some cleaning cloths, a selection of plastic food containers with snap-on lids and a small set of assorted hand tools.

"Where have you been?" Mel asked as soon as she walked in.

"Just up to Amsterdam to do a few bits and pieces. How was the office?" Julia answered.

"There's a bit of an atmosphere, Jake," Mel said, "I'm starting to feel unwelcome. The DG's assistant came by asking for you, said you hadn't been answering your phone. I'm not going in tomorrow; Freddie's been playing up a bit too so I'm taking him to his kindergarten instead of the crèche. What's going on, Jake?"

"I'm just getting ready to sort out Guido Ricci - it will all be over in a few days, so hang on in there. But I'm glad you're not going back to the office - I need you to come to Italy."

"What?" Mel said.

"I want you to drive my car to Como. I've rented a room in a boarding house and I want you to go there in my car and wait for me. Take your good laptop and make sure you can get on the internet - I doubt there's any in the boarding house. We'll need it."

"And Freddie?" Mel asked.

"Take him too, we can come back slowly when it's all over and maybe take a little holiday in Italy or Switzerland or something on the way."

"What about the DG? He's going to flip if you don't come back when your leave is up."

"I expect he's had my letter, my resignation. That will be why he wants to see me," Julia said.

"You've resigned?"

"I said I would, didn't I?"

"I thought you meant in a few months or something, not right now. Why the rush, Jake?" Mel asked.

"Sometimes it's best not to wait. If the time's right, why not do it now? Enough of this, I'm hungry. What do you want for supper?"

******

The next morning Julia set off in her rented car, first for Antwerp and then for Paris. The transaction with Leo in the bar was swift and seamless. She stowed two briefcases in the trunk of her car and drove west and south for a few hours. Having skirted Brussels, she drove through the dark forests of the Ardennes. She took a few side roads and soon found an isolated and deserted picnic spot, well away from the main road, where she could familiarise herself with her purchases.

She opened the heavier briefcase first. Inside was a small semi-automatic pistol, a lightweight and compact Glock 19. She unwrapped the weapon and cleaned off the excess oil with one of the cloths she had bought before loading the magazine and inserting it in the handle. She didn't know why, or even if, she needed it, but Ferdinand had often said that it was better to be over-equipped than under-equipped. Julia walked into the woods and found a small clearing around thirty to forty metres across. She stopped and listened. She could hear no movement or voices. She took aim at a knot in the bark of a tree and fired a pair of shots. The report from the pistol wasn't loud, but it was penetrating. She inspected the tree and was pleased to see that the rounds had hit pretty much on target and tightly grouped. She picked up the shell cases, replaced the spent rounds and walked back to the car.

In the second briefcase was the crossbow. It too was compact and lightweight, made of carbon fibre and with only a thirty-five-pound draw pressure on the bow. She hadn't handled a crossbow before and it took her a while to work out how to assemble it and string the bow. The crossbow she had chosen was self-loading and had a six-bolt magazine, but it had to be cocked manually between each shot. Julia loaded six practice bolts and headed back to the clearing. The first six went wide or didn't reach the target tree.

Julia retrieved and reloaded the bolts. Her second attempt was better as she got the feel of the unfamiliar weapon. The third set of bolts were all on target, and she used a fourth loading to work out the effective range and degree of penetration of the bolts. She didn't want to kill anyone. Her final trial was with one of the special darts, less than half the weight of the lightest practice bolt. She didn't have many, and unlike the bolts, the darts would not be reusable. She adjusted her aim to compensate for the lack of weight and shot at the tree from five metres. The dart hit where she had aimed it, and it stuck in the tree bark. Perfect. She dismantled and repacked the crossbow and went back to the car. She ate a sandwich and resumed her journey to Paris.

Chapter 47

Julia had found Antoine Durand's home in a commuter village, conveniently situated on the eastern side of Paris, by mid-afternoon. It was a normal house on a normal street. The driveway in front of it was empty, but the gates were open. Julia waited for a while. The new pistol, loaded and ready to use, was in her handbag.

Before long a small Renault drove up and pulled onto the driveway, parking off to one side. A middle-aged woman, elegant but looking tired, carried a bag of groceries from the car to the house and looked at her watch. A few minutes later she was out again and back in the car. Julia waited a little longer. Twenty minutes passed before the Renault came back, this time occupied by two adolescent children as well as the woman. They all went inside, the children arguing between themselves and with their mother quite loudly. Julia decided she had stayed long enough and went off in search of a place to spend the night.

She was back outside Durand's house a little after six. A couple of hundred metres away in the heart of the suburban village there was a café-bar, not overly inviting, where she planned to meet Durand when she saw him come home. He arrived around thirty minutes later. She watched him park and stretch wearily. She called his phone. She watched him pick up.

"Oui, Durand," he said.

"Hello Antoine, remember me? It's Julia Kelso."

"What do you want? I have nothing to say to you!"

"But I have something to say to you, Antoine," she said calmly.

"I am busy," he snapped.

"No you're not, Antoine. You're outside your nice little house where your wife and two kids are waiting, if they've stopped squabbling yet. Go to the café-bar in the village. Go now, I'll see you there."

Durand looked up and down the road. Julia didn't try to hide. She waved a hand at him as he glared at her. He looked furious, but nevertheless he turned and walked back towards the village centre.

By the time she arrived he was seated at a table near the door with a small beer in front of him. He didn't offer her a drink. She sat opposite him.

"Not very hospitable, Antoine," she began.

She signalled to the hovering waiter and ordered herself a glass of white.

"What do you want?" he demanded.

"I've got something for you," Julia said, "assuming you still have that arrangement with Isabelle Meyer-Ricci. You are still seeing her, right?"

"What of it?" he said tetchily.

"Your boy Jeroen Faber isn't too well at the moment. He got attacked in Brussels - a robbery by all accounts. Anyway, he's off work for a while, and even if he wasn't he'd be of no use to you. His access to confidential records has been blocked, permanently blocked. I happen to know that Isabelle's husband, Grand Master Guido, wants to keep the supply of Europol information coming for a bit longer. So I'm going to do you a favour."

"Why?" Durand asked.

"You never know when you might need a favour to be returned, Antoine. I scratch your back, as they say. It suits me if Ricci gets what he wants, for now. Who knows, I may even have need of your services myself in future. You're an attractive man, Antoine," she lied.

"What if I say no?" he said.

"If you say no, two things could happen, maybe three," Julia said, "firstly, you won't be enjoying Isabelle again. Secondly, first your wife and then your bosses will find out exactly what you have been up to with her and why, including a detailed account of the consequences. There are French police widows because of you, Antoine. The third possibility is that I could shoot you dead, here and now or in the street in a few minutes, or tomorrow morning or whenever I want. It took me no time to find you, Antoine - I can do it any time I want. You'll never know."

He stared at her, horrified. Her smile hadn't changed; her tone of voice was calm, relaxed even, and she was saying she could and would shoot him dead.

"But if you do what I want, you'll just have to go and get laid by the lovely Isabelle a few more times. By the way, Antoine, let me warn you that if you try to back out or double cross me, everything I just said *could* happen *will* happen, no doubt, no ifs or buts. Only by the time you are dying in the gutter you won't know if it was me or one of your colleagues, friends of the officers who died because of you, who put you there."

"What do you want me to do?" he asked.

"Arrange to see Isabelle, no sooner than four days from now and no later than six days. When you see her, give her this." Julia slid an envelope across the table.

"What is it?" he asked.

"You'll recognise it. It's just like the ones you got from Jeroen Faber, only this one is much more important to Ricci. It is close to home. Isabelle will undoubtedly give you a special reward when she sees it. I hope you're up to it."

Julia left her wine untouched and she stood to leave. She looked at him but said nothing. He stared at her, his expression a mix of fear, loathing and lust. She realised that she had aroused him, and she was both pleased and revolted.

Julia was back in the house with Mel late the following day. Mel was preoccupied and they didn't speak much. The next morning, her purchases safely stowed in the garage of her house, Julia returned her rental car to Schiphol airport after a brief stop at the large cancer hospital not far from the airport. As she had expected, there was a shop near the main entrance that sold all manner of things to make life easier, or at least less bad, for cancer sufferers. She wanted wigs, hairpieces, and she soon found two that were the right size for her, one a deep dark brown, the other a sort of mousy colour. Neither looked anything like her own startlingly bright blonde hair.

She took the train to Amsterdam Centraal Station. She walked to Ursula Klein's workplace and waited in the café opposite. Ursula emerged as expected, carrying a plastic shopping bag. Julia followed her to a different restaurant and waited until she sat down. Julia approached, an envelope in her hand. Ursula placed the plastic bag on the table and opened it for Julia to see. Inside were nine glass vials alongside a small, circular plastic pot about the size of an ash tray. She did have the goods with her, after all.

"These are the doses you asked for," Ursula said. "The ones with the red dots are for the heavier male, the white dots are for the female. The unmarked ones are for the fit men. Understand?"

"Thank you," Julia nodded.

"And in the plastic pot are the white phosphorous pieces, they are in water. Make sure they are always covered, if they are exposed to the air they will combust violently. Be very careful with it."

Julia slid her envelope across the table to Ursula, who opened it and looked inside. She seemed to be able to count the notes without touching them. Ursula nodded and pocketed the envelope. Julia picked up the plastic bag and left.

She took a taxi to the used car lot. Her new car was ready, cash changed hands and she was soon on her way home, ready for the next act.

Mel was out somewhere with Freddie. Julia turned on the oven and opened its door. Soon the kitchen was uncomfortably warm. She drew some lines on a couple of the plastic food containers and filled them with water. Using a sharp knife she made tiny holes on the side and lid of one, and slightly bigger holes just on the lid of the other. Water in the container with the hole on the side drained too quickly. She went upstairs for an hour and when she returned she saw that the water level in the remaining container was slightly lower. She checked again another hour later and marked the water level. She reckoned that in a similar temperature it would take around thirty hours for enough water to evaporate. It would have to do.

Chapter 48

Julia called Niall Morton in Budapest. He had set up the 'training exercise' as they had discussed on the drive up to Vienna. He had recruited a small team from the Hungarian security service, the *Alkotmányvédelmi Hivatal* or simply the 'AH', to act as his attackers. The 'hit' was to take place at an AH urban surveillance training facility where it would be filmed as if captured on CCTV. It was all set for the day after next, and Julia would have the required footage, edited to look like a Hungarian news broadcast, the day after that. All she would need to do was add the desired date, which was simple enough.

"I'm going to head off in a couple of days," she said to Mel over coffee in the kitchen. "The rent here is paid up until the end of next month. When are you planning to come to Italy?"

"I might as well go at the same time as you," Mel said, "I'll need an overnight stop somewhere though, Freddie can't do six hundred miles in one hit."

Julia spent the rest of the day and all of the next trying to relax. She went for a long run, took in a movie, had coffee at the beach in Scheveningen. She even went to the *Rijksmuseum* in Amsterdam, but still she felt tense, anxious. She didn't know how Ferdinand had coped; she felt completely alone and isolated. Back at the house she packed two cases, one for the villa, one for the boarding house and the return to - the return to where? London, she supposed, or maybe home, to Scotland. She didn't have much stuff, and the few bits and pieces she had left in the house were not important to her.

The crossbow, the bolts and darts, and the vials from Ursula Klein went into the villa bag, along with one of the hairpieces. As an afterthought, she added a small backpack, easier to manage if she needed to make a run for it. Her laptop, passport, bank cards and wallet went in the 'home' case. The gun she kept with her, and the white phosphorous, now in a larger sealed food container filled almost to the brim with water and tightly wrapped in a plastic bag, was propped in the glove box, wedged in with socks and books. A sharp-pointed knife lay next to it. The spare petrol container went in the trunk with her cases. She kept the envelope containing the 'story' in her overnight bag, which was always with her. She stowed it all in her 'new' car inside the garage at the house.

They set off in convoy, but Mel soon outpaced the slower Volkswagen and Julia lost sight of her before they reached Utrecht. The journey on the autoroutes and autobahns was tedious and Julia was glad to pull off as she neared Basel. She had to refuel, and Mel was already at the hotel by the time she arrived.

"How was he in the car?" Julia asked Mel.

"Good as gold mostly. I only had to stop once. I turn the radio up if he starts yelling, but that does seem to make him yell louder too. Can you amuse him while I take a shower, I think he might have wee'd on me."

"The joy of motherhood, Mel, it reminds me why I never did it."

Freddie was quiet, so Julia made a quick call to Isabelle.

"When are you going back to the villa?" she asked Isabelle, "I'd like to see you, we need a chat I think. I can be there in two or three days."

"You shouldn't call me unless it's urgent, Julia," Isabelle scolded, "I have some meetings but I plan to be back by the weekend, Friday probably. Send me your vehicle details when you have them so I can tell security to let you in."

She cut the call. Julia seethed for a few moments but found that Isabelle's attitude had merely strengthened her resolve. Isabelle would be going down too, Julia reminded herself.

The next day they drove through Switzerland. The distance was shorter than the previous day, but their speed was lower. The mountain scenery was spectacular, as was the standard of driving in Switzerland, but in a different sense. Both Julia and Mel were quite relieved as they drove on the short stretch of autostrada between the Swiss border in Ticino and the town of Como. Mel thought the boarding house was delightful.

She quickly made friends with the *signora*, who fell in love with Freddie instantly and even helped Mel bring his things in from the car. Julia arrived shortly afterwards to see her friend and the old lady chatting together happily in a mixture of broken Italian and bad English. She felt happy for the first time in a long while, and she told herself to make the most of it.

Julia received the footage of Niall Morton's murder. He sent a link by email and she was able to access the video and download it. She shared it with Mel. Mel inserted an appropriate date, three days in the future, which was when she would send a new link to Jake's phone. The video was very convincing; the special effects worked well and it would take a forensic expert to tell that Niall Morton had *not* been shot seven times by two assassins.

On Friday Julia set off after breakfast. She had sent her car registration to Isabelle but had heard nothing back. She hadn't heard anything from Guido either. She arrived at the villa and waited in her car. The gates swung open and she drove up to the house. The spare fuel container was now on the floor by the back seat, its screw cap loose, barely on in fact, and she could already smell the petrol vapour in the car. Before she got out, she reached into the glove compartment and punched four small holes in the lid of the plastic pot of phosphorous. She hoped that the evaporation would not be too swift.

She took her case and overnight bag from the car and locked it. A butler let her in before she could knock and he showed her to the same suite of rooms. Lunch would be at one, was all he had said. She looked from her window and saw the same tow-truck with her new car on it drive away towards the outbuildings behind the villa. It was as she expected; she just hoped the phosphorous didn't spill.

She changed into a light summer dress and went down for lunch at one. Guido was already on the terrace, a small glass of something in front of him. He looked up, but did not speak.

"Good afternoon, Guido," Julia said politely, "it is a beautiful day."

"It is," was all he said.

"I believe Isabelle will be back today."

Guido just nodded and pointed to the sky. A few seconds later the sound of rotor blades broke the silence. A small crew appeared from nowhere, the cylindrical fire extinguishers on wheels at the ready. Isabelle's helicopter touched down on the lawn and she was on the terrace a few moments later. One of the ground crew took her minimal luggage from the aircraft, which took off again immediately. Silence returned.

Isabelle kissed Guido's proffered cheek lightly.

"Hello Julia," she said, "I see you have made it back."

Julia looked at Isabelle. She looked relaxed, radiant even, and satisfied. Julia recognised the look and knew that Antoine Durand had done his work.

The women exchanged a few words, but Guido kept his reptilian silence as he ate his meagre lunch. As soon as he had finished, he stood up and gestured to Isabelle, who stopped eating and stood as well. She exchanged glances with Julia as she followed her husband into the house.

Julia went back to her rooms and tried to doze but couldn't. She was roused by a splash an hour or so later and went to the window overlooking the pool. Isabelle, in a white one-piece swimsuit, was in the pool. Guido, in a bathrobe was watching her from the terrace. He held a towel for her when she got out and watched as she dried herself. He seemed to be agitated, excited even. This time Isabelle led the way back to the house and Guido followed.

Chapter 49

Julia was hot and bored. The afternoon heat was rising and there was nothing she could do. She changed into a swimsuit and went down to the pool. A few dozen cooling lengths helped, and when she was done she sat on the terrace in the shade of a handy parasol. She closed her eyes and leant back in her chair.

"Are you enjoying yourself?" It was Isabelle, also dressed for swimming.

"To be honest, I'm getting restless. I came here to talk seriously, and all you two do is fob me off and keep me at arm's length."

"You can't blame us, Julia. Guido is naturally suspicious, and so am I. You are police, after all," Isabelle responded.

"So is Antoine Durand; so was Duncan Traynor. I don't doubt you've got others who do things for you in return for whatever. But, Isabelle, I'm not like them. I'm not a messenger, a runner. We can all be of more use to each other if we work together; I've got ideas and skills, but I need to have a clearer insight into your business. I think I can guess, but I'd rather hear it from you and Guido."

"Well what do you think it is, Julia?" Isabelle asked.

Julia sighed. "I think you are asset strippers and tax evaders. I think you're fleecing investors and governments, and I don't have a problem with that. I also think you've set up a network, this 'Order' as you call it, to give you a big enough supply of useful fuckwits, expendable helpers who can be thrown to the wolves if necessary to keep the heat off you. I don't have a problem with that either. But I also think that your business is getting complicated, that it crosses too many borders these days, which is why you need to disempower international collaborative agencies and efforts. Which is how I came to notice you. Nobody else has, at least not yet."

"Very imaginative, Julia," Isabelle said drily.

"But accurate, yes? By the way, I said that nobody else has figured it out yet. Please don't take that to mean that you can just take me out and everything will be fine. I'm not one of your fuckwits, Isabelle, I've left traps. If anything happens to me, or if I don't do certain things to a set timetable, all the information I have will be released to the authorities, the media and the entire world."

"So Julia, if you are correct, what is it that you think you can do for us?"

"I can get you help that knows what it's doing and that can make it impossible to trace your deals and transactions. I can lay false trails that will keep the cops on the wrong foot forever. I can deflect the heat if it gets too close by finding and framing some sucker to take the drop for you. How's that?" Julia almost convinced herself.

"What would you want in return?"

"Equity, Isabelle. I want partnership with you and Guido. I'm not getting any younger, none of us is, and I want to spend a lot of time in obscene comfort."

"You are a straight talker, Julia, but are you a truthful one?" Isabelle said.

"That's sort of what Guido said. I told him I'd give him proof when you got back here."

"What proof?"

"I'll tell you when I tell him, Isabelle. Now, I'm going for another swim, Are you coming?"

"I'm not sure Guido could cope, but yes."

"Sorry, what does that mean?" Julia said.

"I'm sure you will find out for yourself in due course, Julia. Guido likes to watch and imagine, I'll say no more."

The two women swam side by side at a steady pace. Isabelle was a good strong swimmer, but not as fit as Julia. She tired and slowed after fifteen minutes. They had been chatting from time to time as they swam, probing each other for hints and details, almost as if they were becoming friends.

"A drink, Julia?" Isabelle asked.

"Why not, it's almost five."

Isabelle summoned the butler and a bottle of champagne appeared. It was expensively good and deliciously chilled.

"You like the good life, don't you Isabelle?" Julia asked.

"Of course, as do you, it's just that I am more accustomed to it than you are. It will come easily to you, I can tell."

"Will Guido come down to dinner?" Julia asked.

"I think not. He gets overtired when I've been away, or rather when I come back," she let a sly smirk cross her lips.

"Can I ask a personal question?" Julia said.

Isabelle just nodded.

"What do you see in him?"

Isabelle smiled wearily.

"He has needs, I can fulfil them; I have needs, he can fulfil them," Isabelle replied.

"That's all? A mutually beneficial transaction?"

"Don't pretend to be shocked, Julia, it has always been so unless you are one of the lower classes. All proper marriages are mutually beneficial, aren't they? Aristocrats, princes and princesses, titans of industry, financial giants, they all marry strategically. Only simpletons marry for love."

"Fair enough, Isabelle, but isn't it helpful, or less awful, if your strategic spouse is at least a little bit charming and attractive, nice to be around?"

"And you think Guido isn't?"

"I've seen nothing to suggest otherwise," Julia said.

"I said to you in Brussels that a woman can achieve more in an hour in the bedroom than most men can in a lifetime. It's true, especially if you are able to close your eyes and think of someone else."

Julia threw her head back and laughed. To her surprise, Isabelle did too.

******

Guido appeared at breakfast the next morning. He was as incommunicative as ever, but eventually he spoke as he rose to leave.

"Come to the office at ten, please," he mumbled, "both of you. But swim first."

They did as they were told. After ten minutes in the pool Isabelle called a halt.

"That will do, Julia, he will have had enough as we get out."

"What do you mean?" Julia asked.

"He watches, he gets aroused. With someone new, the sight of her body in a wet swimsuit out of the water is often enough. If it isn't, I will attend to things when I get upstairs. I will see you at ten."

Julia felt disgusted but tried to disguise it. She wasn't sure she had fooled Isabelle.

At ten she was outside the office when Isabelle arrived. Julia had an envelope in her hand, her phone in her pocket and nothing else. Isabelle had a compact briefcase. At ten precisely the door clicked and Isabelle pushed it open. The women sat opposite him at the large desk.

"So Julia," he began, "what of your proof?"

"Has Isabelle given you the package? The one she just got from Antoine Durand."

He nodded. Colour drained from Isabelle's face.

"It's from a case downloaded by Jeroen Faber from the Europol system, but why Antoine chose to hold it back I don't know. I have it too."

She slipped her envelope across the table. Guido opened it and studied the contents. He looked up.

"You can see that it is the same as Isabelle's. It concerns a Europol Joint Investigation involving Hungary and Italy, but unusually there is also participation from a non-EU member state, Liechtenstein. There has been some high-level intergovernmental dealing going on. The Hungarians are aware that foreign money, mostly Russian but not exclusively, is finding its way via the Hungarian banking system into certain financial institutions in Liechtenstein. The Italians have also discovered that money from Italian banks is ending up in the same institutions in Liechtenstein, but that the origin of this money is unclear. It seems to come from nowhere. There is a British policeman, a liaison officer, in Budapest who has worked it out. He has infiltrated the Hungarian end of the criminal network on behalf of the Joint Investigation.

"He has worked out that the Italian money is coming from a large number of small- to medium-sized businesses that are being taken over by a smaller number of larger businesses. According to the Europol papers, he has done some checks and has an answer. The answer isn't there, though. I removed it; the Joint Investigation has not been told. His answer is that all the smaller companies have been stripped of assets and the taxes they owe have simply not been paid. He has put a figure on it, on the companies he has identified, and it is a large one. If the Joint Investigation is given that information, it is inevitable that the Guardia di Finanza and the Italian state prosecutors will be told and given the evidence. It will be the big case they have been waiting for to take down the companies behind the takeovers, and the man, or man and woman, behind them. Are you following me? Good.

"I know what you would intend to do with the information Isabelle has given you, so I've done it for you. My proof, if you think it is still needed, is on my phone. May I turn it on?"

"Go ahead," Guido mumbled.

"There's a good signal in here so I shouldn't need the internet. Here we go, it's coming in. Before I travelled to Italy, I contacted people I know of and put them in touch with the principal targets in Hungary. I told them that the British officer had infiltrated their gang and was a danger to them. Yesterday, they resolved the issue. I have footage from this morning's Hungarian TV news. Watch."

Julia handed over her phone. Isabelle rose and went to look over Guido's shoulder at the phone. Guido watched as apparent CCTV footage, rebroadcast, showed two men close in on a third, draw weapons and open fire. The victim went down, blood clearly spraying and oozing from his many wounds. The caption read: Niall Morton, *rendőri összekötő Brit Nagykövetség Budapesten.*

"I don't do Hungarian," Julia said, "but I'm guessing that says 'police liaison, British Embassy Budapest. That's what Niall Morton did. I knew him, he was the infiltrator. He was going to take you down, Guido. There's my proof. I'm in it as deeply as you are now."

Guido passed her phone back. He stood and went to the bulky desktop computer that sat on a side table. He sat in front of it as it started up. Julia could see that it was quite old, and when the screen came alive it was obviously not using the latest software. Guido went to the internet and found an Italian news site. Julia hoped that Niall had been able to get his Hungarian contacts to plant the story of the assassination of a British official in Budapest in the media as they had planned. It seemed he had. Guido grunted and turned the computer off.

"Very well, Julia," he said, "we can talk."

Chapter 50

Guido Ricci nearly smiled. Isabelle's face was white and she looked uneasy.

"Not so pretty close up, is it Isabelle?" Julia said. "That's the reality of what you've been doing."

"I know that, Julia," she replied, "but I do find violence distasteful. Tell Guido what you want."

"I want a share, Guido, "Julia said, "I've a good idea what your business is, and I'll help you grow it if the terms are right. I've collected enough useable information about what you're doing to set the dogs on you if we can't come to an agreement. As I told Isabelle, if anything happens to me, or if I'm prevented from leaving here when I choose to, that information will be made public, starting with the Guardia di Finanza and *La Stampa*."

Guido stared at her, his eyes black and cold.

"You are impertinent, Julia, and spirited. I did not take you for a hothead," he whispered.

"But I'm not, Guido," she replied, "I'm as cold and calculating as you are, but I get things done myself. I don't need your Order. Now, shall we talk about business?"

He nodded slowly. He took a bunch of keys from his trouser pocket and passed it to Isabelle.

"The master file, please," he said to her.

Isabelle went to a large tapestry drape that covered most of one wall. She pulled a cord and it drew back, revealing a bank of three metal safes. The central one had the most impressive looking locks. Isabelle used two of the keys to open it, one in each lock, turned simultaneously. The safe door opened. Julia could see inside and was surprised at how little it contained. On one shelf there was a small black notebook and a single mobile phone, she assumed it was the one Mel had identified as the key to communications with the Order's Regional Masters. On the higher shelf there were two box files and one beige cardboard folder. It was this that Isabelle took from the safe. She closed the door but did not relock it. She handed it to Guido.

"Your assumption is more or less correct, Julia," he said. "We have several master companies, holding companies if you like, which we rotate frequently. It is like one of those seaside games with shells and a pea. Isabelle has her own business in Strasbourg, which has acquired several small law firms throughout Europe. We use those to form and dissolve companies, the holding ones and the smaller ones we buy and drain. I control it all from here, but Isabelle attends to the details."

"And the Order, Guido?" Julia asked.

"As you said, it is useful. Not everything can be done remotely or on paper, as you have just demonstrated. Dressing it up as some kind of meaningful cult, steeped in mystery and tradition, keeps the brothers loyal and discreet. I don't like to leave here very often these days, but from time to time I have to go to a gathering or to meet a potential Regional Master, sometimes a new recruit. In the past, I used to have a higher profile, but such things attract attention and jealousy."

"How many brothers are there?" Julia asked.

"It varies," Guido said, "some are quite old when they join and don't last long, others prove to be unsuitable. It is more difficult to find new brothers these days, our numbers are falling. Today, there are eighty-nine brothers, not counting myself and Isabelle. You will need to join too, Julia, there will be an initiation ceremony for you and two other new brothers in Rome in a couple of months. Isabelle will prepare you."

"What do the brothers do for you, for us?" Julia asked.

"They are our eyes and ears, our arms and legs. Our messengers and couriers," he said.

"Our killers?" Julia asked.

Guido glared at her.

"No," he said, "they do not kill for us. We find others to do that for us if and when it is needed."

"Who decides when it is needed?"

"You decided, didn't you?" Isabelle joined in. "You decided that it was necessary to kill the British policeman in Budapest. We do the same, for the same reasons - to protect ourselves and the Order, and our business. Wars are declared for similar reasons and always have been, we are just more focussed and effective."

"I see the sense in that," Julia said, "selecting specific threats for elimination. But the Europol operations you sabotaged, they weren't specifically targeted, were they?"

"They were different, certainly," Isabelle answered, "but they were strategic. We had information, thanks to Faber and Antoine, that we could use to discredit Europol. We didn't act ourselves, unlike you, we merely made sure that one or other of the brothers got that information to the people who would want to act on it as they wished. The criminals being investigated wanted the information; we gave it to them indirectly. The outcome was perfect."

"You mean the disparaging media coverage, the damage to Europol's reputation?" Julia asked.

"Of course, but not just Europol's. We've done similar things to damage the reputation of any cross-border agency that threatens our business."

"Only cross-border?" Julia queried. "Just so I'm quite clear."

"Yes," Isabelle continued, "there are more traditional ways to deal with threats that are contained within one state, simpler ways."

"Bribes," Julia said.

"Exactly. Why hire lawyers when you own the judge?" Isabelle said.

"You should look at this, Julia," Guido interrupted, passing the folder across.

Julia opened it. It was a slim file, maybe a dozen sheets of paper, each one covered with neat tables and charts. There must have been the names of four- or five-hundred companies in seven or more countries, all set out with their hierarchical relationships indicated. At the very top of the first page was a gold star, representing the centre - Guido and Isabelle.

Another page, not attached to anything else, was a tally of the balances of hundreds of bank accounts in several countries, all expressed in US dollars. The final total was staggering.

"That one is updated daily," Isabelle said. "Until today, Guido and I owned half each. From tomorrow we will own one third each of what we make going forward, and you will own the other third. You will be a rich woman, Julia."

"But you will need to work for it," Guido said softly.

"Oh, I will," Julia said, "may I study this at length?"

"No," Guido said, "it stays in this room, and it is old business. You will concern yourself only with new business, once you are sworn in as a brother."

"Will I meet the other brothers?" Julia asked.

"Some, in due course," Guido said.

"How do you communicate with them?" she asked.

"We have a telephone," Isabelle said, "it is kept in this room as well. It has the numbers of all the brothers in it, and it has never been used for anything else. There is a regional structure. A Regional Master will be able to contact all brothers beneath him in his region, and he can contact the Grand Master, Guido, but only in a dire emergency. No brother knows the identity of more than two others, apart from the Regional Masters, it is a well-tried structure."

"It is," Julia agreed, "but you know who they all are, I take it."

"Of course," Guido said, glancing at the two box files in the safe. "I think that will do for this morning. I will rest before lunch."

He remained seated. Isabelle returned the folder to the safe, locked it carefully and closed the drape. She returned the keys to Guido, who put them back in his trouser pocket. Isabelle glanced at Julia and turned to leave the room. Julia rose and followed. Outside Isabelle turned to face her.

"I do hope you know what you are doing, Julia," she said, "you have crossed a line. There is no going back now."

"I crossed a line a long time ago, Isabelle," Julia said, "and I know exactly what I'm doing. See you at lunch."

Chapter 51

Alone in her suite of rooms, Julia took her bag to the one place that wasn't covered by Guido's nosy cameras. She sat at the small table and lined up the glass vials beside the lightweight hollow darts, which were actually made for use as veterinary tranquilisers. She carefully filled each dart's cylinder with the hypodermic syringe Ursula Klein had provided. Once a dose was loaded, she charged the air cylinder at the back of the dart chamber so that the dart was pressurised and the liquid would be injected into the target when it struck. It was a fiddly process, but after the first couple of darts she developed a smooth technique. Soon she had six darts lined up, one loaded for Guido, one for Isabelle, and the remaining four for anyone who got in her way.

Next, she checked her pistol. When she had arrived at the villa the first time she had been surprised by the lack of security checks once you were past the main gate. She thought it probable that Guido didn't want his sanctuary invaded by security guards, so he put all the effort into keeping people away rather than searching them when they got inside. She was grateful. The Glock was fully loaded, with a spare magazine at the ready.

Finally, she assembled the crossbow and put the bowstring in place. She cocked it and tested the mechanism. It was smooth and almost silent. She loaded the crossbow magazine with the six fully charged darts and slipped a further six standard bolts into a small pouch. The magazine was loaded so that the dart meant for Guido would be the first to be shot, with Isabelle's lined up to be second. Julia hoped she would be able to use them in the right order. She had thought about just relying on the pistol to control Guido and Isabelle while she did what she needed to do, but there was too much of a risk. She might actually have to fire the gun, which would presumably bring the security guys to the house at a run.

She laid out her planned escape outfit. Black running pants and a black hoody. Dark trainers, the dark wig, the backpack. She cursed herself for forgetting to include a ski-mask to cover her pale face. She moved quickly and hung it all in the wardrobe, ready for use in a hurry.

Prepared, she changed into her still damp swimsuit in the bathroom, donned a robe and went down to the terrace. Lunch would be served in thirty minutes. Over lunch she would ask if she could see Guido and Isabelle in the office for a pre-dinner meeting. She wanted the light to be fading when she made her move.

Outside the sun was fierce and the hot air was still. She hoped that the water covering the phosphorous in her car wasn't evaporating too rapidly; she needed another few hours. The terrace was deserted, so she dropped her robe and entered the pool. She swam calmly and rhythmically for ten minutes or so before she became aware of shapes on the terrace. Guido and Isabelle had arrived. She took her time and emerged from the pool slowly, playing on Guido's senses as she towelled herself and slipped into her robe. It was too warm for it, so she left it undone, the clinging front of her wet swimsuit on show. She looked at Guido and imagined a forked tongue flickering out from between his thin lips.

Lunch came. As ever, it was simple but exquisite. Chilled dressed seafood with a crisp Pinot Grigio, fresh fruit, rustic bread. They ate as Julia and Isabelle tried to make light conversation; Guido, as ever, was silent. But as the meal ended he spoke.

"Julia, we would like to continue our conversation later. You should leave tomorrow I think, at least for a while. We can discuss this later. Can you come to the office at five-thirty?"

"You must be psychic, Guido," she said, "I was going to suggest the same to you."

"Good, now why don't the two of you stay a while, and when you have digested you can take another swim."

He almost smiled again before rising from the table. He walked away, leaving Julia and Isabelle alone.

"He likes you, Julia," Isabelle said with a smirk, "take care not to upset him too soon. Coffee?"

******

The afternoon passed slowly and Julia was tense. When it was time she slipped the robe on over a dry swimsuit, putting the pistol, spare bolts and her phone in the patch pockets. She was able to conceal the compact crossbow beneath the robe, holding it firmly so there was no risk of the loaded dart falling out. The crossbow was already cocked and ready to shoot.

At five-thirty the office door clicked and Julia pushed it open. Guido and Isabelle were already inside.

"Excuse the casual attire," Julia said lightly, "I thought I'd have another swim in your gorgeous pool when we're done."

Isabelle smiled, but Guido sat perfectly still.

"What did you want to talk about, Guido?" Julia asked.

"You, Julia. I do not think you are being honest with us." Guido said quietly.

"Really? Why's that?" she asked, playing for a little more time. She was still standing.

"That bit of street theatre in Budapest. I called the British Embassy there myself; they denied that any such incident took place."

"Well, they would, wouldn't they?" Julia said, "they aren't going to admit that one of their people with diplomatic status was infiltrating organised crime, let alone admit he was killed while doing it."

"I want more proof, Julia, incontrovertible proof," he said.

"Alright," Julia said, loosening her grip on the front of her robe, "try this."

She raised the crossbow to waist height and shot across the desk at Guido. The dart flew straight and true, slapping into his chest. Julia could see the plunger on the dart's syringe moving steadily, inexorably, as the drugs were going in. She re-cocked the weapon in an instant and turned it on Isabelle, letting the next dart go as soon as it was lined up. Isabelle, bewildered, gasped as she felt the brief stab of pain and fell backwards to the floor.

Julia turned back to Guido. His face was pale, almost grey, his eyelids were flickering as his head lolled to one side. Spittle drooled from the side of his mouth.

Inside a minute, both Guido and Isabelle lay still, both taking shallow breaths. Julia took a few cable ties from her voluminous pockets and quickly tied Guido's wrists to his chair. Isabelle's she tied behind her back. She felt that Isabelle would present the greater threat as and when she woke up, and she was likely to come round sooner than Guido.

Julia reached into Guido's trouser pocket and pulled out the keys. She drew back the drape and struggled to find the correct keys for the safe. Once it was open, she took the beige file. She took photographs of every page with her phone camera, emailing them to Mel as she went. When she was done she put the file to one side. Isabelle was starting to stir, groaning quietly.

She pocketed Guido's mobile phone and the black notebook before grabbing the two large box files. They were bulky and there were too many documents to photograph in the time she had available. She checked Guido's phone and was surprised to see that there was no password or PIN code needed to open it. She turned it off again and repocketed it. She slipped the slim beige folder into one of the box files and picked them both up.

Guido too was starting to stir. Julia took the ties that secured the drape and made cloth gags from them. She tied one firmly around each of their mouths.

She turned to leave the office, moving rapidly. She locked the safe shut and then locked the door behind her, keeping Guido's keys. She ran up the stairs as loud alarm bells started to ring outside the villa.

Chapter 52

Julia flew up the stairs to her rooms. She hurriedly drew the heavy curtains, leaving her sitting room in virtual darkness. In a few moments she had donned the dark wig and her escape clothes, tying her shoelaces tightly. She shoved the box files, Guido's phone, the black notebook and his keys in the backpack and put it on. With the pistol in the pocket of her hoody and the crossbow, cocked and ready, in her hand she took a deep breath and headed back downstairs.

As she hit the last step, the butler appeared to block her way, yelling at her with his arms outstretched. She launched a kick at his stomach and as he lay on the floor she shot one of the darts at him. It struck his chest and he looked astonished.

"Sorry, *mi scuso!*" Julia muttered as she re-cocked the crossbow.

She ran to the front door. As she opened it she was confronted by a large man in a dark uniform and wearing body armour. It was one of the security men. He reached for his pistol as Julia sent another of her crossbow darts into the small gap between the top of his armoured vest and the chinstrap of his helmet. The effect was almost instantaneous as the powerful sedative entered his bloodstream. The hand reaching for his weapon was fumbling, uncoordinated; he staggered and fell to his knees, trying to focus his attention on Julia. After just a few seconds he slumped unconscious. Julia didn't waste any time.

The security guard had used an electric buggy to get to the house and the key was still in it. Julia jumped in and sped off towards the main gate. In the buggy mirror she could see flames leaping up the roof of the outbuilding behind the villa, where her incendiary-rigged car had presumably been taken. She saw panicking figures running towards it. Two men were pulling the wheeled extinguishers laboriously up the slope towards the fire.

The gate was looming large. Only two men were left on guard, the rest seeming to have run to try to deal with the fire and check on the state of the master and his wife. As Julia's buggy neared the closed gates one of the men went into a hut to answer a ringing telephone while his radio was shouting incoherently in his ear. The second guard turned to the buggy, which was coming to a halt.

He looked confused as he failed to recognise Julia; he had been expecting to see his colleague in the driving seat, not a much smaller figure with dark hair and dressed head to foot in black. He approached, shouting instructions. Another of Julia's darts hit him in the neck, and like the previous one it went to work extremely fast. The man was on the floor in seconds, seemingly struggling for breath. Her next dart, the last but one, slapped into the neck of the man on the phone. He reached to touch it, as if stung by a wasp, before pitching forward. Julia reached past him and pressed a button to open the gates.

She drove as fast as she dared in the unstable buggy. When she was a couple of kilometres down the hill she pointed it into the woods and let it roll into a tree. From the road she could hardly see it. She started jogging downhill.

Fifteen minutes later she was at the waters' edge, having ducked into hedges to avoid being seen by the four fire engines and two police cars labouring up the slope towards the volcanic glow emanating from the remote villa at the top of the hill. Julia slowed to get her breath back, and at a fast walk she went towards the cafés and bars where the lads with speedboats hung out. She was reaching for her phone to call the one whose card she had taken when she saw him lounging in the warm evening air. Julia went up to him. A few minutes of smiling negotiation was all it took, and soon she was in a speedboat bound for Como.

******

Back at the villa, Isabelle had come round first. She was furious. She was able to get to her feet, but that was about it. She couldn't reach the gag in her mouth or free her hands, and she couldn't get out of the office. The doors were locked and would stay that way until someone with a key unlocked them or broke them down. She hefted a table lamp behind her back and awkwardly tried to smash a window. It didn't work, but it did attract the attention of one of the remaining security guards. He ran towards the villa, jumping over his fallen comrade and the equally fallen butler in the hall.

It took three of them twenty minutes to break the door down, by which time Guido was also conscious. The guards quickly cut the cable ties and removed the gags and braced themselves for the verbal onslaught they knew was coming. It came from Isabelle.

"Useless fools!" she roared at them, "get that idiot from the *carabinieri* on the phone; he's about to earn all that money we've been paying him. I want that bitch found and stopped! I want our property back. Get him here now!"

They ran away while she turned her attention to Guido, who was breathing heavily and didn't look at all well. She wasn't sympathetic.

"You're a complacent moron, Guido," she hissed at him, "how many times did I tell you to have back-ups made? Put some faith in technology rather than your superstitious reliance on bits of paper. They can't be hacked, you said. No, but they can be stolen and that's what has just happened. Kelso is going to destroy us, Guido!"

Isabelle fetched her phone from her room and called Antoine Durand.

"Get to the villa now," she instructed him, "we have an emergency."

Guido looked surprised.

"Durand?" he queried. "Isn't he in France?"

"No, Guido, he is nearby, in Como. He will be here in thirty minutes. He must catch Kelso for us, and deal with her."

"Have you been seeing him?" Guido asked, with an almost pained expression. "Without telling me?"

"What do you think, Guido?" She snapped. "He's good in bed and he makes that small part of my life bearable, unlike you!"

She was interrupted by the arrival of the *maggiore*, the regional commander of the *carabinieri*, the paramilitary police. He was perspiring heavily and smelt of alcohol.

"We have been robbed, Major, by a terrorist." Isabelle said, without any preamble. "She has stolen important business documents, including some that have details of our working relationship with you! It is imperative that she is found and stopped, and that the documents and other possessions are returned to us immediately. She is British, around my height, and she has very blonde hair. Her name is Julia Kelso, and she claims to be a police officer. She is armed and dangerous. Do you understand?"

"Yes, *signora*," the Major said.

"Then why are you still here?" Isabelle shouted, "get on with it!"

Half an hour later she had a similar conversation with Antoine Durand, who had expected the call from Isabelle to have a more pleasant and rewarding outcome than a wearing drive up the narrow lakeside road from Como. He had never been to the villa before, but finding it was not difficult, not now. The glow from the fire could be seen from a long way away.

"There are roadblocks already in place, Isabelle, at several points on the road up from Bellagio. I think they are too late, though. She is fit; she could have made it to Bellagio on foot long before you alerted the police."

"So find her, Antoine. You are a detective! I want her dead, but I want our documents back first. She doesn't have a vehicle as far as we know. I think she must have set the fire in the outbuilding using the vehicle she arrived in. She stole one of ours, but it won't have gone far. Don't let me down, Antoine!"

Chapter 53

By the time Antoine Durand set out from the villa and the *carabinieri* Major had his roadblocks in place, Julia was in the boarding house with Mel Dunn and Freddie. Julia had already emailed the pages from the beige file to Mel, and now she handed over the phone, the notebook and the box files. It took Mel nearly all night to photograph the contents of the box files and notebook, and to download all the contacts from the phone. By dawn, the whole lot had been sent by email to Mel and Jake's accounts.

"Right," said Jake, who had been dozing on a sofa, "I don't think Isabelle and Guido are going to take this lying down, so it's best we get the hell out of here. I'll feed Freddie while you pack your stuff up. Mine's all ready. I want to leave within half an hour."

An hour later they had crossed the border into Switzerland. Julia had dumped the crossbow, the remaining bolts and one dart in the lake from the boat as they were speeding towards Como the night before. She had kept the pistol, though. Julia drove while Mel slept; Freddie was also sleeping in his car seat in the back.

Meanwhile in Bellagio, Antoine Durand had been giving some thought to how he would arrange to escape from the villa if he was in Julia Kelso's shoes. He would go by boat, almost certainly. It took him an hour and quite a few Euros to find the young man who had transported her to Como the night before. After some persuasion at gunpoint, the young man told Antoine everything, including the exact spot in Como where he had dropped her.

Antoine made his way to Como and surveyed the landing spot. It would have been dark when Kelso arrived, but nevertheless he might be able to find some images or clues as to where she had been. He gave up after two hours as he thought of something else.

He called a friend of his who worked for the Italian border guard. They had collaborated on a smuggling case a few years ago and had stayed in touch. Antoine asked if there had been any movement across the Italian border into Switzerland in the previous twelve hours by a woman named Julia Kelso?

In another hour he had his answer. A car, make, model and Dutch registration provided, belonging to a Julia Kelso, resident of the Netherlands, had crossed from Como into Ticino shortly after eight that morning. It was now midday; she had at least four hours head start.

Antoine drove into Switzerland before one. He pulled out his identification and chatted to the Swiss police manning their side of the border post. One of them remembered the vehicle, the female driver being very attractive. There was also another woman and a young child in the car, nothing suspicious. The driver had said they were on a touring holiday. They were heading for Lugano.

Lugano isn't a large city, even if it is the largest in the canton of Ticino, but it is quite complicated. Its winding hillside streets hid countless small hotels in which a fugitive could hide. He chose to focus on the railway station. Just because they had a car, it didn't mean they would keep using it.

Julia was having a similar thought. It was a very long and arduous drive to get almost anywhere, apart from

Italy, if you started from Lugano. She left Mel and Freddie in the small hotel they had chosen on spec and walked towards the more touristy part of town, near the casino and the lakeside. She soon found the sort of people she was looking for.

A young Dutch couple were waiting tables in a lakeside café. She got talking and found out they were students on holiday, but they had been robbed in Milan. They were working to earn enough money to get home to Amsterdam in time to go back to college.

"I'm on vacation too," Julia said," I've been driving but I'm getting fed up with it. I want to take the train but I've got my car. If I give you petrol money and enough for food and lodging, would you drive it back to The Hague for me?"

They readily agreed. Julia signed a letter authorising them to drive her car and gave them an envelope full of Euros. She gave them the keys and told them where the car was. Everyone was happy.

Julia walked back to the hotel and roused Mel. She explained in a few words that they were continuing by train, and within the hour they were at Lugano central station. Julia bought them tickets for the next fast train to Zurich and they had coffee while they waited. Antoine Durand waited too.

It takes less than two hours to cover the distance between Lugano and Zurich, a fraction of the time it would take by road. Mel was happy as she could feed and change Freddie easily and keep him entertained. Julia spent the entire journey scanning faces of other passengers, looking for signs of interest.

At Zurich they changed trains for Basel, where Julia decided they should stay the night in a hotel near the station. Freddie was starting to get restless. From Basel they could get a train to Amsterdam via Frankfurt and they would be home the following evening.

"So much for a relaxing holiday," Mel complained.

It was late afternoon by the time they got to Basel. Julia was stiff and tired, and the short walk from the station to the Alexander Hotel was a welcome relief. The late afternoon air was pleasantly warm. They hadn't noticed Antoine Durand at the station, and they didn't know they had lost him in the rush-hour throng. He was furious; so near yet so far. Antoine spent an anxious night in the vicinity of the station, assuming that Basel wasn't Kelso's final destination and that she would be continuing by train sometime soon. The scrupulous Swiss police were constantly on the lookout for waifs, strays and vagrants, especially around train stations, and Antoine found it hard to get much rest.

He got his break around seven the following morning. He was cold, tired and hungry, and the station buffet had just opened. He saw Kelso across the concourse, looking rested and relaxed. She wasn't carrying anything as she walked towards the ticket office. She engaged the clerk in conversation for a while, proffered a card from her wallet and was given a sheaf of tickets in return. He let her go, and when he was fairly sure she was clear of the station he approached the same clerk. Fifty Euros bought him the information he wanted, and he got himself a ticket to Frankfurt on the same train that Kelso had booked, although she had bought tickets all the way through to Amsterdam from Frankfurt. He handed over his overworked credit card to the ticket clerk, hoping that it wouldn't be declined. It wasn't.

After eating whatever breakfast he could afford after parting with his last fifty Euro note and not trusting his credit card any further, he waited near the platform for the nine a.m. Frankfurt train.

He watched them board, Kelso, the other woman and a small child. He saw them take their seats, the women opposite each other at a table for four. He boarded and took a seat in the next car, from where he could see the door of the toilet the two carriages would share.

An hour into the journey, after the train left Freiburg, he saw her. Julia Kelso moved towards the toilet. He waited until she went inside but made his move as she pushed the door closed. He shouldered it, taking her by surprise. In the cramped toilet he drew his service weapon, his bulk pinning her against the handbasin. Overcoming her initial shock, she let herself go limp against him. He pushed harder to support their combined weight.

"I wasn't expecting to see you here, Antoine," she said as lightly as she could.

"You've made Isabelle very angry, Julia, very angry indeed. She wants her property back, just for a start."

"And you think I've got it, whatever it is?"

"You know full well you have it. I want it!" He was almost shouting above the noise of the train.

"Well it's not in here, is it?" She pushed back against him, not too hard, just to give herself a bit more room. "Look, Antoine, we can come to an arrangement. Isabelle is finished, so is Guido, but I'm not. Come in with me and I'll give you everything you got from Isabelle, and more. You won't be sorry, I promise."

"You are a liar, Julia. I trust Isabelle, not you," he shouted.

"Then you are a fool, Antoine!"

"Give me what she wants, it's in your backpack, I'm sure of it. Two files, she said, some other papers, a notebook, a phone and some keys."

"That's very specific, Antoine. What's in those files?" Julia was taunting him, playing for time and a little more space.

He was getting angry; he drew a fist back to punch her and that gave Julia the space she had been looking for. She fired once from the pocket of her hoody, the barrel of her Glock almost touching Antoine's stomach. He gasped and twitched in pain and astonishment.

"I said you were a fool, Antoine," she said as she shifted his slackening weight to sit him on the toilet seat. His face was grey, his breathing rapid and shallow. Her shot would have gone up through the top of his stomach and into his diaphragm, into a lung, possibly his heart. It was a killing shot at that range. He coughed weakly; some blood trickled out of his mouth.

"I hope she was worth it, Antoine," were the last words he heard.

Julia left the toilet compartment, feeling Antoine's weight push the door closed behind her. The next stop was Karlsruhe in about an hour.

"That took a while," Mel said when Julia went back to her seat.

"There was a problem," Julia said, "Antoine Durand was on the train; Isabelle set him on us to get her things back. He's in the toilet, and he won't be coming out."

"You killed him?" Mel asked.

"It was him or me, and if he'd killed me, you would have been next. Maybe Freddie too.

"We have to get off at Karlsruhe," Mel said.

"No we don't," Julia insisted, "we stay on as planned. As far as I can tell, there's no CCTV in the carriage or covering the toilet door, so we sit tight and we didn't see anything."

The stop at Karlsruhe was brief, and no one checked the toilets. The train continued towards Frankfurt, and it was nearly there when an irate passenger complained to the train guard that the toilet wouldn't open. The guard tried it and agreed. He hung a sign on the door saying it was out of order in three languages.

Chapter 54

They arrived at Amsterdam without any further anxieties or incidents. At Amsterdam Centraal Station Julia rented a left-luggage locker and deposited her backpack, and its contents, before locking it safely. She pocketed the key and went off to find Mel and Freddie. Her hoody, complete with its bullet hole, went into a carrier bag and then a rubbish bin outside the station. They were all tired, so a taxi all the way home was in order.

Once inside, with Freddie sorted out and large gins dispensed, Mel opened her computer to look at the international news. The discovery of a murder victim on a train between Frankfurt and Berlin was noted, but not given too much attention. Similarly, the large fire at an Italian millionaire businessman's home got a mere handful of mentions. That would probably change soon, Julia thought.

Mel spent the evening sorting the information she and Jake had accumulated into a series of internet posts. Some would go to the new social media phenomenon, others to financial websites. Details of the Order and its members, with the right parts emphasised, were destined for the tabloid press or its equivalent. All of it would go on to the Dark Web and to the Guardia di Finanza, all the affected police services, the FBI, Interpol, and of course Europol, where it had all started. They discussed the timing, deciding that releasing the data in separate chunks over several days would have a better impact than releasing everything all at once. They agreed a timetable, starting the next day.

While Mel was tidying up the release schedule and content, Julia wrote long letters to Niall Morton and Errol Spelman. She wasn't going to entrust them to email. Each one told the entire story of Guido and Isabelle Ricci's crooked businesses. She set out their scheme to discredit international cooperation by trashing cross-border efforts and investigations, with a lot of emphasis on EU institutions and agencies including Europol. That was why the Jamaican informant and Errol's cover had been blown, using one of Ricci's stooges, a 'brother' in 'the Order', to feed stolen information to Adda. That had set Adda off on his witch hunt, and Ricci had fed him the final pieces naming Errol through another one of his stooges in London. That stooge, in blissful ignorance, was Duncan Traynor, the ex-cop who should have known better than to get involved in secret societies at his age.

Julia had been half-tempted to go into a fuller confession about her own participation in bringing the Ricci operation down, but she resisted. She concluded by saying she had resigned from law-enforcement and would be moving on in a few weeks. In a while she would send one of them a further note, together with a left-luggage locker key, detailing the physical evidence that was available and telling them where to find it. It could form the basis of a prosecution, but knowing how things worked it could take several years before the Ricci's appeared in any court.

In the meantime, Julia had said, Guido and Isabelle Ricci would be taken out of business by being subjected to local and global ridicule, the tactic they had relied on to protect their own dirty dealings. The way this would happen would become apparent very soon.

She signed off, thanking them both for their friendship and support over the past few years, and wishing them well.

With some sadness, she sealed the letters and put them to one side to be posted the next morning.

******

In the villa above Bellagio, Isabelle and Guido Ricci were still reeling from the shock of the past few days' events. The outbuilding had been completely destroyed, along with several very expensive vehicles. Fire engines had gouged the lawn beyond salvage, scuds of soot floated on the surface of the pool. Worse still, the calm sanctity of the villa had been violated.

They were unable to open the safe; the keys on Guido's key ring were the only ones, and they weren't about to get a locksmith to break into it. Isabelle guessed, but didn't categorically know, that Kelso had taken the files, notebook and phone and had instructed Antoine Durand to retrieve them at all costs. She hadn't heard from him in days.

Guido sat at his desk, almost catatonic in his still silence. He was overwhelmed. Seeing him like this, Isabelle finally realised what an inadequate man her husband, at least in name, really was. She despised him more than ever, but until this matter was settled and she had their information back, it seemed she was stuck with him. There was a chance that he could reconstruct enough of the information, minus the pointless 'Order', to enable their enterprise to continue. Her conversations with the duplicitous Kelso had actually given her some ideas about a less arcane structure to protect their business interests.

She went to her room and locked the door to prevent Guido from coming after her. She took a long bath, and for a while she felt a little more positive. She guessed that Antoine Durand was no longer hers to play with; never mind, there were plenty of others in the pond he came from and fishing for one would be a pleasant diversion from the current circumstances. She was roused by a sudden blood-curdling scream.

Pulling on a robe and still dripping, she ran down the stairs to the office. Guido was howling and staring at a computer screen. He was watching the start of it, the slow exposure of everything he had done, everything he had built, everyone he had bribed, everyone he had recruited to his ludicrous cult. Over the next few days it all came out. The headlines in the next edition of *La Stampa* poked fun at him, the cartoonists cruelly lampooning his reptilian features.

He made a furious call to the editor, only to be told that he was unavailable. He then called his paid journalist on the paper, who put the phone down on him. He went through the contact list on his regular phone; half the calls didn't go through - he had been blocked. He called his chauffeur to take him to see his bank manager, only to be told that firstly, he had no cars anymore, and secondly that the chauffeur had resigned with immediate effect. He called all of his bankers in Liechtenstein. They were unavailable, and unfortunately all of signor's accounts had been placed under audit and could not be accessed until the process was completed. It could take weeks or months.

Guido called for Isabelle, seeking some comfort at least.

"Fuck off and die, Guido," she hissed as she walked to her waiting taxi.

******

It was Julia's last night in The Hague. Her final few days had included several tense and trying interviews with the Director General of Europol and the organisation's chief legal officer. Both of them roundly condemned Julia's unorthodox and, as they described it, cavalier approach, but nevertheless they did admit that the interests of justice had been efficiently served. The meetings ended with Julia's assurance that she would not darken the door of Europol again, and for their part the DG and chief legal officer would do their best to dissuade the *carabinieri* in Italy from pursuing the fugitive who had seemingly been using Julia's name. The fact that the regional commander of the *carabinieri* who had been most assiduous in the hunt for a Julia Kelso had now been named as a corrupt recipient of large amounts of money from the rapidly falling star, Guido Ricci, helped enormously.

Apart from this, the last ten days had gone according to plan. Guido Ricci had apparently been admitted to a special care home in Turin with a severe mental breakdown. He had been arrested by the *Guardia di Finanza* and placed under investigation. His extended family were trying to meet the significant cost of his care from their own meagre resources, Guido never having been much of a sharer.

Isabelle Meyer-Ricci had disappeared and was no doubt scheming away somewhere. Warrants had been issued for her arrest and she was the subject of an Interpol Red Notice.

Julia had signed up with the Secret Intelligence Service and was due to start her mandatory induction at the Fort, as the MI6 training establishment was known, the following week.

Chapter 55

Autumn had well and truly set in and there was a chill in the gritty London air. The few weeks by the sea down at the Fort had been quite interesting, sometimes even challenging, but with a bit more play-acting than Julia thought absolutely necessary. Nevertheless, she was now an officer of the Secret Intelligence Service, following on in her father's footsteps. He was delighted, of course, having always thought it was a natural fit for her; it was just a shame she had wasted so much time in the police toying with mindless ruffians - on both sides of the legal fence.

She had been up to see her parents for a few days, rejoicing in the colours of a Highland fall. She kept things light and deftly deflected probes about her private life, her relationship with Mel Dunn and the boy Freddie, both of whom they had met briefly in London shortly after Jake returned from The Hague.

At last she was actually working. Each morning she strolled from her father's flat, now effectively hers, along the riverbank and over Vauxhall Bridge. Apart from the manic morning traffic it was a pleasant enough walk. She bought a newspaper from the stand at Vauxhall bus station and sometimes a decent coffee from one of the Portuguese cafés across the road from Vauxhall Cross, the somewhat bizarre MI6 headquarters building. She often wondered what it was about its outlandish design that had said 'secret' to its architect.

Mel was due to come for a visit next weekend. Jake found that she missed her more than she had expected, and although Mel would never admit it, Jake suspected that she missed her too. They had made plans to take Freddie to London Zoo for the day.

Jake strolled along as usual that last morning. She had bought her newspaper and coffee, and was waiting for the lights to change so she could cross the road along with the other commuting sheep. Some worked in her building, most didn't - but they did wonder. Hugh had called her the evening before and asked her to come to see him - there was an operation brewing and he wanted her to be part of it. She was starting to be excited.

As she took her first step to cross the road, Julia felt a sharp pain in her side, just to the left below her ribs. She gasped and started to turn as her legs buckled. She saw the back of someone, someone wearing a scruffy anorak with the hood up, hurrying away. Someone screamed, someone else shouted something. Julia was confused; the pain wouldn't stop. In fact it was getting worse and spreading. She felt sick, and then cold. She felt herself slump down on the cold damp tarmac.

******

Hugh Cavendish stood in the Resus Room at St Thomas's Hospital, no more than a mile from Vauxhall Cross. He had tears in his eyes as he watched them work on her. He had known Jake since she was a baby, knew her almost as well as he knew his own children. He had been called by one of the door staff, an ex-soldier who knew that old Cavendish was close to the blonde new girl. He said there's been a stabbing, I think it's the new officer, Ms Kelso.

Hugh had been driven to St Thomas's on blue lights and sirens in his official car and he had been dropped in the ambulance entrance. He pushed his way past the security people, waving his hard-to-read i/d card as he went.

Julia was in a very bad way - critical and unstable, the medics had said. It was touch and go.

She died that lunchtime. She was still unconscious, had tubes in her arms and nose. The Resus Room looked like an abattoir. Hugh Cavendish stood and cried like he had never done before.

******

Three weeks later, on a chilly and wet afternoon on a purple-grey hillside in Perthshire, a small group of people in sombre dress gathered, almost huddled together for warmth. Ralph Kelso stood with his wife, Sarah, as his best friend - the bear of a man that was Hugh Cavendish - read from Julia Kelso's favourite poem in adolescence. It was, incongruously, Coleridge's Kubla Khan, all about stately pleasure domes and mighty rivers. Jake had loved its sound and its imagery. Mel was there, and Abigail from Hugh's office as well as a handful of locals. There was no priest, no prayers - just a poem and people's thoughts.

The light was fading, the drizzle soaking everyone through their heavy clothes. They took turns to take a handful of Jake's ashes and toss them to the ground in the gentle wind. Mel Dunn held her handful for a moment, touching it with her lips before letting the dust fall.

They all stood in quiet contemplation, no one quite knowing when was the right time to break off and move away. Eventually Hugh Cavendish took his old friend by the arm and led him back towards the house.

The small group of friends left her there, where she had grown up and become Jake Kelso, who was no more, apart from in their minds and memories.

Chapter 56 - Vancouver, Canada, 2023.

That's where Jo Calman left it - on that cold bleak hillside in Perthshire on a grey afternoon that Jake Kelso would have called 'driech'. 'It's the end of the story. It's where the moment of madness ends, it's the act of faith', Calman had said.

Of course, in reality no story ever ends, not like that; everything is a continuum, a web of interwoven ups and downs and ins and outs, lives and deaths.

This is Sarah, by the way, although you'll know me better as Mel, Mel Dunn. I changed it some time ago, remember? I have a different surname now too, so I'm not Mel Dunn at all anymore - I thought it best. My new name is private, for now.

Jake Kelso died. I can't believe it was her time, she was still only in her forties, but then again I could never see her being old. I could never see her letting herself be old. In the end it was something sadly ordinary.

She was stabbed by chance, an awful accident of time and place. She wasn't targeted, the police said. Just a random act by someone who needed more care than the community would give them. Two other random women were stabbed after Jake, all by the same person. Like you, I thought it might have been a past enemy, someone whose life and crimes had been ruined by Kelso and Alf Ferdinand, and by me too I suppose. But it wasn't. The killer was caught quickly and will spend the rest of their life in a secure hospital. Is that any consolation? I don't know.

I argued with Calman. I said the story, her story, our story, isn't over; it can't just end with a wet funeral. Jo said: "why not? Lots of stories do. " A fair point, I suppose. Eventually Jo gave in and said I could have a go if I wanted to. So I've got the rest of the book, these last few pages, if you want to know if the story did end there, on that hillside, or if there actually is a bit more.

The funeral - I can't think of another word for it - was small, only a handful of us there. The cremation had already been done, ashes were brought there to be scattered where she'd grown up, where she'd ridden her pony, where she had played and learned about life. Apart from her dad, Ralph the Rake, her mum was there, another Sarah as it happens. Hugh Cavendish too, a few local family friends. I was surprised to see Abigail Ukebe there. She said she had grown to like and respect Julia Kelso after a rocky start - I said tell me about it! We scattered the ashes; there was no ceremony, just quiet reflection. Sarah Kelso held back her tears, Ralph didn't. Afterwards we all went back to the house for tea and things and the few locals started to drift off. When it was just the five of us left, Sarah broke out the whisky and gin and got out albums of photographs. It was a long night.

I don't have any photographs of Jake, but I can see her face and form, every detail, any time I want.

As the evening of the wake rolled on, Ralph, Sarah and Hugh were sort of huddled together talking quietly but emotionally. I was in another corner with Abigail. I hadn't seen her drink before, but she could put it away. They must teach them at spy school or something. She said she was still looking for Ferdinand, as a distraction from her day job. I asked her if she thought he might still be alive, but she didn't answer. She didn't ask me about my relationship with Jake, nor did anyone else. I was just there, accepted but excepted, an incidental friend. I'm glad no one asked, and gladder still that no one knew, or if they did they didn't say anything. Although Hugh Cavendish did say a few strange things; I think he knew or guessed that there was more to the way Jake and I were than it seemed.

I called my sister the following morning. I'd left Freddie with her, and I said I would collect him the following day. I needed to clear my head a little before facing the long drive to Yorkshire and the ferry back to Holland, which I thought of as home back then.

Before we all left, everyone exchanged phone numbers and promised to stay in touch. It always happens, and no one ever does. I felt that the chapter was closed, the whole book even, and that it was time to move on. I had no idea where to or how; that bridge would be crossed in my own good time.

I collected Freddie from my miserable and bitter sister. Since mum died and dad went bonkers and had to go into a home she's been knotted up and at war with our brother. I don't know what about, and I'm not that interested. She's got kids of her own but she goes through their dads rapidly and she's a single mum again for now. Every time she breaks up she swears she's had it with men, but she always goes back to them. Freddie looked pleased to see me and was relieved to be going home. He's alright, my Freddie, he was getting more interesting back then and he's even more interesting now, but more of that later. We stopped at a Premier Inn on the way to Harwich. My sister asked if we wanted to stay at hers, but I could see she was only trying to be polite and couldn't wait to get shot of us.

I was still using Jake's car and living in her house in The Hague. She had gone back to London but said there was no rush to close down Holland, not until I had decided what I wanted to do. She had squared it with the landlord.

Then she got herself killed. I was still there, still undecided about what to do and where to go. In some ways, we could have stayed and sometimes I think we should have. Freddie had liked going to the crèche at Europol and he was enrolled at a kindergarten. He got on well with other kids, but I must admit I found other mums, especially the foreign ones like me, quite annoying. I put off making any decisions, I don't think I was functioning that well to be honest. Jake being murdered like that was a huge shock, more of a shock than I realised at the time. It rocked my world.

So, a few weeks later I got a call. It didn't happen that much. I didn't keep in touch with my sister or brother and hadn't called Hugh or Abigail or Jake's parents. I wasn't working. After the oil trading escapade I was comfortably off and I didn't have the motivation to want to do anything other than be Freddie's handmaid. The call was from Abigail. I think I remember it word for word.

"Mel," she said, "it's Abigail. I'm not sure if I've got news or not, but his passport has been used."

"Whose passport? What passport?" I asked.

"Alf's, Ferdinand's! Remember, I got one for him, one of our special ones. They're flagged on the immigration system until they're cancelled, and the one I gave Ferdinand is still current. It's slipped down the priority list though, and I was only notified this morning. His passport was used at Algeciras in southern Spain a week ago, an arrival on the ferry from Morocco. I'm trying to get any CCTV but the station in Madrid isn't optimistic."

"What does it mean, Abigail?" I asked.

"I don't know, something or nothing. It could mean that the passport was found by someone and sold or given to a migrant - there are thousands of them - or it could mean that….."

"He's alive!" I think I shouted.

"It's a possibility, no more than that," Abigail said.

"A week ago? You said it was used a week ago?"

"Yes, a week ago today. If it is him, he could be anywhere once he's in the Schengen zone. The passport hasn't been used at any British or Irish ports; I checked."

I thanked her and hung up. She promised to let me know if there was any further information. I packed a few things up, filled the car with fuel and went to get Freddie from kindergarten. If it was Alf, a very big if, and if he had been in Europe for a week, another big if, I had a pretty good idea where he would go.

I set off with mixed feelings. Freddie was sleepy for a while, until we were in France, then he started bawling. I turned the car radio up. The last time I was at the house in Charente, I was in a bad place and all my good memories had been wiped. I had hoped I'd never see it again, but if, another very big if, Alf was there, I needed to see him, to know how he was and what had happened to him.

We had to stop for the night at a motel. Freddie was getting too distraught and it just wasn't fair on him to keep going. So it was midday the next day when we got to the house. The gate was closed but the chain and padlock hung loose. I pushed it open and drove in. I didn't want to leave Freddie in the car outside.

The place looked abandoned. The garden, once well-tended, was overgrown. The pool where we had swum and played was murky and green. Only the side of the barn, which Alf had painted over and over again, seemed in good order. It had been a while since the place had been lived in. I looked around, starting with the barn. The door wasn't locked. I pulled it open, just enough to get inside. There was a car, an old one, covered in dust and dents, with foreign number plates I didn't recognise. I touched the grille - it was cool. I turned to leave the barn. As I stepped into the sunlight and my eyes adjusted, I was confronted by a woman.

She was my height, with very dark hair and brown skin. Her eyes, though, were a vivid blue. She was holding a shotgun, and it was pointed at my chest.

"That's Ferdinand's shotgun," I said in English.

"What?" was all she said, also in English.

"The gun. It belongs to the person who lived here; he's a friend of mine."

"Who is Ferdinand?" she asked.

"He sometimes uses different names. He's this tall," I held my hand just above the level of my head, "medium build, quite good looking in a way. Is he here? Did you come with him from Africa?"

"You know about Africa?"

"Not really. Is that your car in the barn? It has foreign plates. I think it's from Africa."

"Why do you think he's here?"

"Long story, something to do with flagged passports. Is he?"

"Come."

She lowered the shotgun and walked towards the house. Apparently it hadn't even been loaded. I walked up the ramp to the terrace that had been made for me while I was stuck in a wheelchair. I walked into the familiar kitchen. Parts of it had been dusted and washed down; there was a pan of water on the stove.

He was there. He sat in an armchair, saying nothing and hardly moving or blinking. He looked vacantly at the window but not through it. I went to him and took his hand. It was painfully thin.

"Alf? It's me, Mel."

He looked up. A flicker of recognition and the beginning of a smile, then confusion.

"How have you been, Alf?" I asked gently.

"Alf?" he croaked. I fetched some water for him.

"It's what we call you, remember? Alan Lourenço Ferdinand, A L F, Alf."

A brief smile and a small nod.

"Mel?" he said, haltingly.

"He needs to rest," the woman said. "Come, let's sit outside and talk. I'll make coffee when the water's hot. There is no power or hot water, so I must use the gas cooker."

"I'll show you where the oil tank and boiler are, and how to turn the electric on," I remembered where everything was, of course.

Twenty minutes later, we sat outside. Ferdinand was snoring softly in his chair. Then she started.

******

"I am Sakina," she said, "my father is a doctor, and I am nearly one as well. I completed four years of medical school and my father taught me the rest; he says I am as good as any doctor, given our circumstances. We live in the desert.

"My father is French and he was in the military; I think it was the Foreign Legion but he doesn't talk about it. He was serving in North Africa, the desert of southern Algeria and further south too, well into the Sahel. He says he fell in love with the bleakness and the beauty of it. He also fell in love with a woman, a Tuareg. They met several times, never alone, and they communicated in their own way. My father negotiated with her father and a deal was struck. They married; she moved around with him - he was almost as nomadic as her family was. He practiced medicine, treating the tribespeople who wandered across the desert. He devised vaccine programmes, treated wounds, removed appendixes and cysts, did the occasional amputation when needed. He trained as a

surgeon but was a good all-rounder too. He still is, although he is getting old now, and the people trust him. There is very little in the way of health care in the desert, just a few clinics run by western charities and churches.

"He could not save my mother, though. She contracted a virus; I don't know which one or how she got it. He got it too, but he survived. She didn't. She died of fever in our small house, a permanent one somewhere in Mali near Timbuktu, and we buried her beneath the tree that gives a little shade beside it. I go there whenever I am home, and so does my father. He always said it was my mother's wish that I too became a physician so I could help heal the people, her people, and mine too now.

"I'm telling you this because it is an important part of the story. The clinics I mentioned sometimes have trained surgeons, but most don't. My father is a surgeon, first and foremost, and the clinics often send for him if they have a case they can't handle or there is an urgent need for surgical intervention. Local people cannot afford to go to the hospitals in the bigger towns in Niger or Mali or Chad, even if they could make the journey. Most of them still travel by camel, or sometimes in old pick-up trucks.

"We were at our house in Mali, where we also have a small clinic and an operating room. One day a truck arrived from Niger. It belonged to one of the charities, one which we knew and had worked with. He was in the back, your friend. They said he had been found, barely alive, by the roadside in the south of Niger not far from the Nigerian border. Someone had taken him up country to the charity's clinic and they did what they could for him. They hydrated him, kept him cool and clean, gave him anti-inflammatories and analgesia, but he had severe head injuries. They thought he would inevitably die if the pressure in his skull could not be released. So they brought

him to my father, despite the risks of the long journey. He was going to die anyway if they did not get a surgeon for him.

"*By the time my father saw him, he was within moments of death. He was very sick indeed. My father did not hesitate. There is a very old and quite primitive procedure known as trepanning. Holes are drilled through the bone of the skull to release pressure. It is very risky and not practiced in hospitals these days. My father knew how to do it from his time as a surgeon in the army; he did it several times on the battlefield.*

"*Your friend survived the procedure, but only just. We used most of our supply of opiates to keep him sedated for a few weeks. He was too sick to be moved again, not now there was a chance of his survival. When we brought him round he was confused. He could not talk and he had no memory of anything. He did not know his name or how he came to be in Niger. He had no papers, no possessions of any kind except a dirty old sleeveless jacket, which was the only thing he seemed to recognise. When he was fully conscious he started to panic unless he could see this filthy thing, otherwise we would have put it on the fire.*

His recovery was slow. For almost a year he couldn't walk further than from his bed to the toilet, just a few metres. He sat up for a few minutes every day, slowly increasing bit by bit until he could spend a whole morning sitting up. At first he could take only liquids so we made him a special soup, then he could eat some bread and eventually a little fruit. He slowly regained some strength, but he still could not talk. We tried to talk with him. He was obviously a European so we tried French, German, Spanish and English. He seemed to recognise English and a little French as well.

"*The wound in his head from the trepanning healed well, but there will always be a weakness unless he gets a metal plate put in. We could not do that where we were. He was still fainting and collapsing quite frequently, as my father expected, but over time these episodes became fewer. Eventually he tried to talk."*

Sakina paused to drink some coffee.

"Where did you learn English?" I asked.

"My father taught me. He also taught me French and my mother taught me Tamasheq, the language of her people. I also studied at medical school in England for a while. I shall continue.

"When he started to try to talk it was clear he had forgotten almost everything, so we taught him to speak again as you would a child. We first taught him to read, then we put labels on everything. We taught him children's rhymes. We decided on English as he seemed more receptive. A few months on and he was making short sentences and taking part in simple conversations. He still had no memory of his past or the events which led to him being in his situation.

"About once a year either my father or I have to go to Europe to get medicines and provisions. We have a supplier in southern Spain who gives us reasonable prices. My father went that year, and I stayed home to look after your friend, who by now had a name we had given him, and to run the clinic. He seemed to relax a little when it was just the two of us. But as he relaxed he started to have dreams, sometimes nightmares, as his past began to return. I would hear him crying out in his sleep, or sometimes leaping out of bed screaming at someone or something. When my father returned after about a month I told him what had been happening. He said these were good signs, that his brain was repairing itself. He did warn me though. He said that the person who eventually came back would not be the same person who had been under our roof and in our care for all those months. I

should prepare to be surprised, and not necessarily in a pleasant way.

"But it was okay. He helped around the house. He became reasonably articulate and was friendly and polite. He wasn't curious, though, he didn't ask where he was or how he had come to be there. It was as if he just accepted the situation as his new reality, his new normal.

"The big change happened just a few months ago. His filthy old jacket finally fell apart. He was trying to wash it and it just disintegrated. He was distraught but couldn't say why. He just started weeping uncontrollably. Then among the pile of wet rags I saw a plastic pouch, like a sealed envelope. He looked at it in a puzzled way and gave it to me. He asked me to try to open it. I did, it was quite easy.

"Inside the pouch was a British passport and a lot of money in American dollars, thousands. He looked puzzled, then over the next few days it was like seeing lights come on in his head. He stared at the passport for hours, looking at the photograph. It was obviously him, although he had changed a lot in the intervening time, but he did not recognise or respond to the name in the passport. For several weeks when he wasn't helping us with the house or the clinic, he paced around the house and around the small village, deep in thought.

"One day he said to me that he needed to get to France, and could he come with one of us the next time we went to Europe. And that's what happened. A couple of months ago, I told him I would be making the trip this year and he should come with me. He was delighted, but also a little scared I think. When the time came we set off in the car we keep for these trips. It's old, but it works well enough and was built for this sort of travel, even if it's not so comfortable. It's a long and arduous drive. Food and water are in short supply as we need to carry a lot of fuel, but we managed by being disciplined. He didn't talk

much, which was fine. I am used to doing the journey by myself. It was just nice to have someone in the car with me.

"We drove on Algerian roads towards Morocco. There is a lot of security there, looking for Islamist terrorists. They took no notice of us, just a few stops to solicit small bribes, and it was an uneventful journey to the coast. We got the ferry to Spain. He gave me all the money from the pouch, said it would pay for the provisions and medicines, but could I drive him to western France, to Charente. And here we are. The journey has been hard for him; he's exhausted and disorientated. I'm glad you've shown up. I can't stay too long and I don't want him to be on his own."

Just at that moment, Freddie started to wail. I'd left him on his own too long, distracted and consumed by the reappearance of Ferdinand, albeit in a much-reduced form. It would take some getting used to. I went to the car to release my son, Ferdinand's son, and to start to think about how I was going to introduce them to each other.

******

In some ways the house was familiar, in others it was completely alien. The presence of someone who looked like Ferdinand but did not act like him didn't help with any sense of normality. Sakina made supper while I took care of Freddie. Ferdinand dozed in his chair, waking occasionally to look around and smile from time to time. He looked old. His hair was sparse and grey, cropped short. His skin, although tanned from the Saharan sun, had a pale, almost pasty, undertone. His eyes were the same shade of brown but seemed less vibrant, almost dull. Above all, his expression was mostly vacant, like there was no one home. I was worried.

We ate together at the large dining table, Freddie perched on my lap. Alf looked at the child frequently but didn't comment. I chatted as casually as I could manage to Sakina, who understood that I was trying to act as if everything was fine. After supper I put Freddie to bed in what used to be Alf and Jake's room, while Sakina put Ferdinand to bed in the ground floor room that had been my torture chamber for all those months, a lifetime ago. Afterwards, I sat with her on the terrace, sipping some Armagnac I'd found in the back of a kitchen cupboard.

"Will he always be like this?" I asked her.

"It is hard to tell, but probably not. I expect him to improve, to be more functional. It may take months, even years, or it could happen suddenly tomorrow. My father has seen many cases of traumatic brain injury; no two are the same but the outcomes tend to be similar. You should know that such injuries can be life-changing, and most are likely to be life-shortening. Alf, as you call him, was strong and fit, healthy, but he suffered repeated injuries as far as we can tell. He's been conscious for more than two years and has made good progress given his starting point. You should be aware of some possible signs, assuming you intend to stay with him for the foreseeable future."

To be honest, I hadn't even thought that far ahead, but then what else would I do?

"What sort of signs?" I asked.

"Rapid and extreme mood-swings are quite common, as are bouts of severe depression. Forgetfulness, of course, changes in habits. Sometimes compulsive gratification behaviours - eating, drinking, sex, thrill-seeking. He may get crushing headaches and muscle pains, cramps. He could get any of these things, or all of them or none at all. I just don't know, but they are all possible. One thing that is definite,

though, is that he cannot fly on aircraft for the time being, not until he has been examined thoroughly and he has had all the appropriate scans. The risk of pressure fluctuations in his brain while the trepanning holes are still open could be fatal. The skin has healed, but the bone underneath won't have regrown."

I listened and had another drink. I knew I'd have to think about it.

******

Sakina stayed for a week. I cleaned the pool and started the filters; I stocked up on food and drink. Sakina liked to spend time with Freddie. She told me she was not married and had no children, and neither situation was likely to change any time soon. She said being at the house with us was like a holiday, but the day came when she had to leave. She was a bit tearful as she said goodbye to Alf, who was also tearful. He had come to depend on her, which I understood. I stood on the terrace beside Alf, holding his hand as we watched Sakina drive off.

"Just us now," I told him, "but if it's any consolation, my cooking has improved."

He smiled at me and squeezed my hand. I think he was finally remembering me.

"Who is he?" Alf asked, meaning Freddie.

"He's our son, Alf, our little boy. You're his dad, I'm his mum. He's called Freddie."

"Freddie? Why Freddie?"

"After you, Alf. It works as well for girls as boys, so he's Freddie. It's what we, Jake and me, called him all the way through."

"Our son?" he asked.

"Yes, Alf, from that time on the ship, the last time. He's two and a bit. You'll need to get to know him, you have a lot to teach him."

"The ship? The Doris?" He smiled to himself.

I was thrilled that he recalled the name of the ship, the old tanker he'd chartered. At least some of his memory was starting to work.

"Yes, the Doris. Do you remember?"

"Not much," he shook his head, "just bits, pictures. I want to remember. I think I remember you now, and Jake too. Where is Jake?"

"She's not here, Alf. I'll tell you about her another time. Now, I'm going for a swim. Will you look after Freddie, make sure he doesn't fall in the pool?"

He nodded. I went inside to change into a sober swimsuit - the days when I wouldn't have bothered seemed a long time ago. He watched me as I swam, and he took little Freddie's hand. Freddie seemed quite happy to climb onto his lap, and Alf hid the unfamiliar discomfort well.

That evening, after Freddie had gone to bed, I sat with Alf and started to tell him the whole story as I knew it, from the beginning. I took it a bit at a time, over several days. He became quite anxious and confused at the dark parts, the fraught moments and acts of violence, the deaths, the pain. The lighter moments, the times he'd spent with me or Jake, or with both of us, also confused him but he smiled anyway. I don't think he could relate to any of it; it was just like I was telling him a made-up story, but over the next weeks and months he would ask questions, seeking clarifications or wanting to add a detail I might have missed.

Seeing him come back from the dark, a step at a time, reminded me of watching Freddie develop. Alf was relearning his life as if it was all new, but unlike Freddie he could not *choose or control how his life would pan out. Alf was stuck with the past; I was too.*

When I told him that Jake had been killed, that she was dead, he went to his room and cried. He didn't come out at all that day, or the next. He took food and drink while I was out or in bed. On the third day he emerged, red-eyed and unshaven.

"Tell me how...how she died."

"She was stabbed in the street in London by a stranger. It was a random event. She didn't see it coming. They took her to hospital but they couldn't save her."

"What a waste," Alf said, starting to cry again.

"You loved her, Alf, you still do. Try to remember her how she was, how she was with you. It hurts, but it will help, believe me." I told him.

We spoke about Jake, Julia Kelso, a lot from then on. Not for long, but often. The effect of the news of her death seemed to have shocked Ferdinand out of his torpor, and for brief moments, increasingly frequent, he was a bit more like his old self again.

One day he said he needed to see Roisin. I was surprised that he remembered who she was, and more surprised that he knew what he wanted to see her about.

"I want us to leave this place," he said to me, "there is somewhere else we can go. It is far away, but it is new, no bad memories. I need to speak to Roisin about it."

I called her and explained as best I could that Alf was not dead after all but had survived, and that I was with him in France. She arrived by train from Paris the next day, having taken the first flight out of Dublin that morning. I picked her up at the station in Poitiers. She was puzzled by the presence of Freddie, and by the time I'd explained it all we were approaching the house. Alf sat on the terrace, a rug over his bony knees.

They embraced like old friends and he made a show of fetching her some coffee and pastries. She told him about his friend Eugene Flynn, her uncle, who wasn't doing so well and had round-the-clock carers to look after him.

"I told him I was coming to see you," Roisin said to him, "and he said to tell you the chess board is always ready. He misses you."

Alf and Roisin spoke as if I wasn't there. I didn't follow all of it, and neither did Alf, but she took lots of notes. She stayed one night and I took her back to the station the following day.

"I'll sort everything out, Mel," she said, "don't worry about a thing. Just take care of him and the little one."

We spoke for a while about Kim Morris and Flora. Kim had been a police sergeant who was savagely attacked by a gang of people-traffickers. Roisin had given her sanctuary at her home near Cork, along with her twins and Flora, a Serbian girl who had herself been trafficked to be a sex worker. The kids were grown now and were away at university; Kim had done remarkably well and was still reasonably and unexpectedly healthy. Roisin suggested that Kim and Flora could come to the house to look after Alf while I went to finalise our departure from The Hague. I should get ready to go if I was going to stay with Alf.

A few weeks later, with Jake's house returned to the landlord and her car sold, Alf, Freddie and I boarded a smallish cruise ship at Bordeaux and set off for Canada. Alf was now Declan Walsh again, with a new Irish passport to prove it. I had passports for me and Freddie, and after a week at sea we arrived in Halifax, Nova Scotia. The formalities were quick and we boarded the coast-to-coast train the following morning.

Five days is a long time to be stuck on a train with a toddler and a grown man who wasn't all there some of the time, and by the time we arrived in Vancouver I was close to screaming. I parked Freddie and Alf in a hotel and, hoping he was having a good day, I left Alf in charge while I went to get a hire car and some head space.

The ferry ride from North Vancouver to Nanaimo was spectacular and invigorating. I was relaxed and happy as I drove us across the island to Tofino, closely following Roisin's very precise directions. By early afternoon, we arrived at the house, our new home, overlooking the Pacific Ocean and as far west as I'd ever been in my life. It was stunning, and very scary. I had told my sister I was going away, and she didn't seem that bothered. Nor did my brother, although he did say he hoped I was going somewhere nice where he would like to go on holiday.

Alf explored the new house as if he'd never seen it before. He seemed delighted to find a bright red Jeep Wrangler in the garage, its battery on a trickle charger and its tank full of fuel.

"I got this for Jake," he said, remembering. "I thought she would like it."

"She would have loved it, Alf," I told him, "I love it too."

We settled in. Freddie went to nursery three mornings a week and eventually to the local primary school. Alf pottered in the garden and took walks on the beach. Sakina's gloomy forecast about Alf's future behaviour proved to have been mostly inaccurate; he was fairly steady mood-wise, but sometimes very quiet and quite remote. He grew to be very attached to Freddie and we all got along just fine, but the old spark that had once been there didn't flicker again. We lived separately in the same house, although he did sometimes come into my room and my bed, just to be close, nothing more. Sometimes I went to his too, when I needed to.

During the long winter evenings, or when the Pacific storms kept us indoors, we talked. He asked repeatedly about the things the three of us had done. He went over details, especially his own part in whatever piece of mayhem we were discussing. He said he couldn't believe that he had been capable of the deception, the violence, the duplicity he had enacted. I reassured him as much as I could, saying that the act had been necessary, both for his own survival and the success of whatever project it was.

"Why did we do it, Mel?" he asked one night.

"We did it because we believed in justice, Alf," I answered, "and because justice sometimes doesn't work, it's sometimes corrupted. We believed we were doing the right thing."

"Were we, though? What did it do to us?"

"It made us alive, Alf. It was what we were meant to do. I need to believe that, to keep the faith, to make the cost of it all worth it."

We went to school things, Christmas plays, art exhibitions, parents' evenings, stuff like that. When Freddie went to school full-time I joined an online college with some residential courses in Victoria to learn about the environment and the First Nations, then I got summer jobs on the whale-watching and bear-spotting boats. I didn't need the money but I did need something to do. I met people, some were almost friends, I had some sort of personal life as me, not as Freddie's mum or Alf's carer. I think I was happy; we all were.

Alf got himself a bike. He didn't like to drive anymore, and he'd cycle into town most days. He got to know a few people well enough to have a coffee or a beer with, but he didn't really make friends. Neither of us did. Real friends take a lot of time and effort, and honesty. Our honesty would have been too much for most people, so we kept it to ourselves and put up with our own company.

313

One day Alf told me he'd bought a boat. We went to see it and took it out on the Sound; it was great. The boat was small but comfortable, with a decent engine and a cosy cabin. He spent a lot of time in it, out on the water. And that was where he died.

Alf had gone out on his boat. He had a favourite route around Clayoquot that took about three hours. I dropped Freddie at school and took Alf to the dock. I watched him get the boat ready. Before he set off he did something strange. He came to me, hugged me and kissed me, right on the lips. He said: "I do love you, even though you told me I wasn't allowed to tell you, after that first time." He kissed me again and smiled, then he got into the boat and set off.

He hadn't come back to the dock by late afternoon. The search and rescue guys found him the next day, still in the drifting boat, sitting upright in the cabin looking totally calm. He was dead, stone cold. The autopsy said natural causes, a brain haemorrhage that he would have known almost nothing about. Natural causes, maybe, but he had been killed by what we had done, the three of us. Now I was the last one standing, and even then only by chance.

We left the island not long after that. I had inherited the house and quite a bit of money and we could afford to go just about anywhere, but Canada seemed to work. Freddie was growing up and he needed a bigger pond to swim in, and I've never been a natural island dweller. We bought a house in Vancouver, in an inner-city suburb that has recently started to be up-and-coming, which is where we still live now. Freddie is at college, school he calls it. He asks me a lot about his father, about Alf. It's sometimes hard to know what to tell him.

Maybe one day I'll just let him read Jo Calman's books, and when he's finished I'll tell him it is all true. Every word. But I might find some parts quite hard to explain...

Last week I was summoned to see his school principal. Freddie is a bit of a star, very athletic and really quite academic too, so I was surprised to get the call. An incident had happened on the ice. Freddie was playing hockey - he's on the school team - and two of the opposing side ganged up on one of the smaller players on Freddie's team. Freddie's player got quite badly hurt, broken bones, concussion. In the dressing room afterwards Freddie was wiping the floor with the bullies, both of whom were battered and bruised, and he had to be pulled off them.

The principal said that while he appreciated that Freddie should be praised for seeking justice, that really wasn't the way to go about it.

I wonder where he gets that from?

The End

Other books by Jo Calman

The Kelso Series:

Book 1: A Transfer of Power

Book 2: A Price for Mercy

Book 3: An Inner Circle

Book 4: An Undeclared Contest

Book 5: An Alchemist's Tale

By Jo Calman and Casey J Smith:

Viktor

All available on Amazon, in some larger bookstores to order, and as eBooks with the Kindle app

or through

www.jo-calman.com

Printed in Great Britain
by Amazon